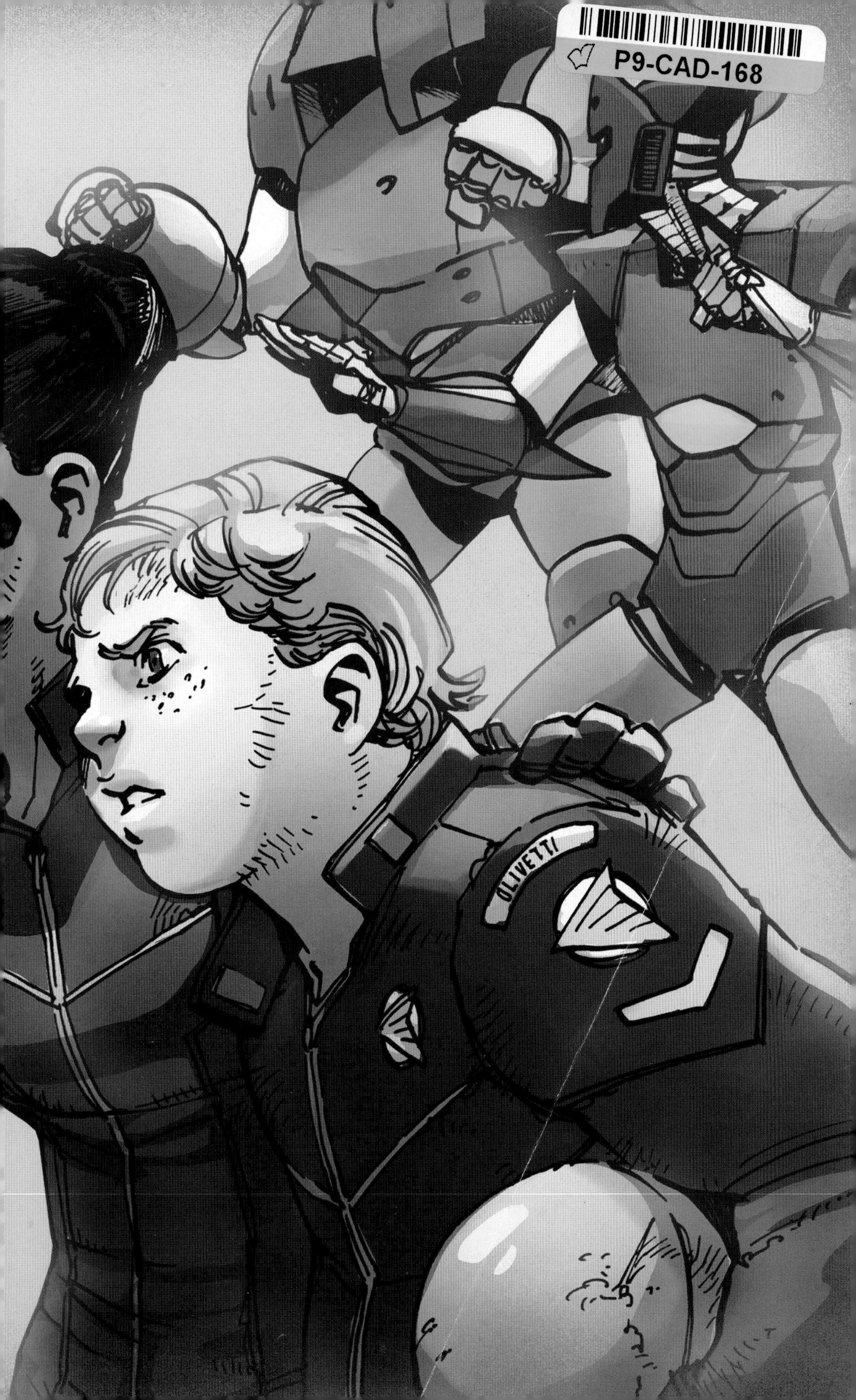
OLIVETTI

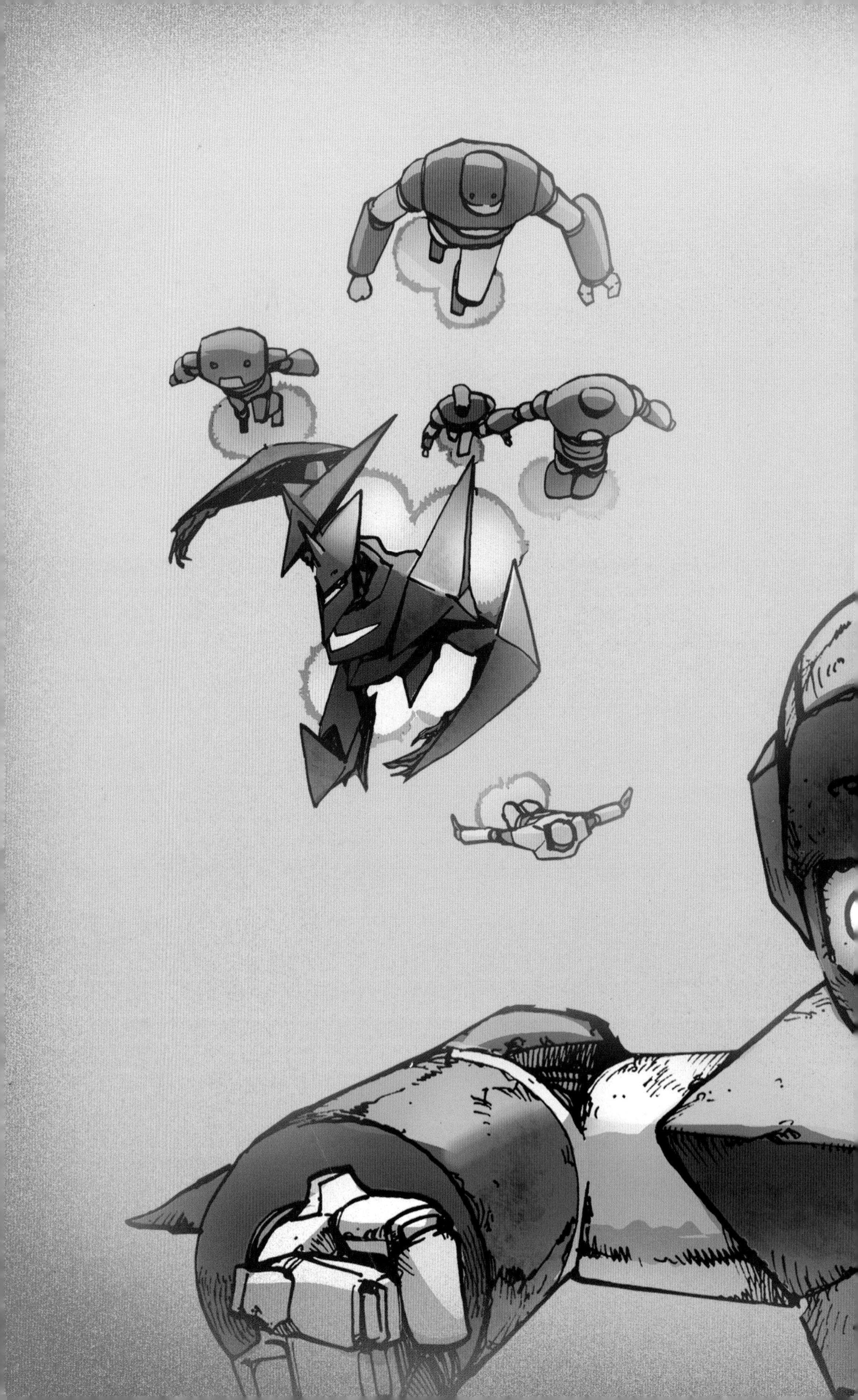

GREG PAK • TAKESHI MIYAZAWA • JESSICA KHOLINNE

MECH CADET YU™

VOLUME THREE

Series Designer
MICHELLE ANKLEY

Collection Designer
CHELSEA ROBERTS

Editor
CAMERON CHITTOCK

Special Thanks
ERIC HARBURN

MECH CADET YU Volume Three, April 2019. Published by BOOM! Studios, a division of Boom Entertainment, Inc. Mech Cadet Yu is ™ & © 2019 Pak Man Productions, Ltd. & Takeshi Miyazawa. Originally published in single magazine form as MECH CADET YU No. 9-12. ™ & © 2018 Pak Man Productions, Ltd. & Takeshi Miyazawa. All rights reserved. BOOM! Studios™ and the BOOM! Studios logo are trademarks of Boom Entertainment, Inc., registered in various countries and categories. All characters, events, and institutions depicted herein are fictional. Any similarity between any of the names, characters, persons, events, and/or institutions in this publication to actual names, characters, and persons, whether living or dead, events, and/or institutions is unintended and purely coincidental. BOOM! Studios does not read or accept unsolicited submissions of ideas, stories, or artwork.

BOOM! Studios, 5670 Wilshire Boulevard, Suite 400, Los Angeles, CA 90036-5679. Printed in China. First Printing.

ISBN: 978-1-68415-337-4, eISBN: 978-1-64144-190-2

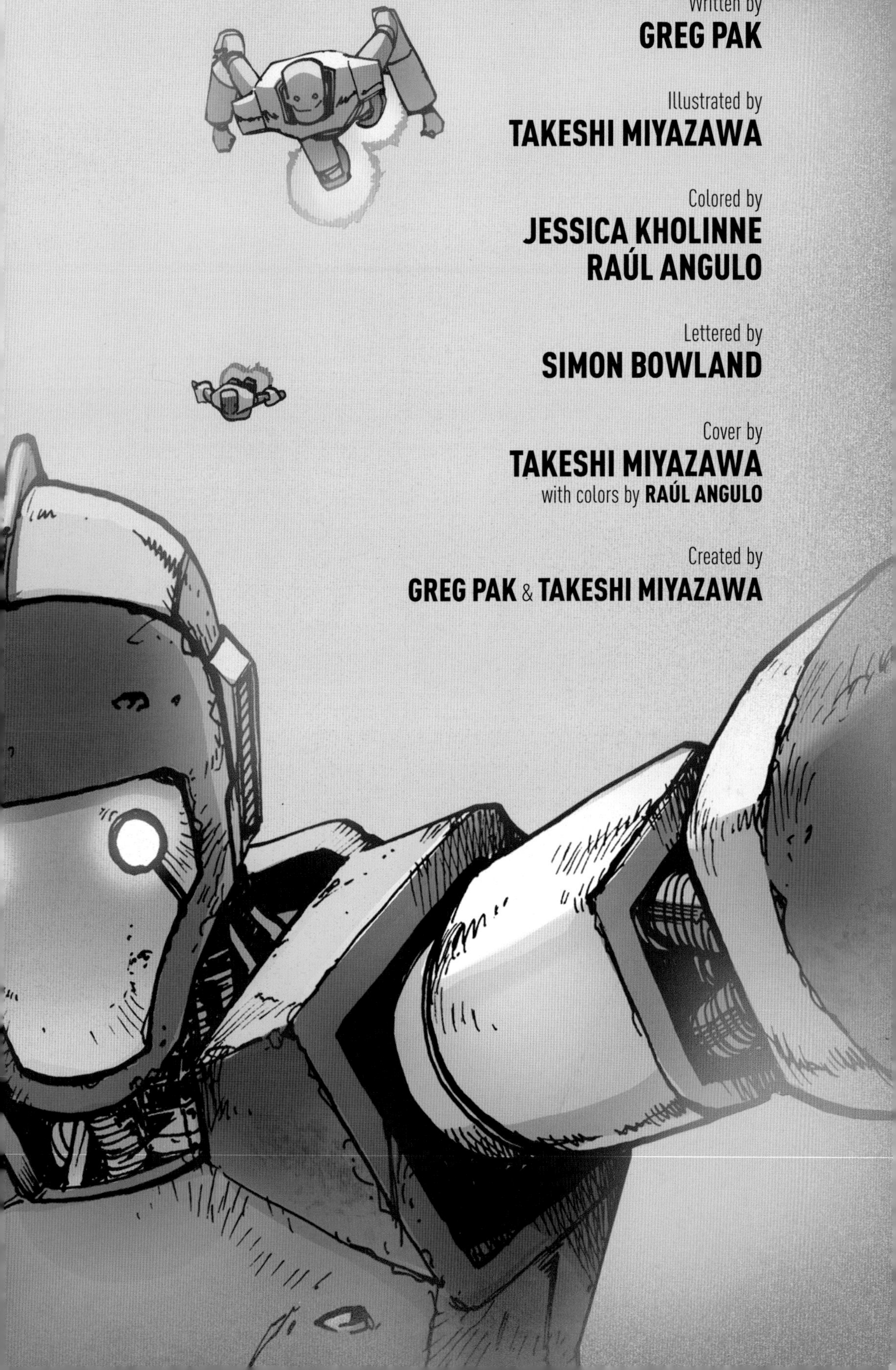

Written by
GREG PAK

Illustrated by
TAKESHI MIYAZAWA

Colored by
JESSICA KHOLINNE
RAÚL ANGULO

Lettered by
SIMON BOWLAND

Cover by
TAKESHI MIYAZAWA
with colors by **RAÚL ANGULO**

Created by
GREG PAK & **TAKESHI MIYAZAWA**

CHAPTER NINE

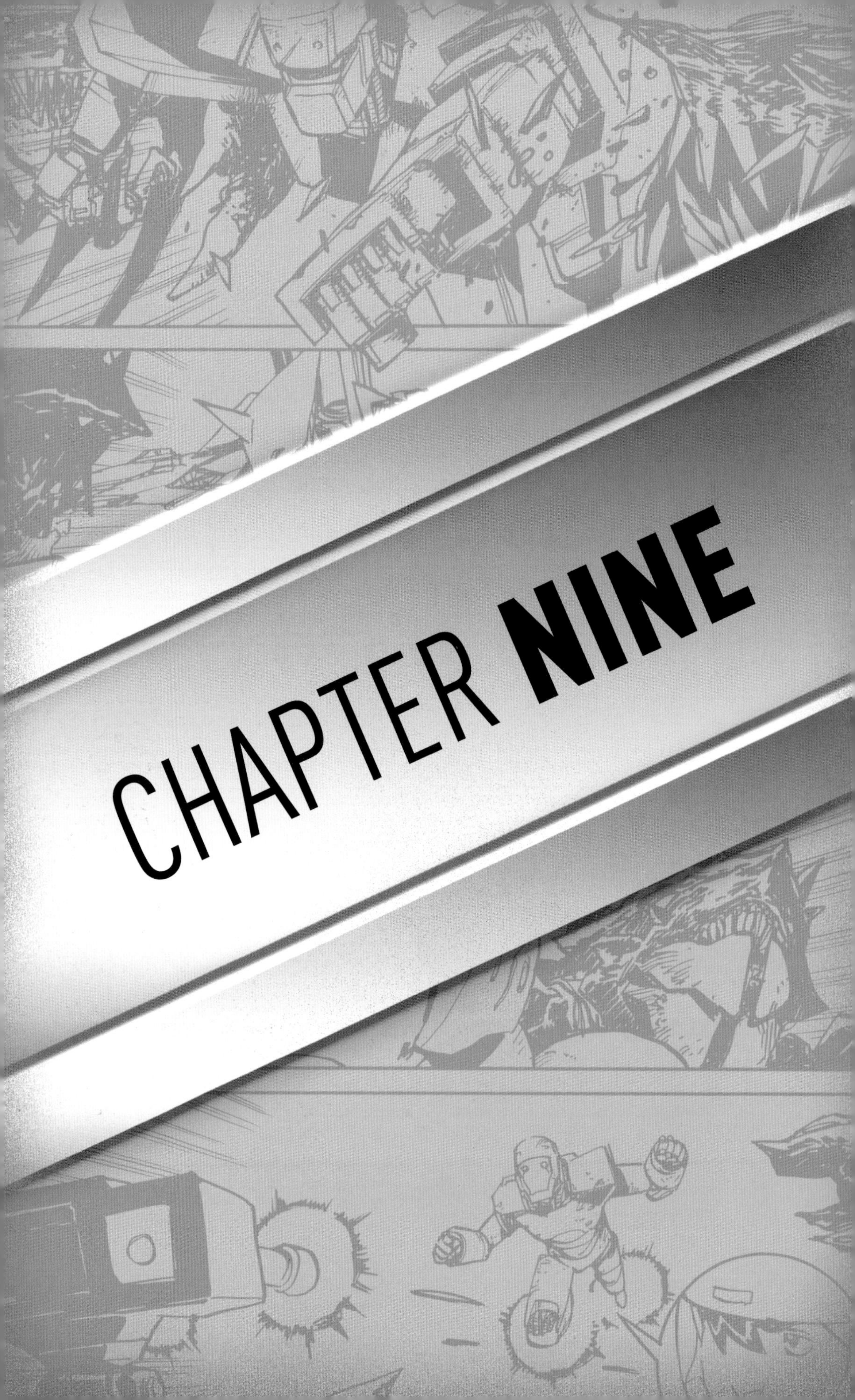

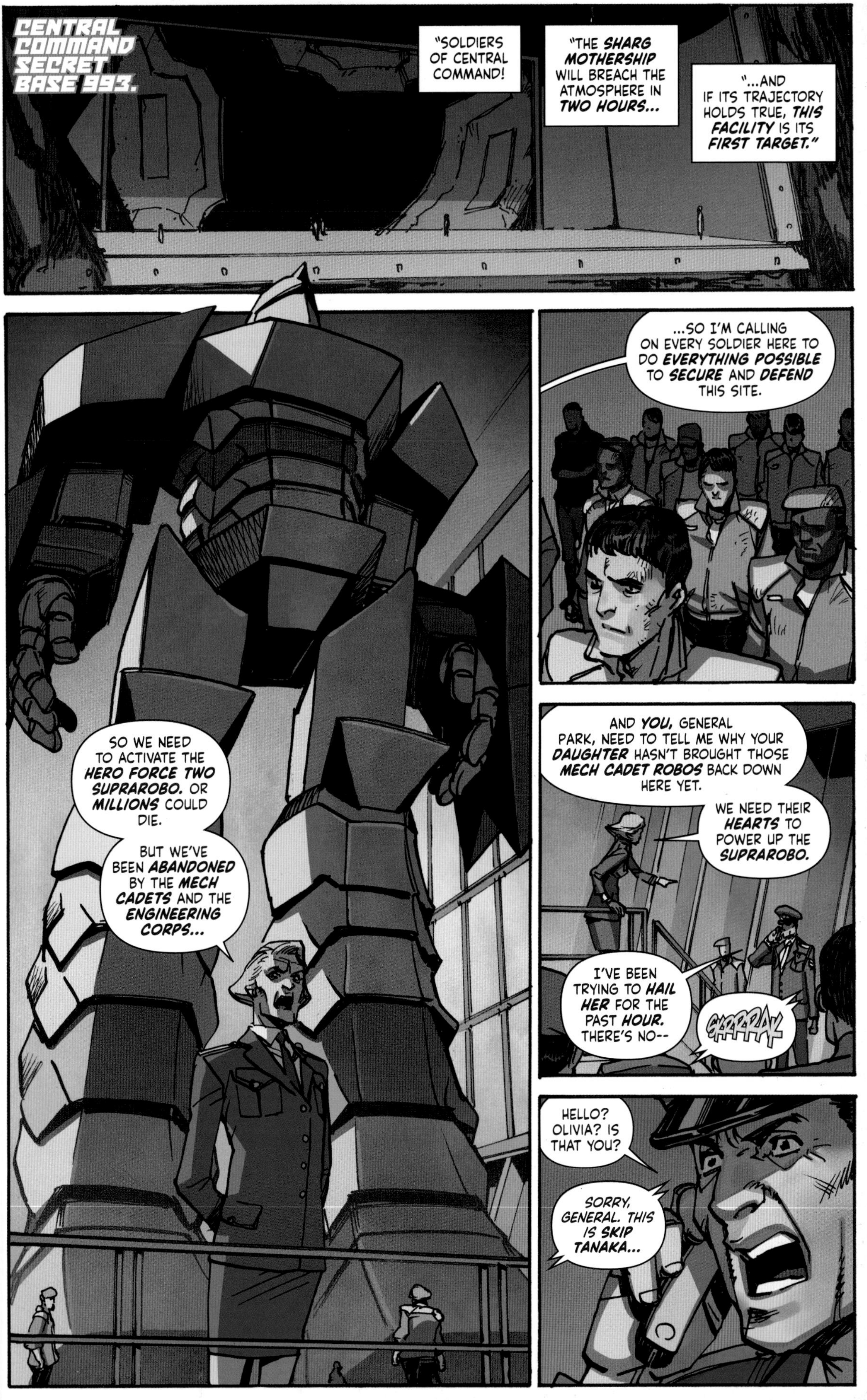
CENTRAL COMMAND SECRET BASE 993.
"SOLDIERS OF CENTRAL COMMAND!
"THE SHARG MOTHERSHIP WILL BREACH THE ATMOSPHERE IN TWO HOURS...
"...AND IF ITS TRAJECTORY HOLDS TRUE, THIS FACILITY IS ITS FIRST TARGET."
...SO I'M CALLING ON EVERY SOLDIER HERE TO DO EVERYTHING POSSIBLE TO SECURE AND DEFEND THIS SITE.
SO WE NEED TO ACTIVATE THE HERO FORCE TWO SUPRAROBO. OR MILLIONS COULD DIE.
BUT WE'VE BEEN ABANDONED BY THE MECH CADETS AND THE ENGINEERING CORPS...
AND YOU, GENERAL PARK, NEED TO TELL ME WHY YOUR DAUGHTER HASN'T BROUGHT THOSE MECH CADET ROBOS BACK DOWN HERE YET.
WE NEED THEIR HEARTS TO POWER UP THE SUPRAROBO.
I'VE BEEN TRYING TO HAIL HER FOR THE PAST HOUR. THERE'S NO--
SKRRRRAK
HELLO? OLIVIA? IS THAT YOU?
SORRY, GENERAL. THIS IS SKIP TANAKA...

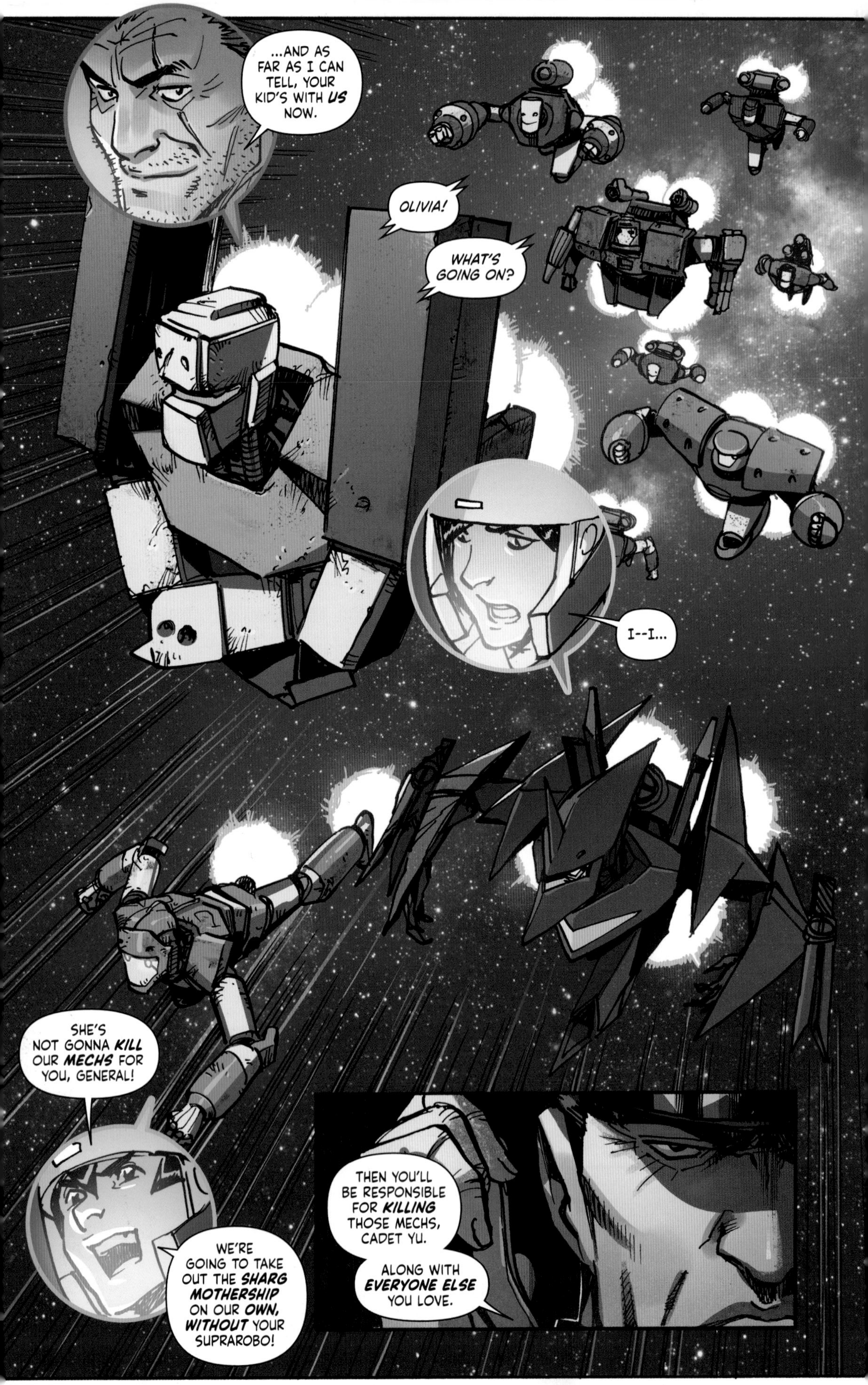
...AND AS FAR AS I CAN TELL, YOUR KID'S WITH *US* NOW.
OLIVIA!
WHAT'S GOING ON?
I--I...
SHE'S NOT GONNA ***KILL*** OUR ***MECHS*** FOR YOU, GENERAL!
WE'RE GOING TO TAKE OUT THE ***SHARG MOTHERSHIP*** ON OUR ***OWN, WITHOUT*** YOUR SUPRAROBO!
THEN YOU'LL BE RESPONSIBLE FOR ***KILLING*** THOSE MECHS, CADET YU.
ALONG WITH ***EVERYONE ELSE*** YOU LOVE.

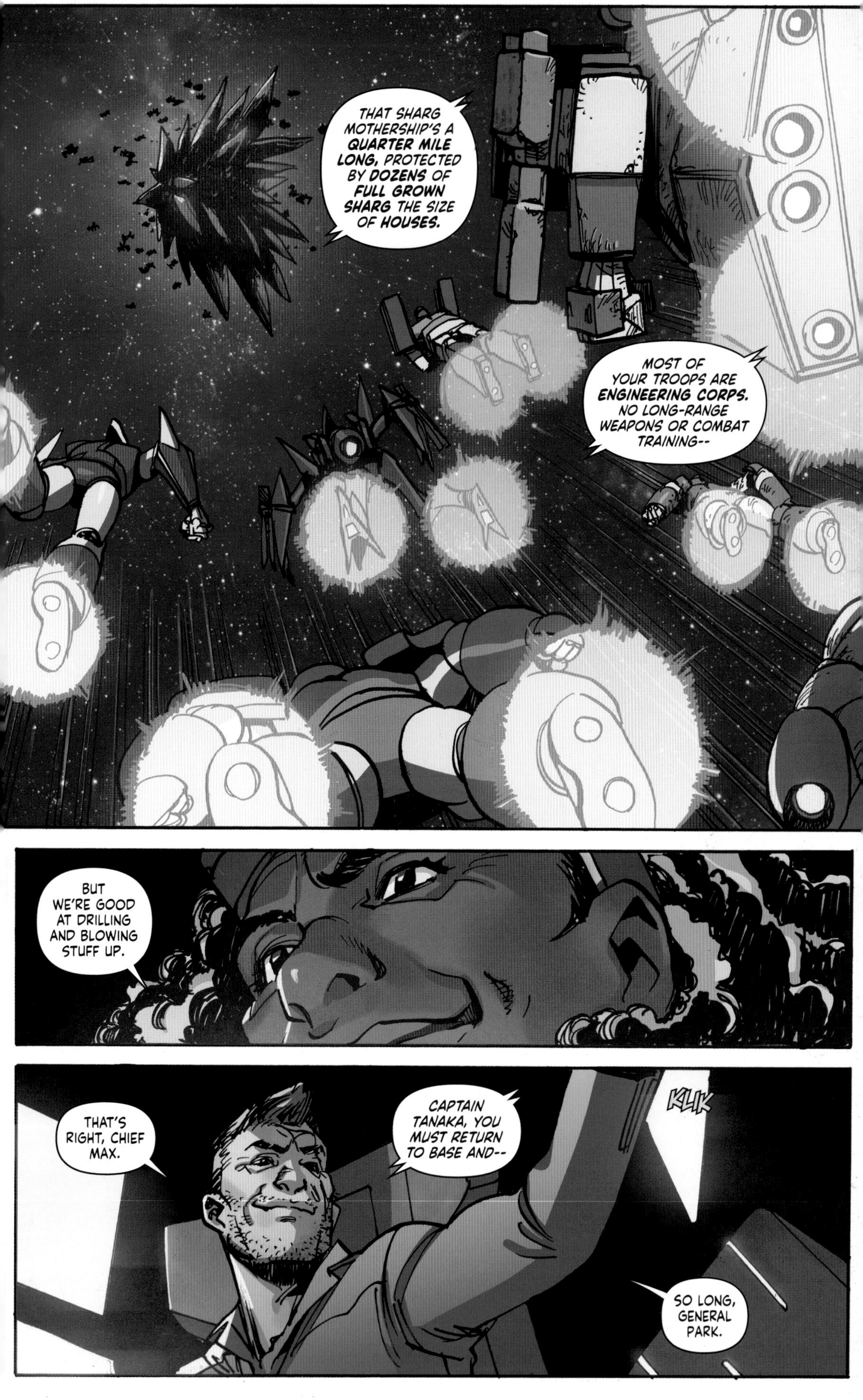
THAT SHARG MOTHERSHIP'S A QUARTER MILE LONG, PROTECTED BY DOZENS OF FULL GROWN SHARG THE SIZE OF HOUSES.
MOST OF YOUR TROOPS ARE ENGINEERING CORPS. NO LONG-RANGE WEAPONS OR COMBAT TRAINING--
BUT WE'RE GOOD AT DRILLING AND BLOWING STUFF UP.
THAT'S RIGHT, CHIEF MAX.
CAPTAIN TANAKA, YOU MUST RETURN TO BASE AND--
KLIK
SO LONG, GENERAL PARK.

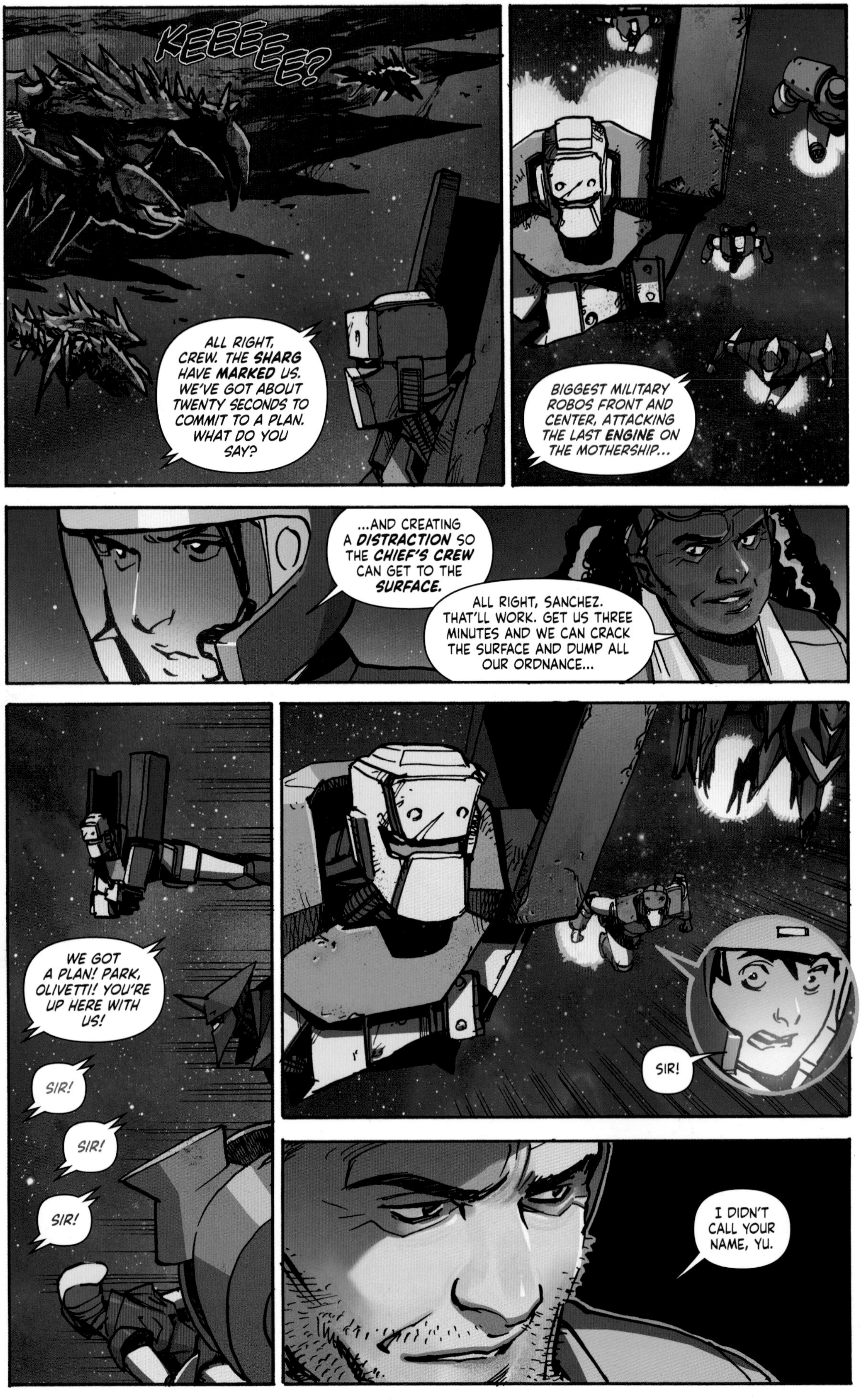
KEEEEEE?
ALL RIGHT, CREW. THE SHARG HAVE MARKED US. WE'VE GOT ABOUT TWENTY SECONDS TO COMMIT TO A PLAN. WHAT DO YOU SAY?
BIGGEST MILITARY ROBOS FRONT AND CENTER, ATTACKING THE LAST ENGINE ON THE MOTHERSHIP...
...AND CREATING A DISTRACTION SO THE CHIEF'S CREW CAN GET TO THE SURFACE.
ALL RIGHT, SANCHEZ. THAT'LL WORK. GET US THREE MINUTES AND WE CAN CRACK THE SURFACE AND DUMP ALL OUR ORDNANCE...
WE GOT A PLAN! PARK, OLIVETTI! YOU'RE UP HERE WITH US!
SIR!
SIR!
SIR!
SIR!
I DIDN'T CALL YOUR NAME, YU.

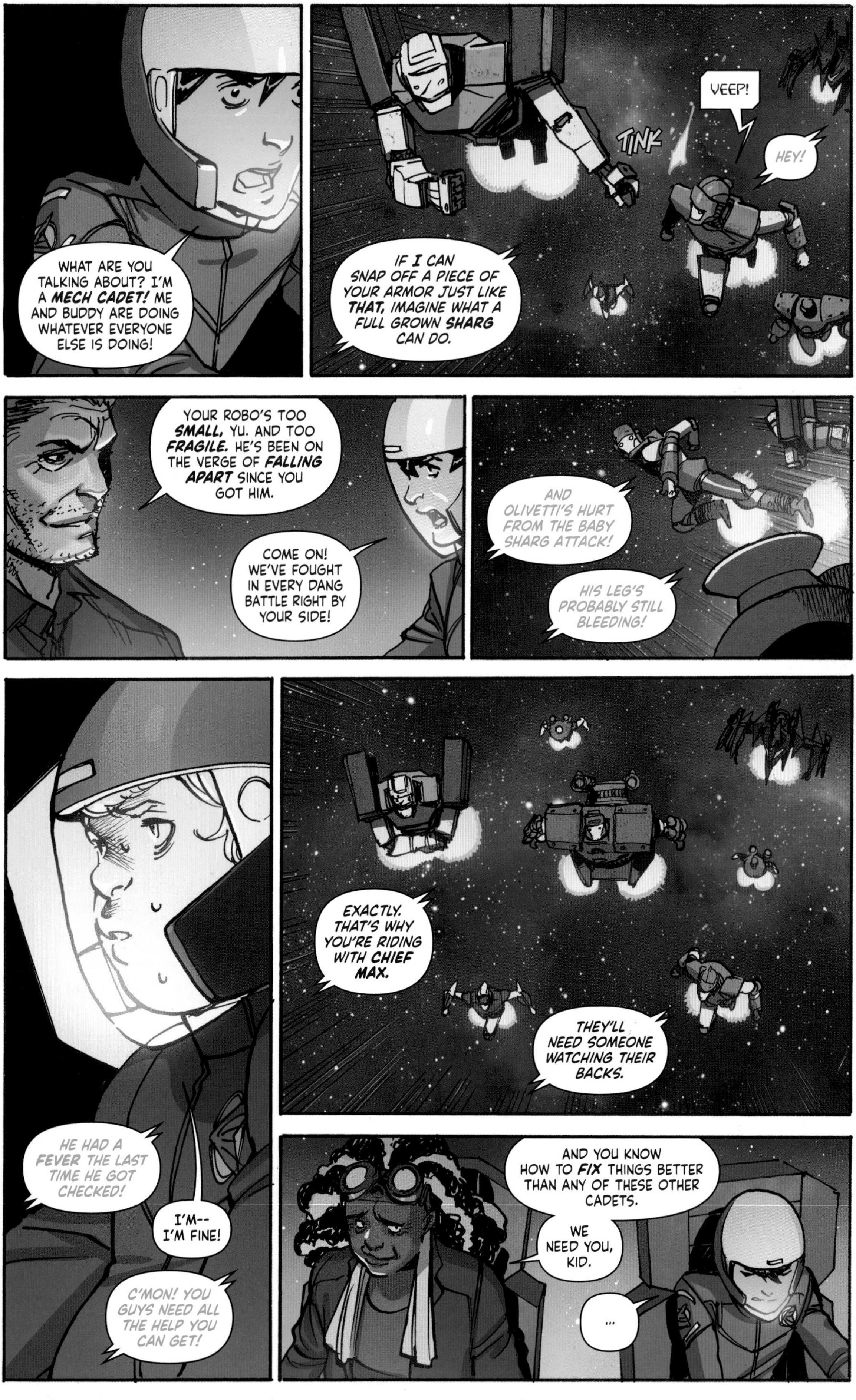
WHAT ARE YOU TALKING ABOUT? I'M A MECH CADET! ME AND BUDDY ARE DOING WHATEVER EVERYONE ELSE IS DOING!
TINK
VEEP!
HEY!
IF I CAN SNAP OFF A PIECE OF YOUR ARMOR JUST LIKE THAT, IMAGINE WHAT A FULL GROWN SHARG CAN DO.
YOUR ROBO'S TOO SMALL, YU. AND TOO FRAGILE. HE'S BEEN ON THE VERGE OF FALLING APART SINCE YOU GOT HIM.
COME ON! WE'VE FOUGHT IN EVERY DANG BATTLE RIGHT BY YOUR SIDE!
AND OLIVETTI'S HURT FROM THE BABY SHARG ATTACK!
HIS LEG'S PROBABLY STILL BLEEDING!
EXACTLY. THAT'S WHY YOU'RE RIDING WITH CHIEF MAX.
THEY'LL NEED SOMEONE WATCHING THEIR BACKS.
HE HAD A FEVER THE LAST TIME HE GOT CHECKED!
I'M-- I'M FINE!
C'MON! YOU GUYS NEED ALL THE HELP YOU CAN GET!
AND YOU KNOW HOW TO FIX THINGS BETTER THAN ANY OF THESE OTHER CADETS.
WE NEED YOU, KID.
...

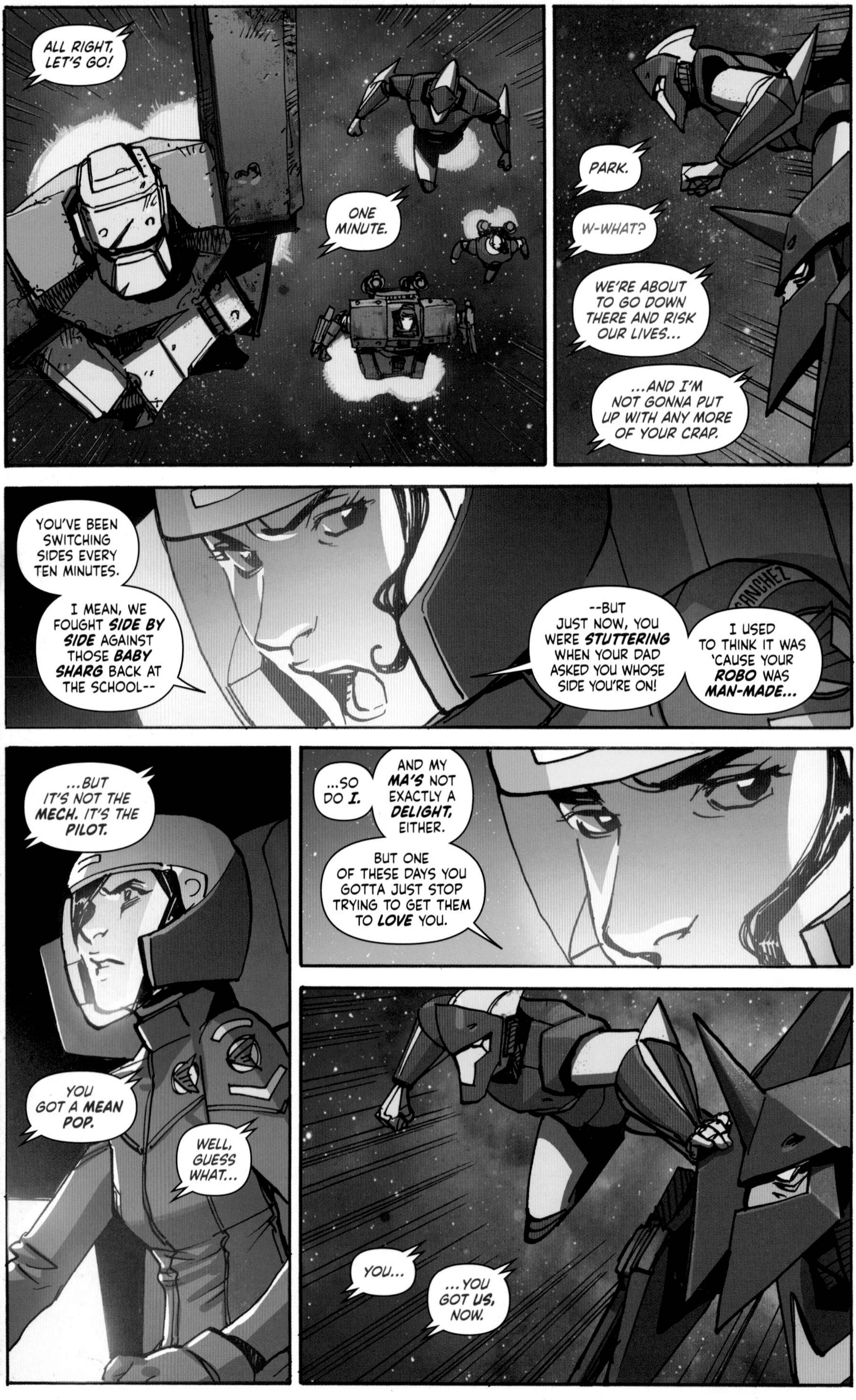
ALL RIGHT, LET'S GO!
ONE MINUTE.
PARK.
W-WHAT?
WE'RE ABOUT TO GO DOWN THERE AND RISK OUR LIVES...
...AND I'M NOT GONNA PUT UP WITH ANY MORE OF YOUR CRAP.
YOU'VE BEEN SWITCHING SIDES EVERY TEN MINUTES.
I MEAN, WE FOUGHT SIDE BY SIDE AGAINST THOSE BABY SHARG BACK AT THE SCHOOL--
--BUT JUST NOW, YOU WERE STUTTERING WHEN YOUR DAD ASKED YOU WHOSE SIDE YOU'RE ON!
SANCHEZ
I USED TO THINK IT WAS 'CAUSE YOUR ROBO WAS MAN-MADE...
...BUT IT'S NOT THE MECH. IT'S THE PILOT.
YOU GOT A MEAN POP.
WELL, GUESS WHAT...
...SO DO I.
AND MY MA'S NOT EXACTLY A DELIGHT, EITHER.
BUT ONE OF THESE DAYS YOU GOTTA JUST STOP TRYING TO GET THEM TO LOVE YOU.
YOU...
...YOU GOT US, NOW.

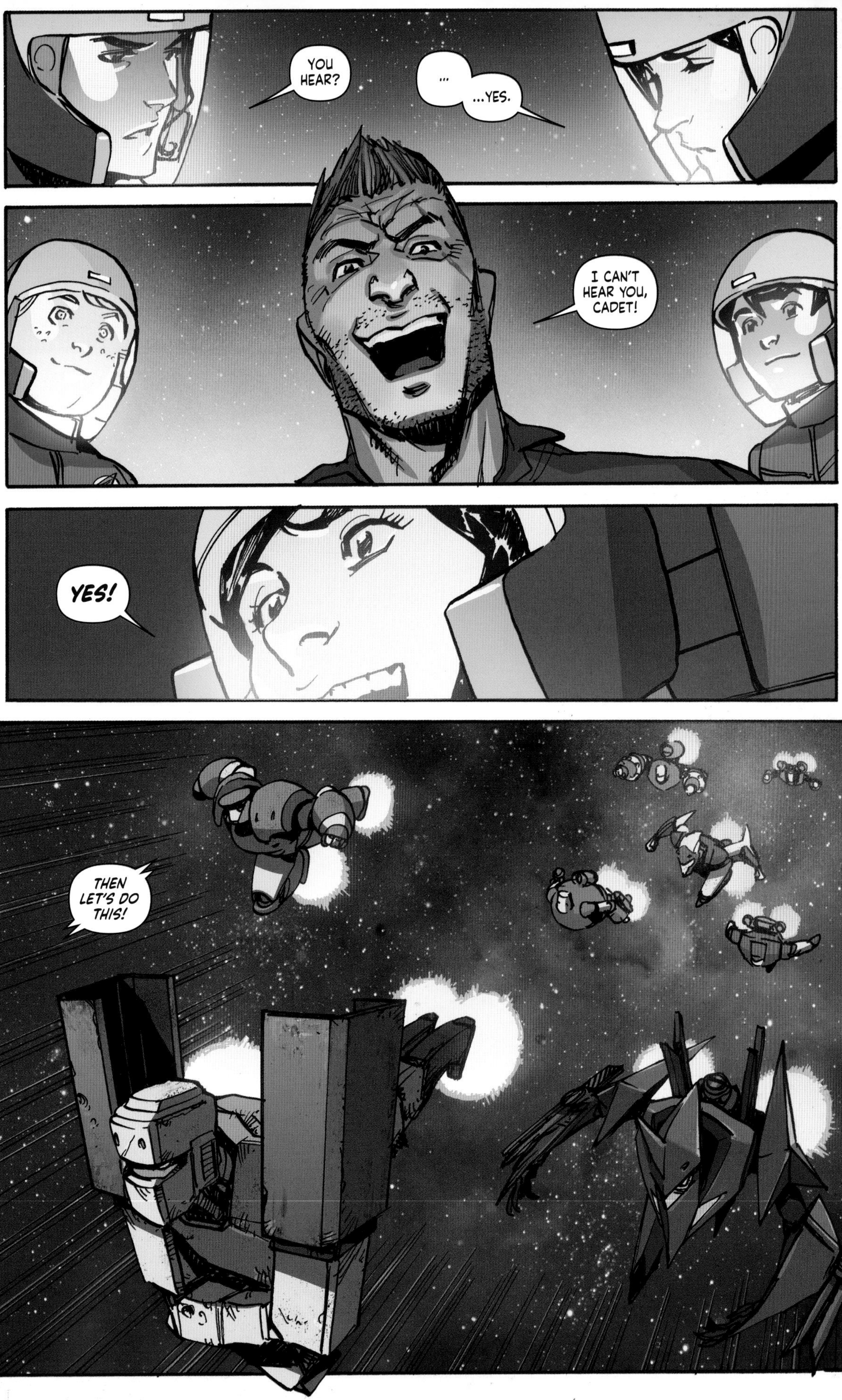
YOU HEAR?
...
...YES.
I CAN'T HEAR YOU, CADET!
YES!
THEN LET'S DO THIS!

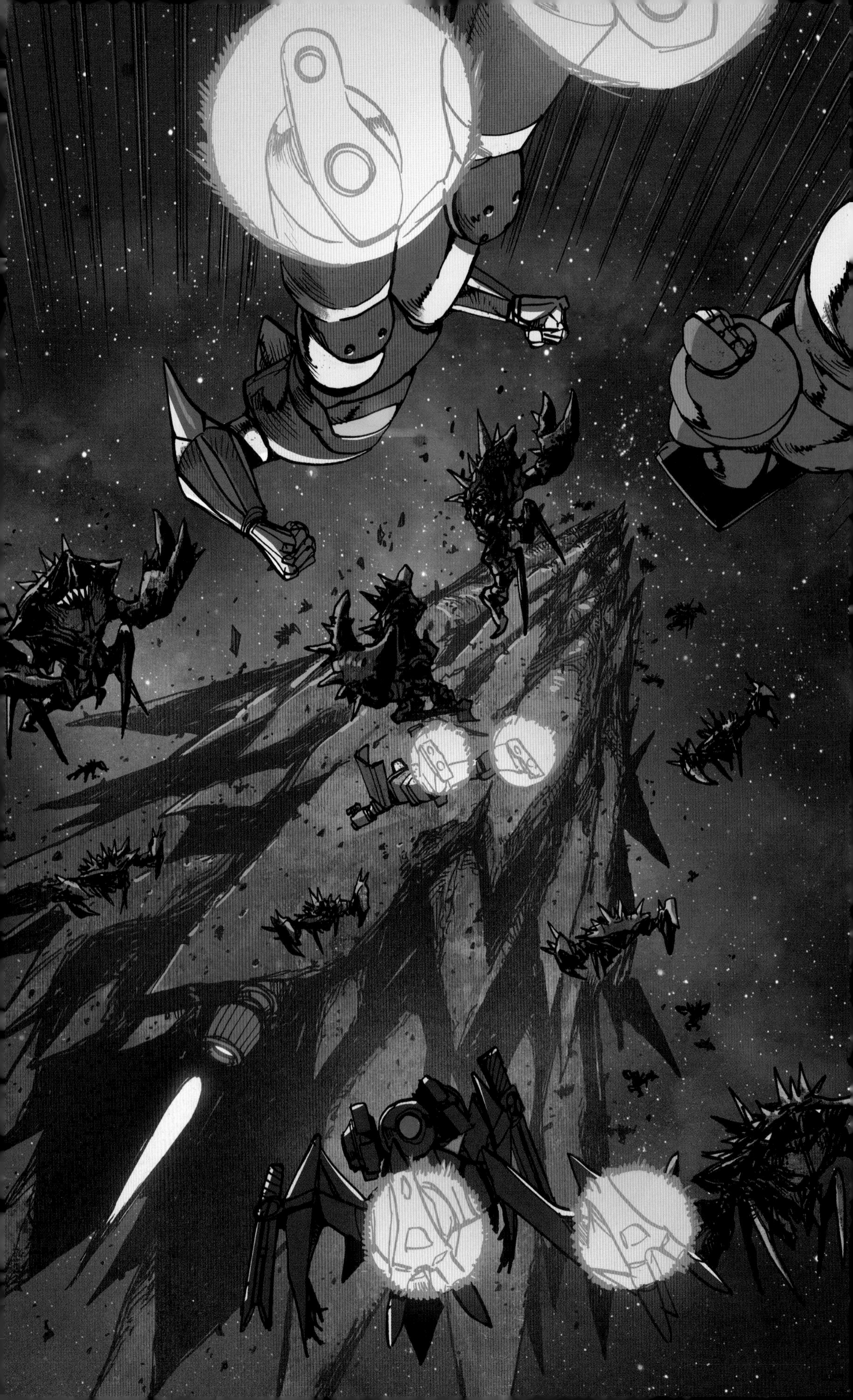

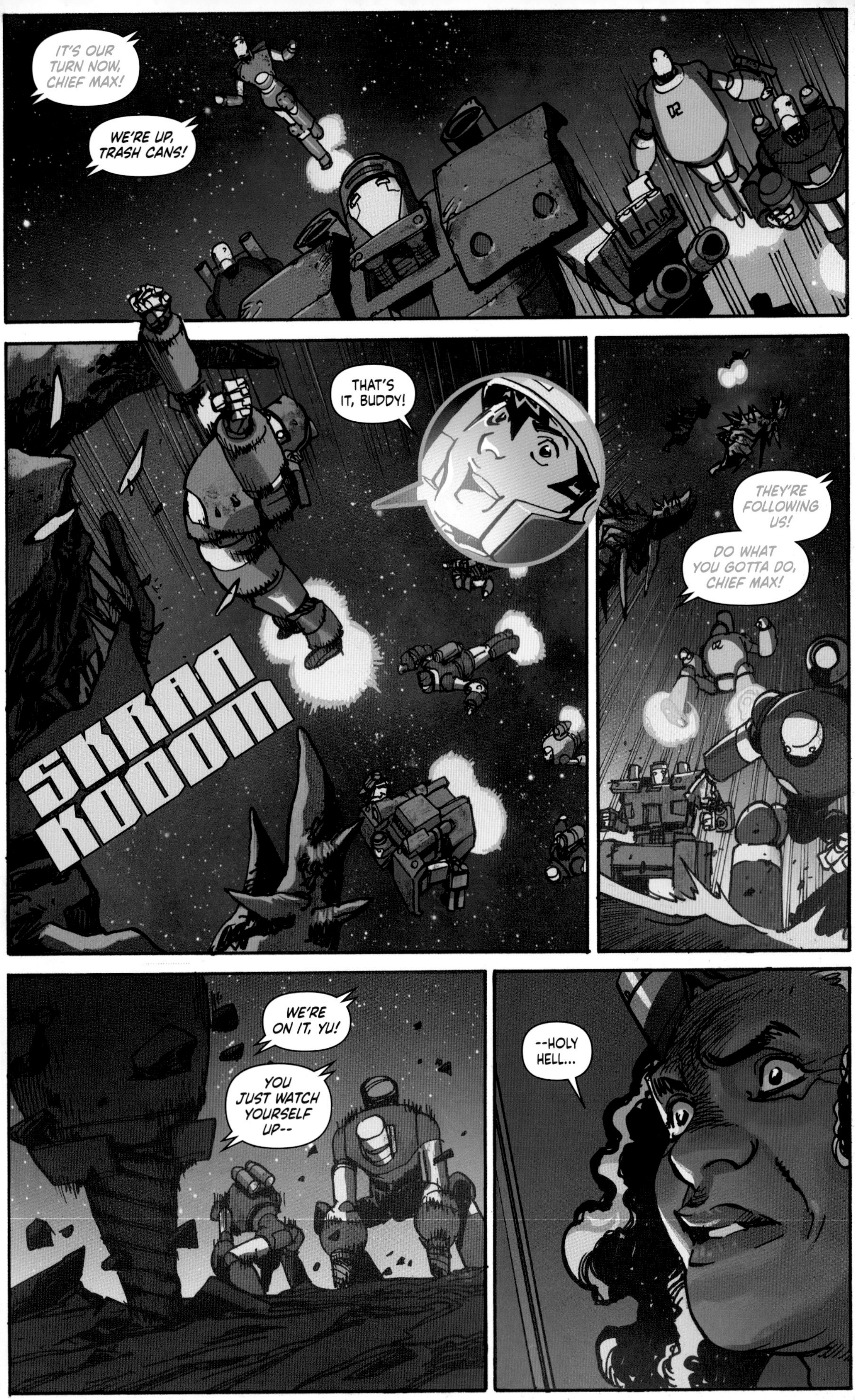
IT'S OUR TURN NOW, CHIEF MAX!
WE'RE UP, TRASH CANS!
THAT'S IT, BUDDY!
SKRAA KOOOM
THEY'RE FOLLOWING US!
DO WHAT YOU GOTTA DO, CHIEF MAX!
WE'RE ON IT, YU!
YOU JUST WATCH YOURSELF UP--
--HOLY HELL...

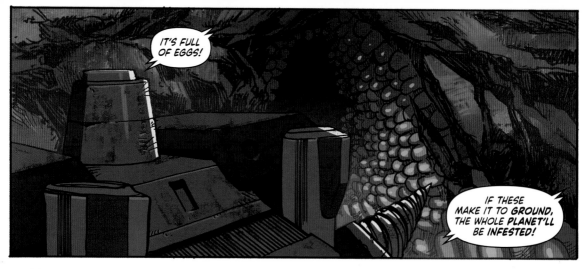

IT'S FULL OF EGGS!

IF THESE MAKE IT TO GROUND, THE WHOLE PLANET'LL BE INFESTED!

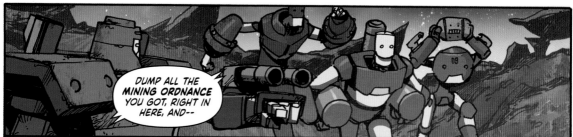

DUMP ALL THE MINING ORDNANCE YOU GOT, RIGHT IN HERE, AND--

KTOOOM KTOOOM

WHAT THE--

MY GOD...

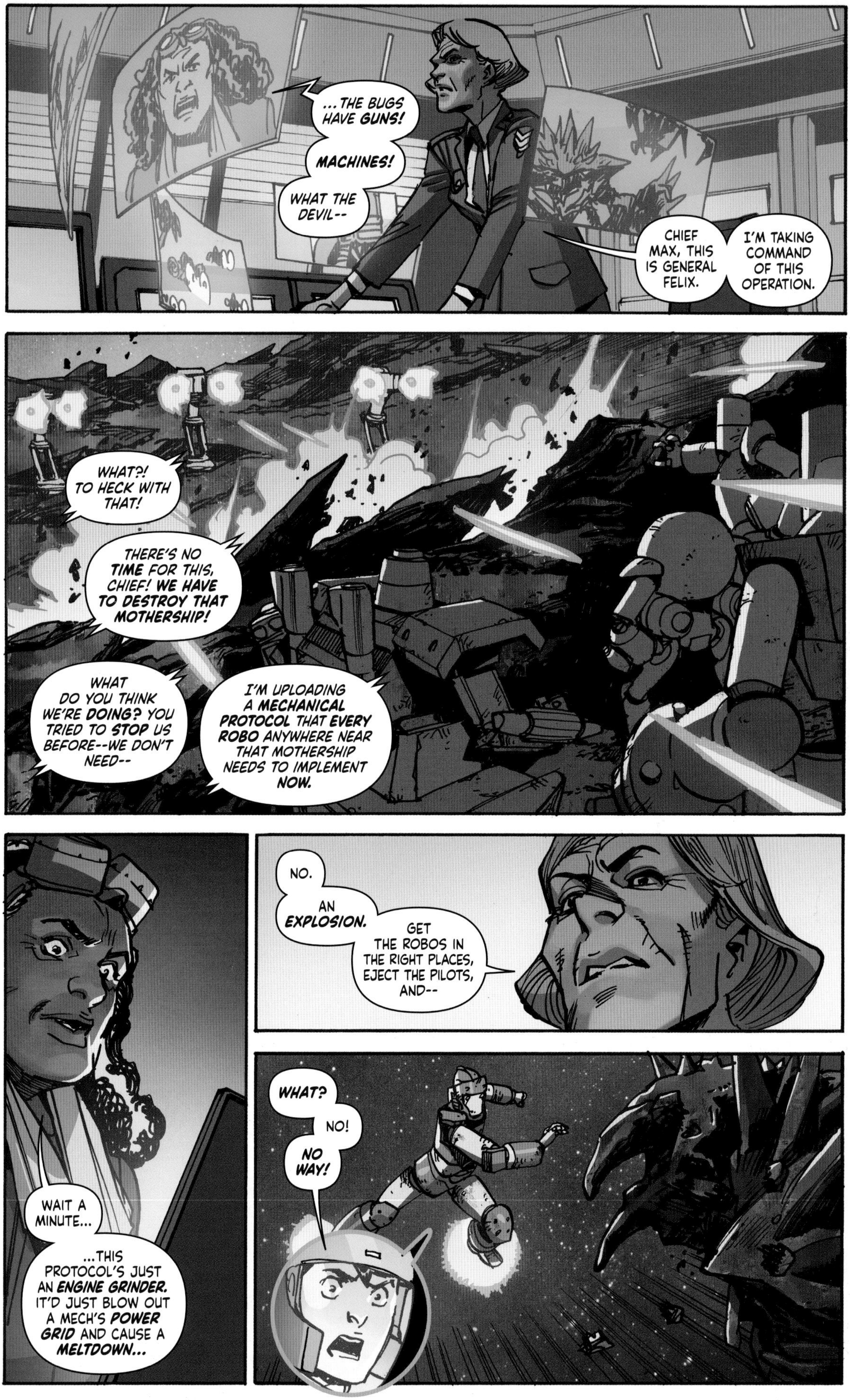
...THE BUGS HAVE GUNS!
MACHINES!
WHAT THE DEVIL--
CHIEF MAX, THIS IS GENERAL FELIX.
I'M TAKING COMMAND OF THIS OPERATION.
WHAT?! TO HECK WITH THAT!
THERE'S NO TIME FOR THIS, CHIEF! WE HAVE TO DESTROY THAT MOTHERSHIP!
WHAT DO YOU THINK WE'RE DOING? YOU TRIED TO STOP US BEFORE--WE DON'T NEED--
I'M UPLOADING A MECHANICAL PROTOCOL THAT EVERY ROBO ANYWHERE NEAR THAT MOTHERSHIP NEEDS TO IMPLEMENT NOW.
WAIT A MINUTE...
...THIS PROTOCOL'S JUST AN ENGINE GRINDER. IT'D JUST BLOW OUT A MECH'S POWER GRID AND CAUSE A MELTDOWN...
NO.
AN EXPLOSION.
GET THE ROBOS IN THE RIGHT PLACES, EJECT THE PILOTS, AND--
WHAT?
NO!
NO WAY!

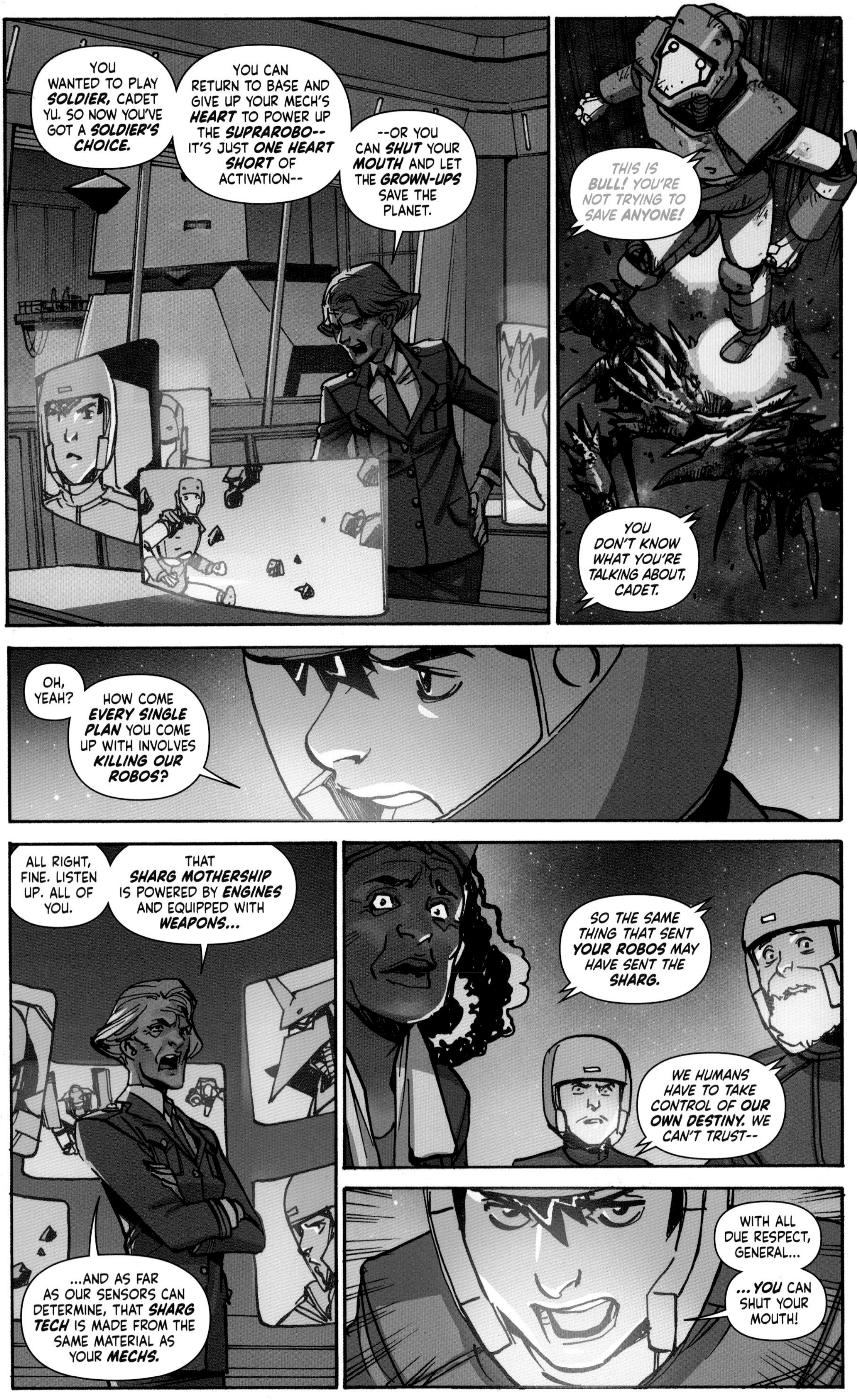
YOU WANTED TO PLAY SOLDIER, CADET YU. SO NOW YOU'VE GOT A SOLDIER'S CHOICE.
YOU CAN RETURN TO BASE AND GIVE UP YOUR MECH'S HEART TO POWER UP THE SUPRAROBO-- IT'S JUST ONE HEART SHORT OF ACTIVATION--
--OR YOU CAN SHUT YOUR MOUTH AND LET THE GROWN-UPS SAVE THE PLANET.
THIS IS BULL! YOU'RE NOT TRYING TO SAVE ANYONE!
YOU DON'T KNOW WHAT YOU'RE TALKING ABOUT, CADET.
OH, YEAH?
HOW COME EVERY SINGLE PLAN YOU COME UP WITH INVOLVES KILLING OUR ROBOS?
ALL RIGHT, FINE. LISTEN UP. ALL OF YOU.
THAT SHARG MOTHERSHIP IS POWERED BY ENGINES AND EQUIPPED WITH WEAPONS...
...AND AS FAR AS OUR SENSORS CAN DETERMINE, THAT SHARG TECH IS MADE FROM THE SAME MATERIAL AS YOUR MECHS.
SO THE SAME THING THAT SENT YOUR ROBOS MAY HAVE SENT THE SHARG.
WE HUMANS HAVE TO TAKE CONTROL OF OUR OWN DESTINY. WE CAN'T TRUST--
WITH ALL DUE RESPECT, GENERAL...
...YOU CAN SHUT YOUR MOUTH!

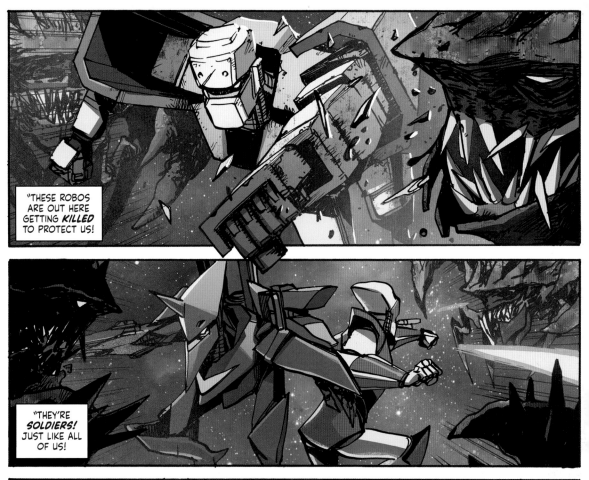

"THESE ROBOS ARE OUT HERE GETTING *KILLED* TO PROTECT US!"

"THEY'RE *SOLDIERS!* JUST LIKE ALL OF US!"

"DON'T YOU *DARE* QUESTION THEIR ALLEGIANCE!"

KTOOOM KTOOOM KTOOOM

NOW *COME ON,* YOU GUYS!

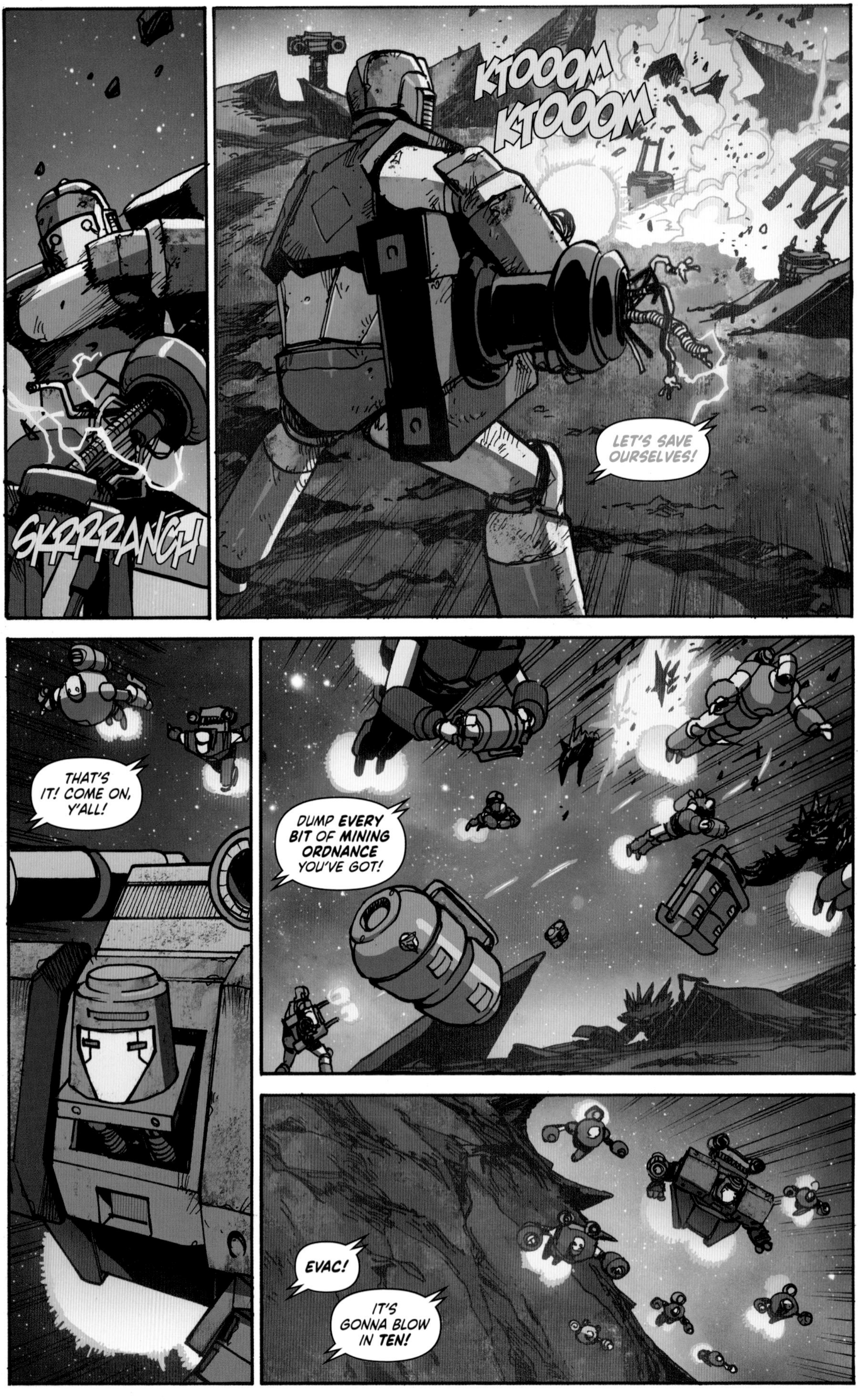
SKRRRANCH
KTOOOM
KTOOOM
LET'S SAVE OURSELVES!
THAT'S IT! COME ON, Y'ALL!
DUMP EVERY BIT OF MINING ORDNANCE YOU'VE GOT!
EVAC!
IT'S GONNA BLOW IN TEN!

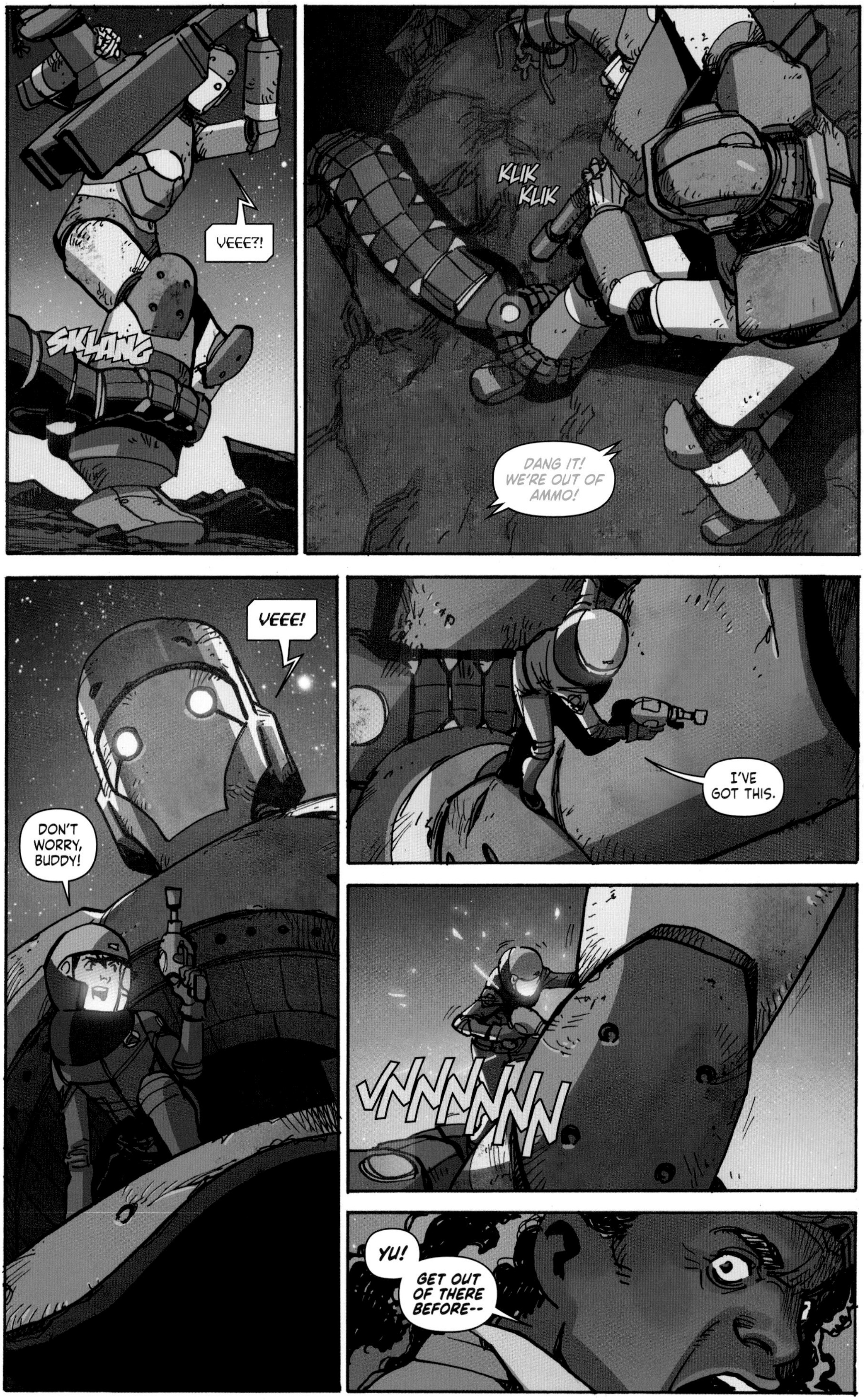
VEEE?!
SKLANG
KLIK
KLIK
DANG IT! WE'RE OUT OF AMMO!
VEEE!
DON'T WORRY, BUDDY!
I'VE GOT THIS.
VNNNNNN
YU!
GET OUT OF THERE BEFORE--

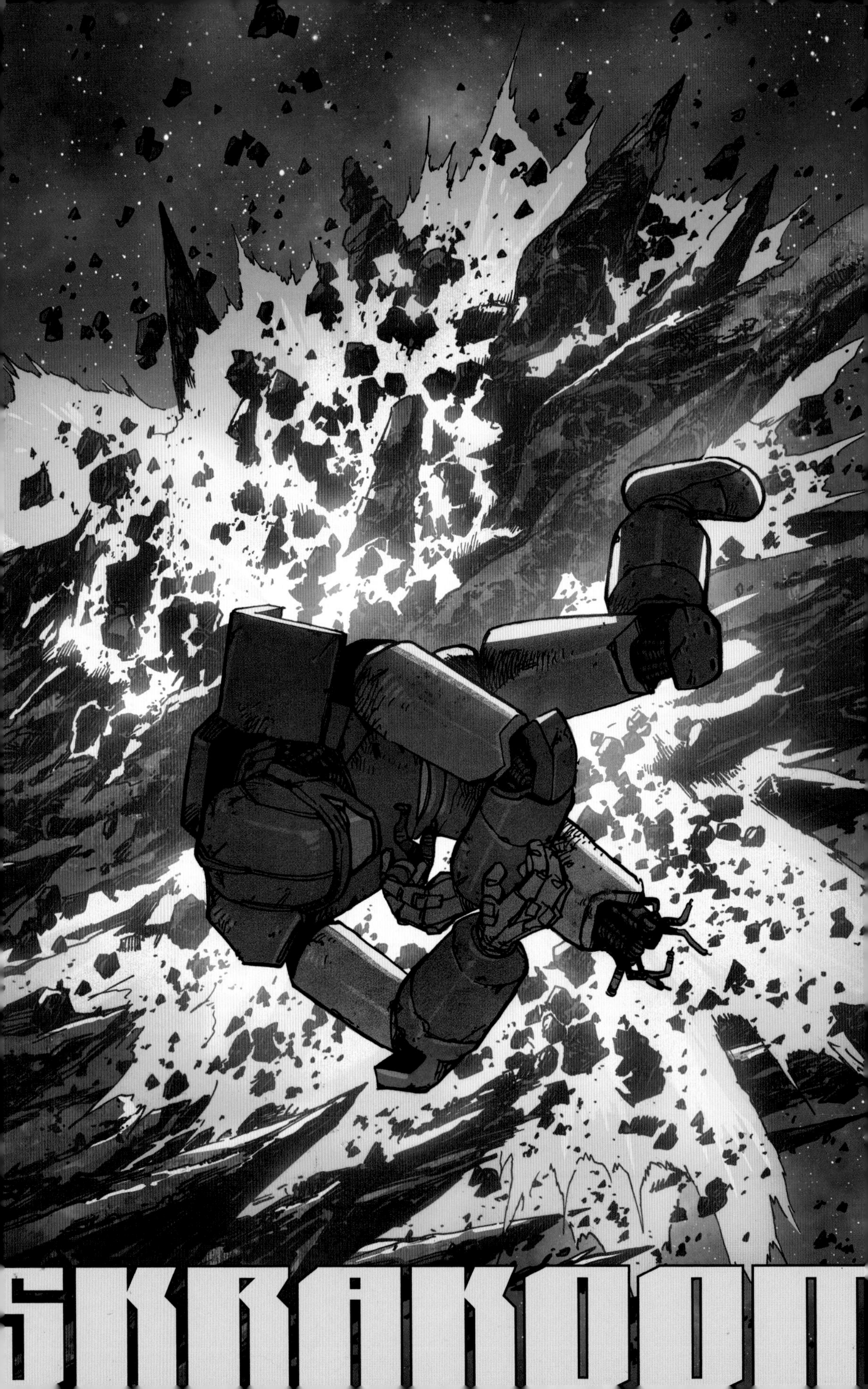
SKRAKOOM

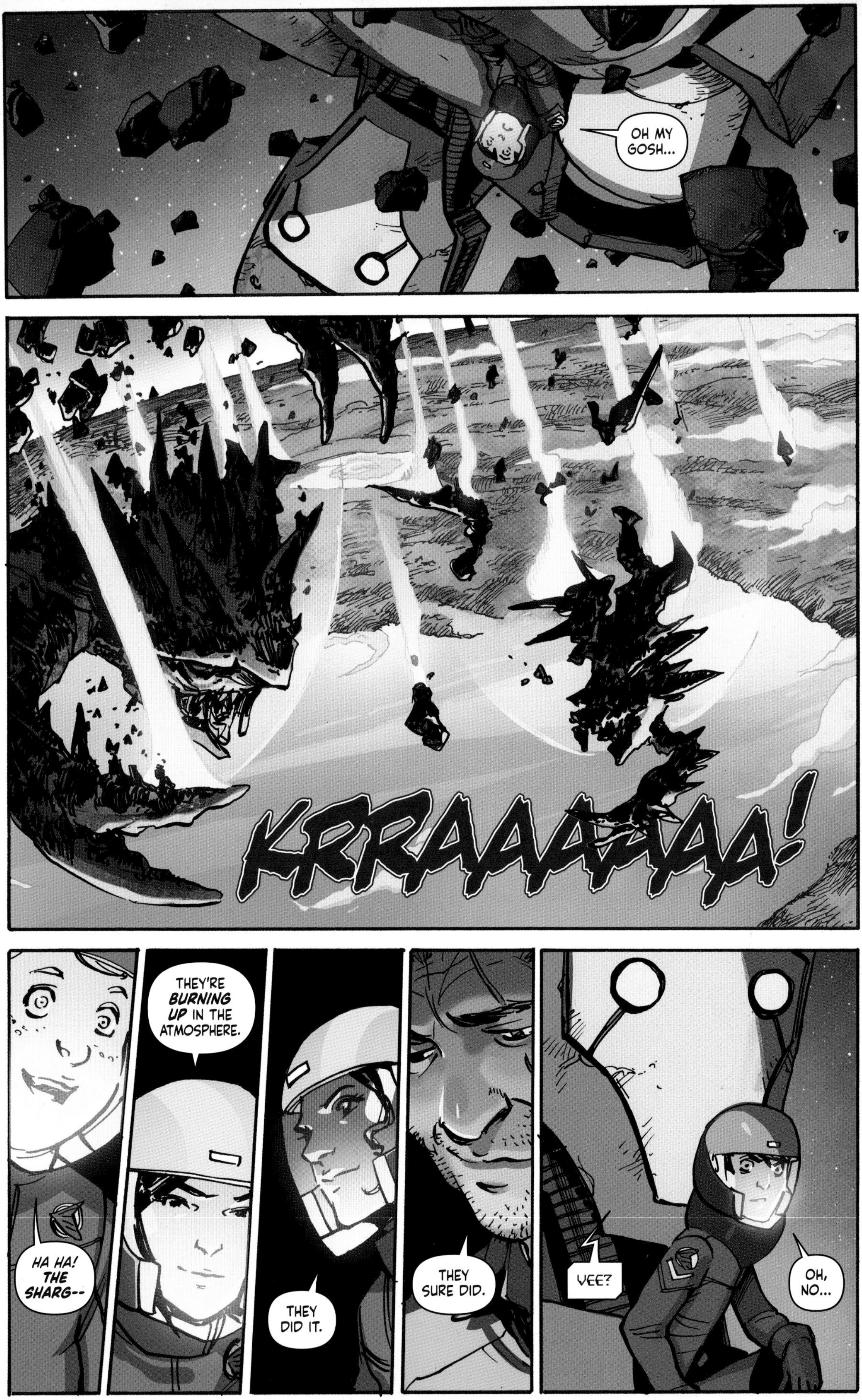
OH MY GOSH...
KRRAAAAAAA!
HA HA! THE SHARG--
THEY'RE BURNING UP IN THE ATMOSPHERE.
THEY DID IT.
THEY SURE DID.
VEE?
OH, NO...

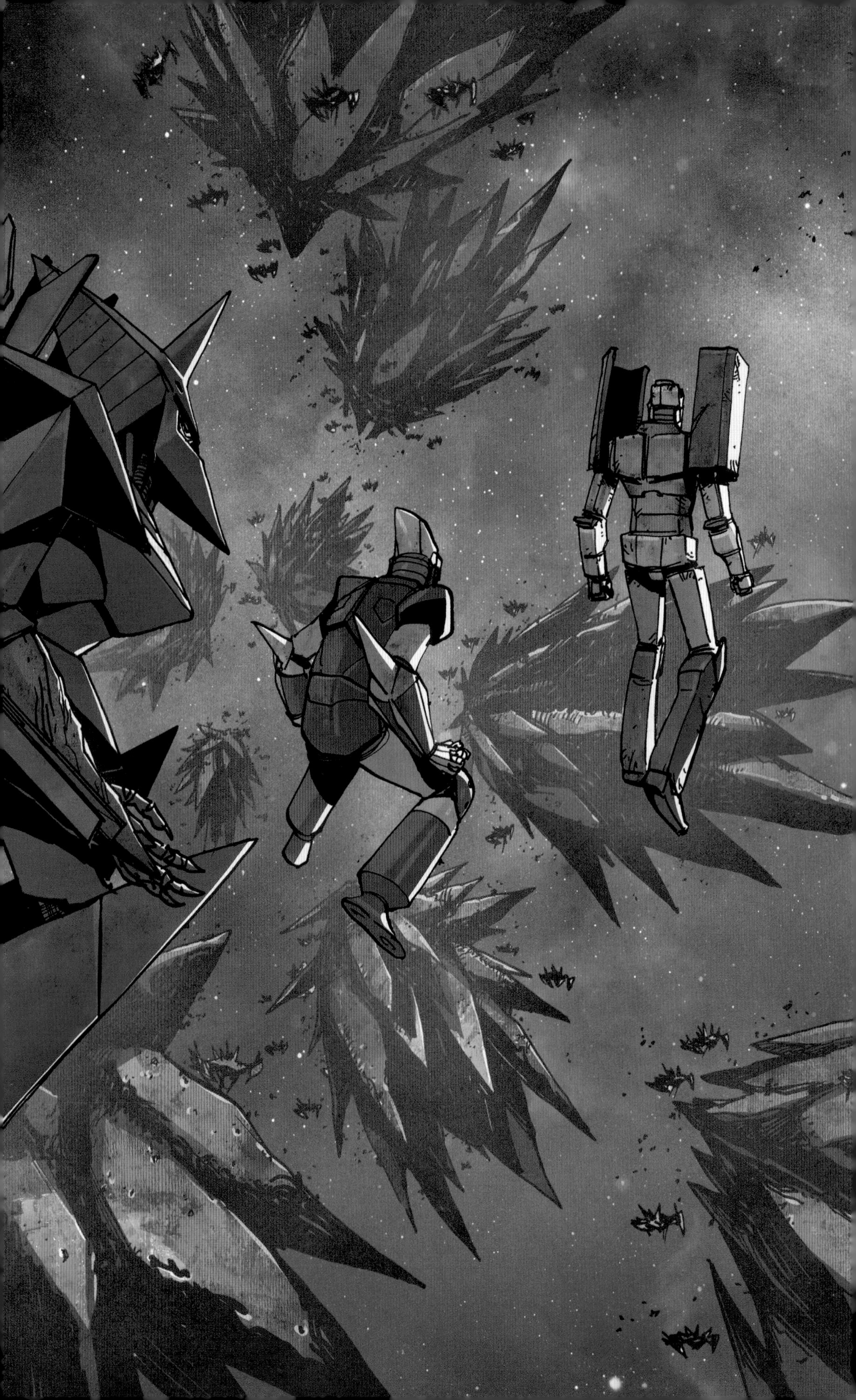

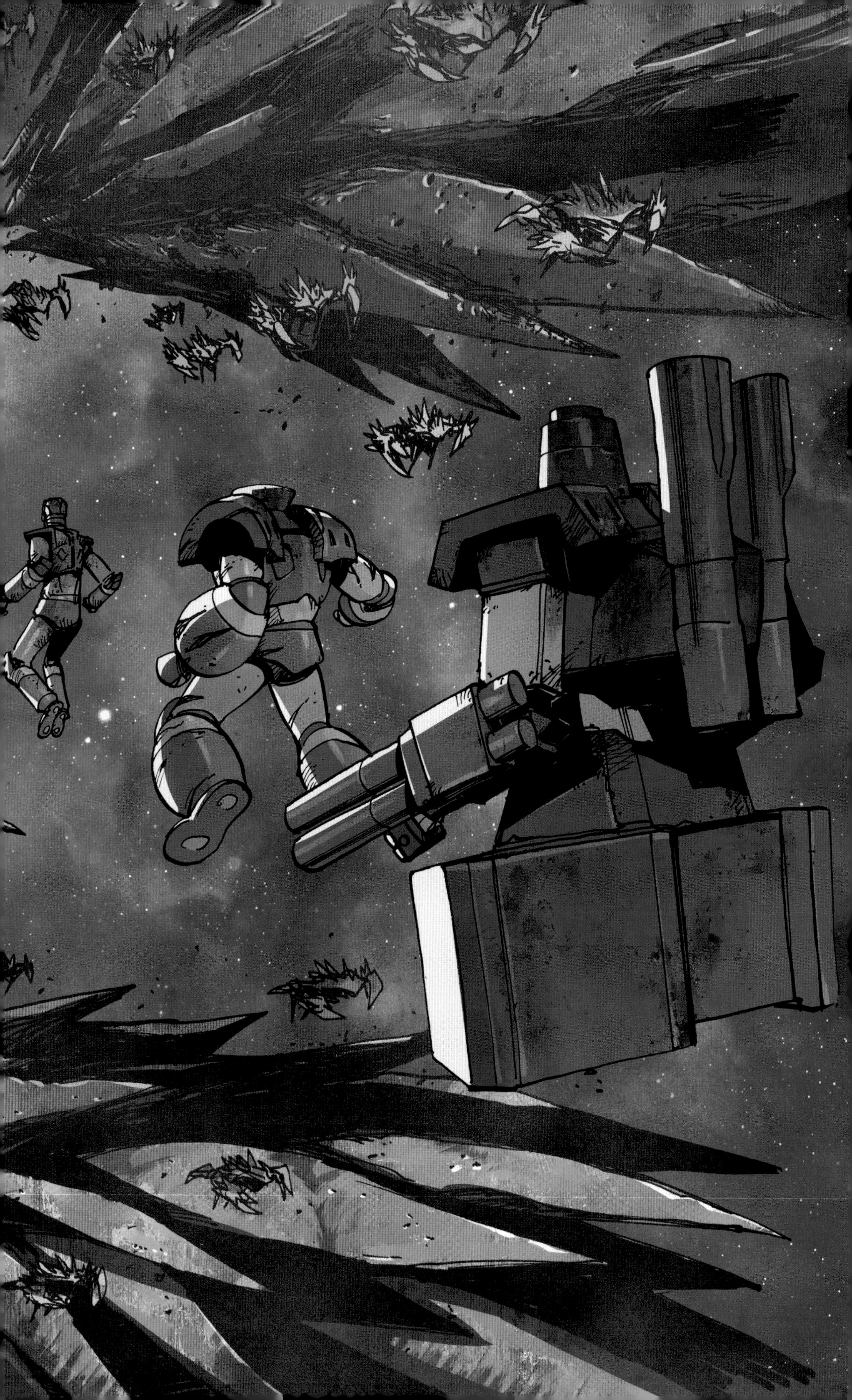

DEAR GOD...

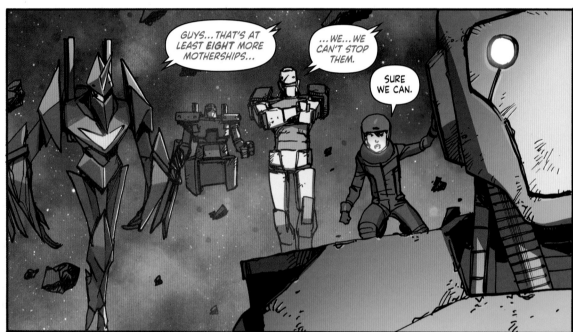

GUYS...THAT'S AT LEAST *EIGHT* MORE MOTHERSHIPS...

...WE...WE CAN'T STOP THEM.

SURE WE CAN.

WAKE UP, YU!

WE CAN'T DO IT THIS TIME!

DAMMIT, PARK! WHAT DID I TELL YOU?

WE ALL PICKED OUR SIDE! NOW WE GOTTA--

THIS DOESN'T HAVE *ANYTHING* TO DO WITH ANYONE'S *FATHER!*

THIS IS JUST--THIS IS JUST *REALITY!*

SKIP! CHIEF MAX! *TELL THEM!*

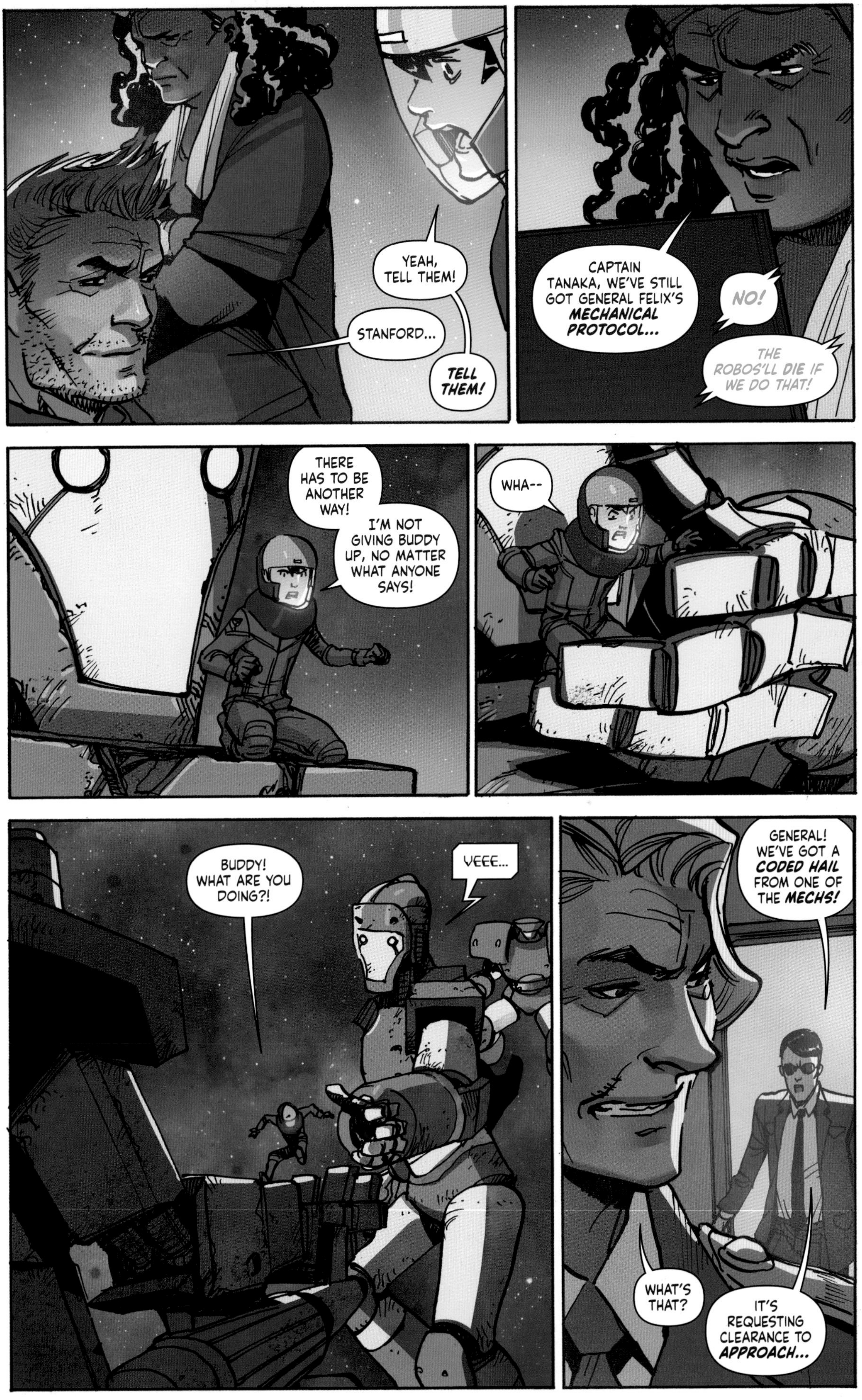
YEAH, TELL THEM!
STANFORD...
TELL THEM!
CAPTAIN TANAKA, WE'VE STILL GOT GENERAL FELIX'S MECHANICAL PROTOCOL...
NO!
THE ROBOS'LL DIE IF WE DO THAT!
THERE HAS TO BE ANOTHER WAY!
I'M NOT GIVING BUDDY UP, NO MATTER WHAT ANYONE SAYS!
WHA--
BUDDY! WHAT ARE YOU DOING?!
VEEE...
GENERAL! WE'VE GOT A CODED HAIL FROM ONE OF THE MECHS!
WHAT'S THAT?
IT'S REQUESTING CLEARANCE TO APPROACH...

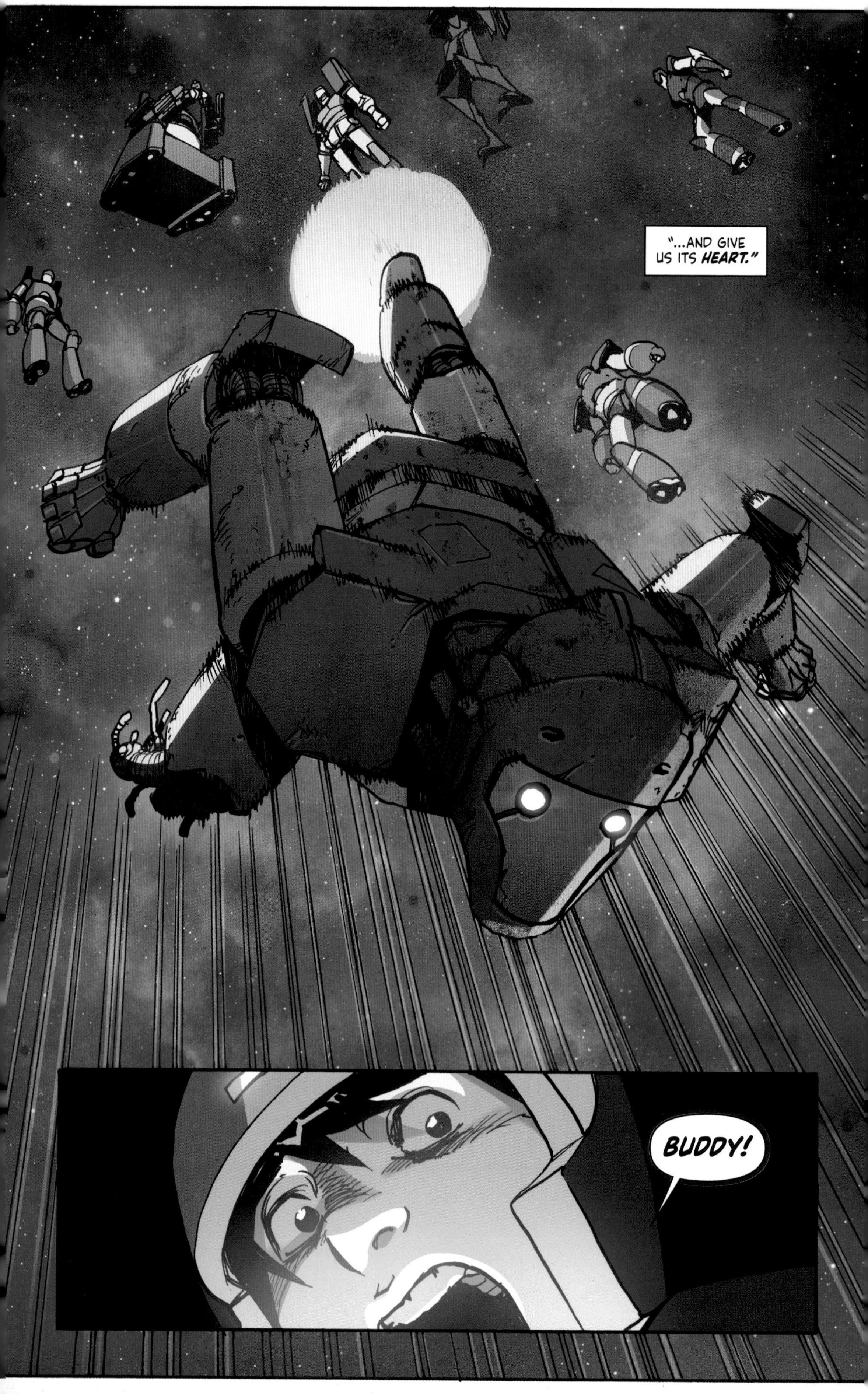
"...AND GIVE US ITS HEART."
BUDDY!

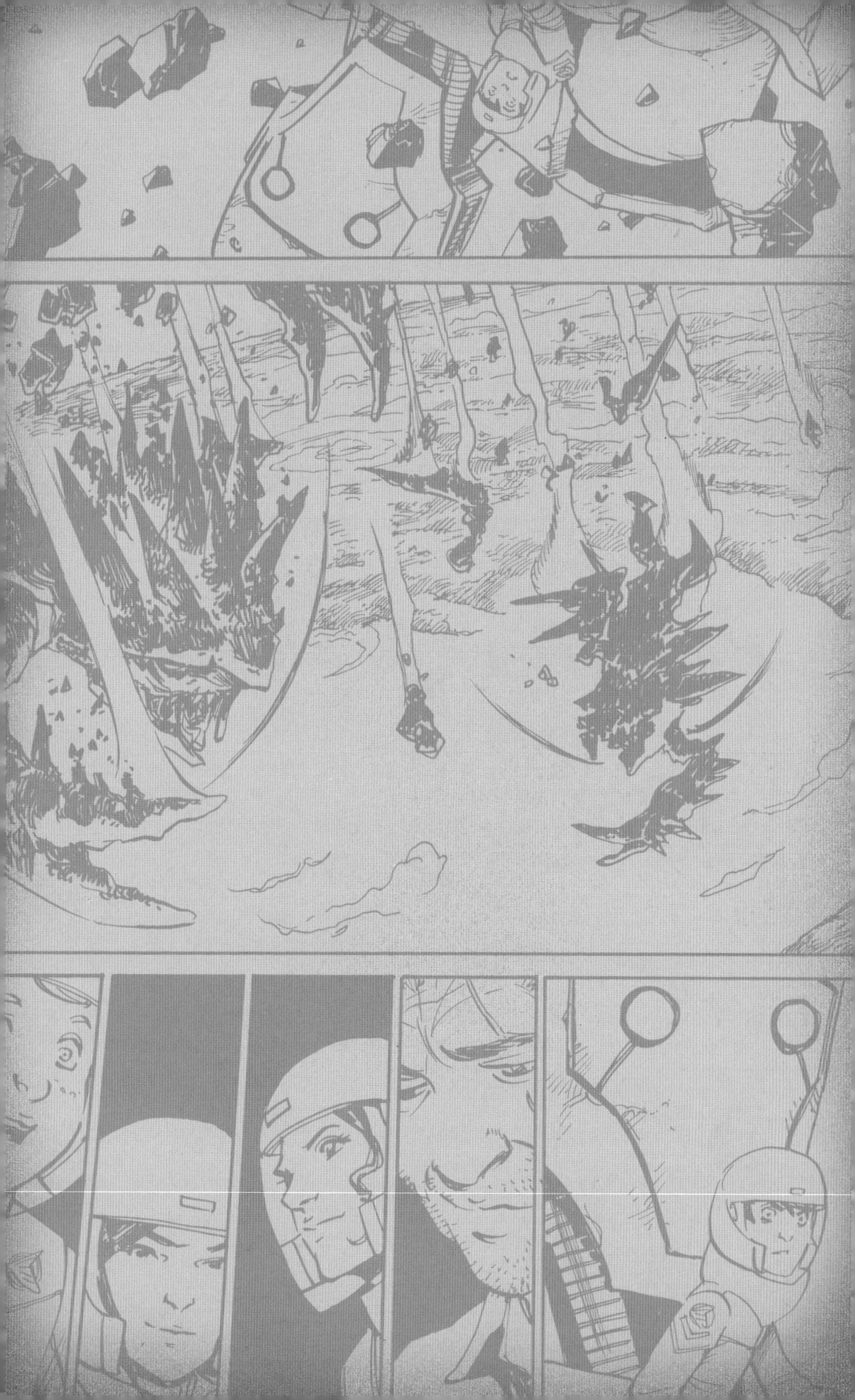

CHAPTER TEN

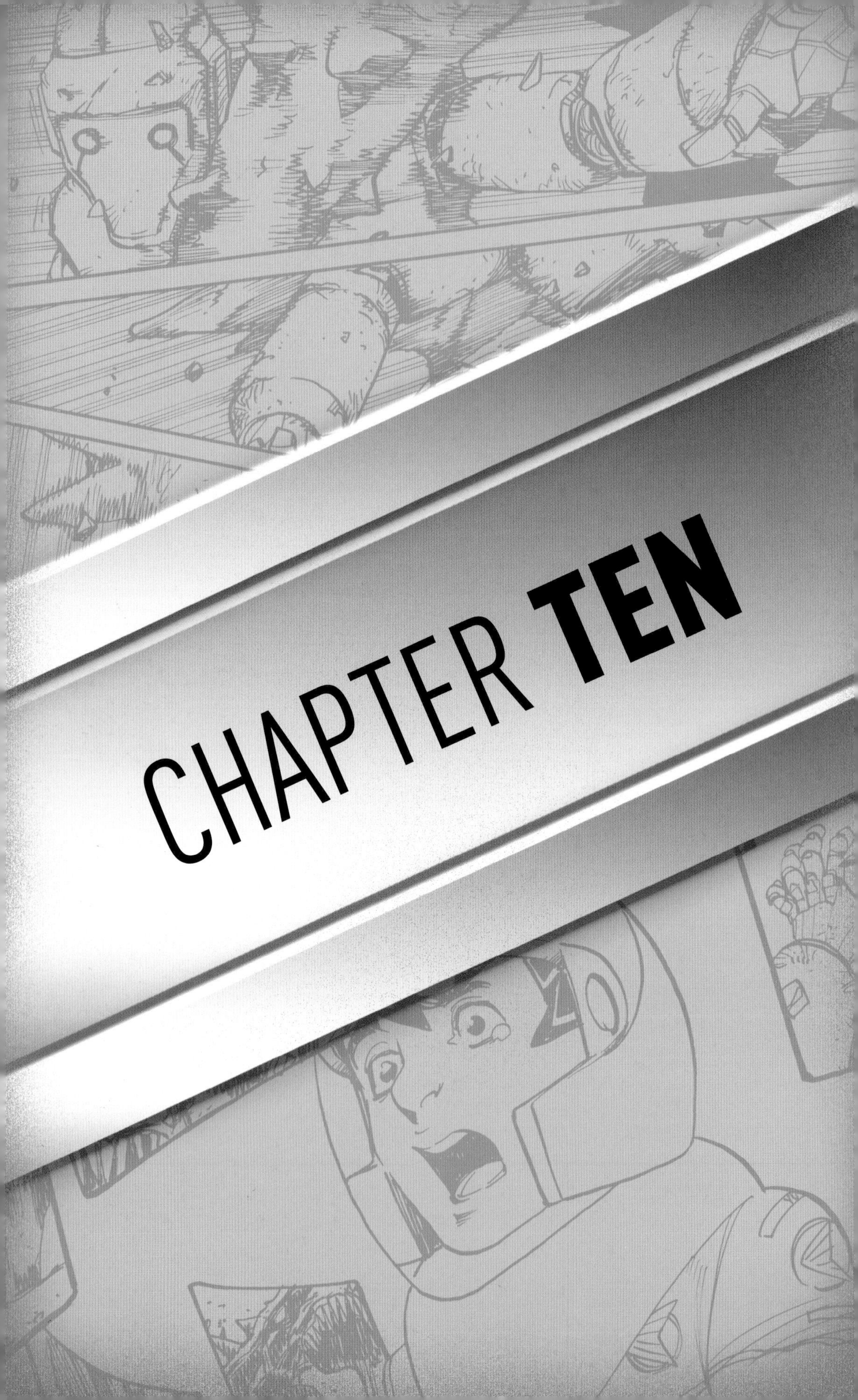

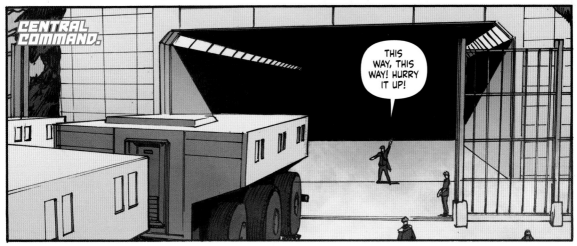

CENTRAL COMMAND.

THIS WAY, THIS WAY! HURRY IT UP!

HEY, NO NEED TO PUSH!

WHAT IS GOING ON HERE?

WE WANT TO SEE OUR DAUGHTER!

MR. AND MRS. SANCHEZ, MR. OLIVETTI. I'M GENERAL PARK.

THE SOLDIERS HAVEN'T TOLD US ANYTHING.

IS SOMETHING... IS SOMETHING WRONG WITH OUR KIDS?

YES.

THEY WENT AWOL WITH THEIR ROBOS. AND EVERYONE ON THIS PLANET COULD DIE AS A RESULT.

BUT NOW WE'VE GOT A CHANCE TO FIX THINGS, IF YOU CAN CONVINCE THEM TO--

SIR!

DAMMIT!

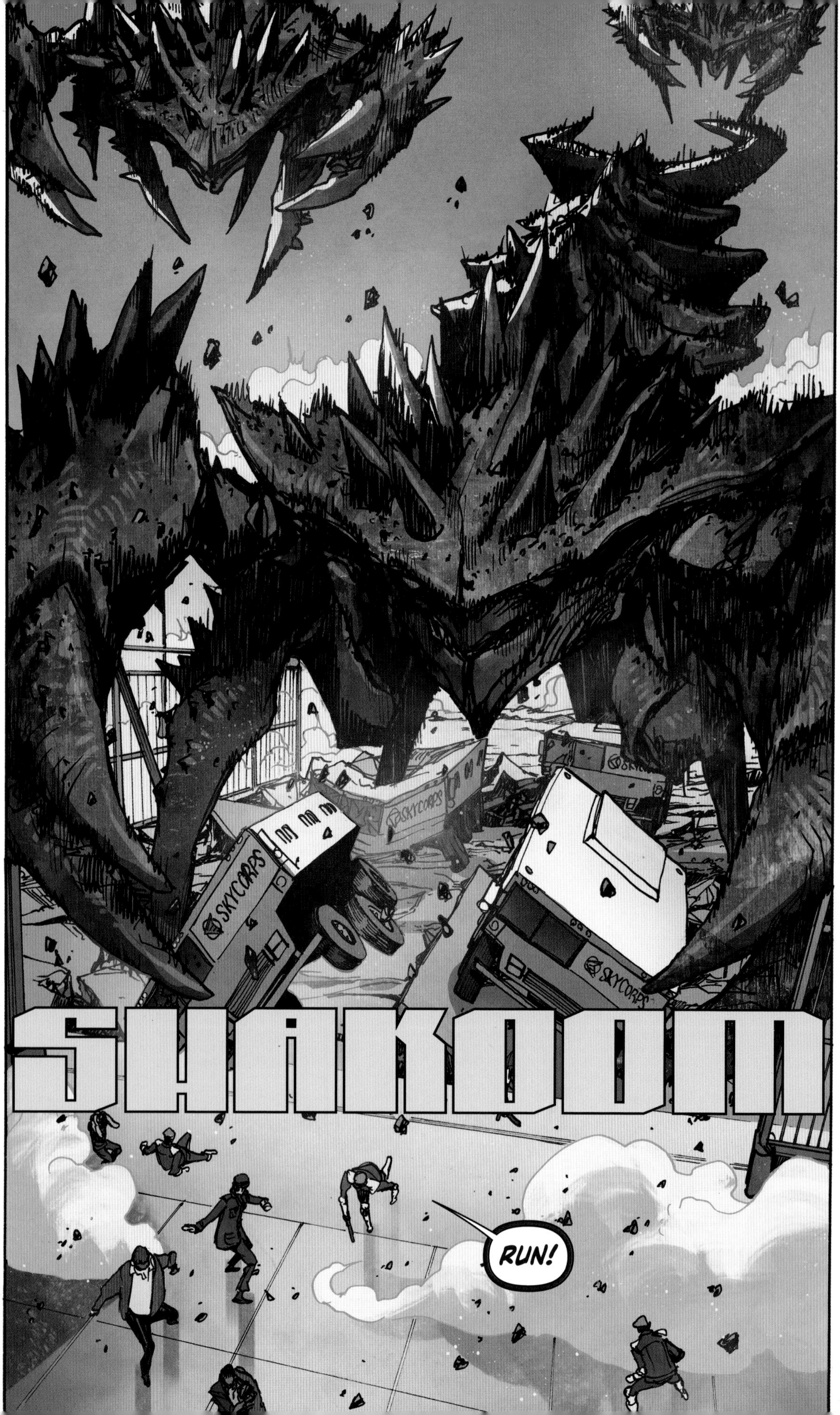
SKYCORPS
SKYCORPS
SKYCORPS
SKYCORPS
SHAKOOM
RUN!

CADETS! THIS IS GENERAL PARK!

YOUR **PARENTS** ARE NOW AT THE FACILITY--

--AND WE ARE **UNDER ATTACK** BY THE SHARG!

WHAT?

DID I **STUTTER**, OLIVETTI?

OUR **PARENTS**?

YES, SANCHEZ! YOU NEED TO RETURN TO BASE **IMMEDIATELY**!

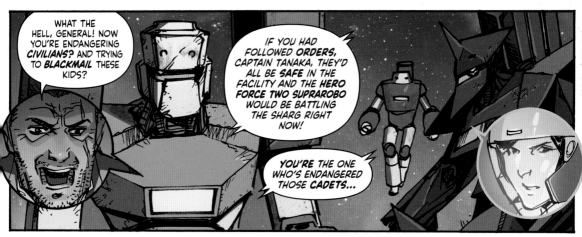

WHAT THE HELL, GENERAL! NOW YOU'RE ENDANGERING **CIVILIANS**? AND TRYING TO **BLACKMAIL** THESE KIDS?

IF YOU HAD FOLLOWED **ORDERS**, CAPTAIN TANAKA, THEY'D ALL BE **SAFE** IN THE FACILITY AND THE **HERO FORCE TWO SUPRAROBO** WOULD BE BATTLING THE SHARG RIGHT NOW!

YOU'RE THE ONE WHO'S ENDANGERED THOSE **CADETS**...

...INCLUDING MY OWN DAUGHTER!

DADDY...

I THOUGHT YOU KNEW YOUR **DUTY** BETTER THAN THIS, OLIVIA! GET BACK TO THE BASE, **NOW**, AND BRING YOUR FRIENDS WITH YOU!

WE NEED THOSE MECHS' **POWER CORES** OR WE'RE ALL **DOOMED**!

IT'S TOO LATE, DADDY...

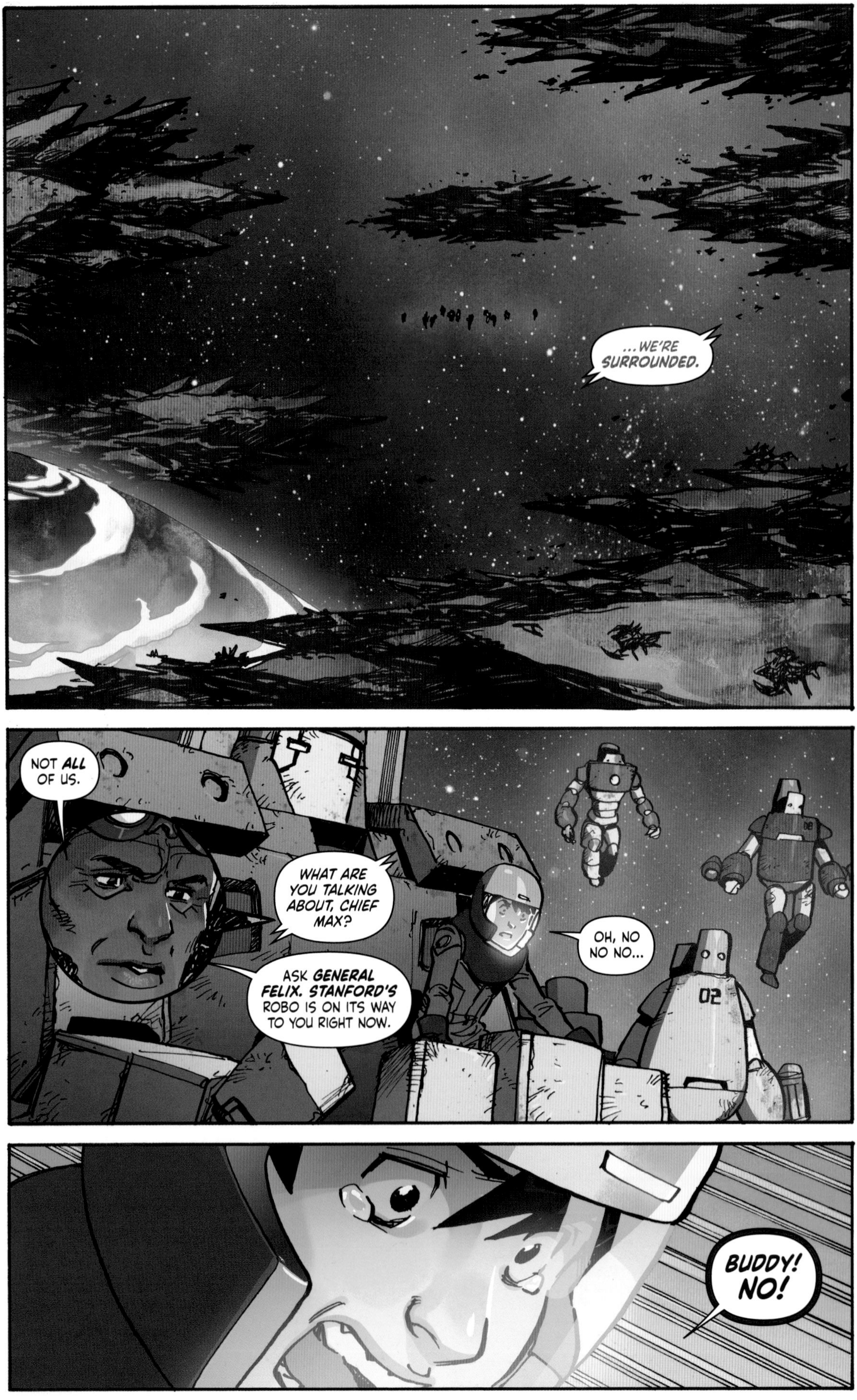
...WE'RE SURROUNDED.
NOT ALL OF US.
WHAT ARE YOU TALKING ABOUT, CHIEF MAX?
ASK GENERAL FELIX. STANFORD'S ROBO IS ON ITS WAY TO YOU RIGHT NOW.
OH, NO NO NO...
02
BUDDY! NO!

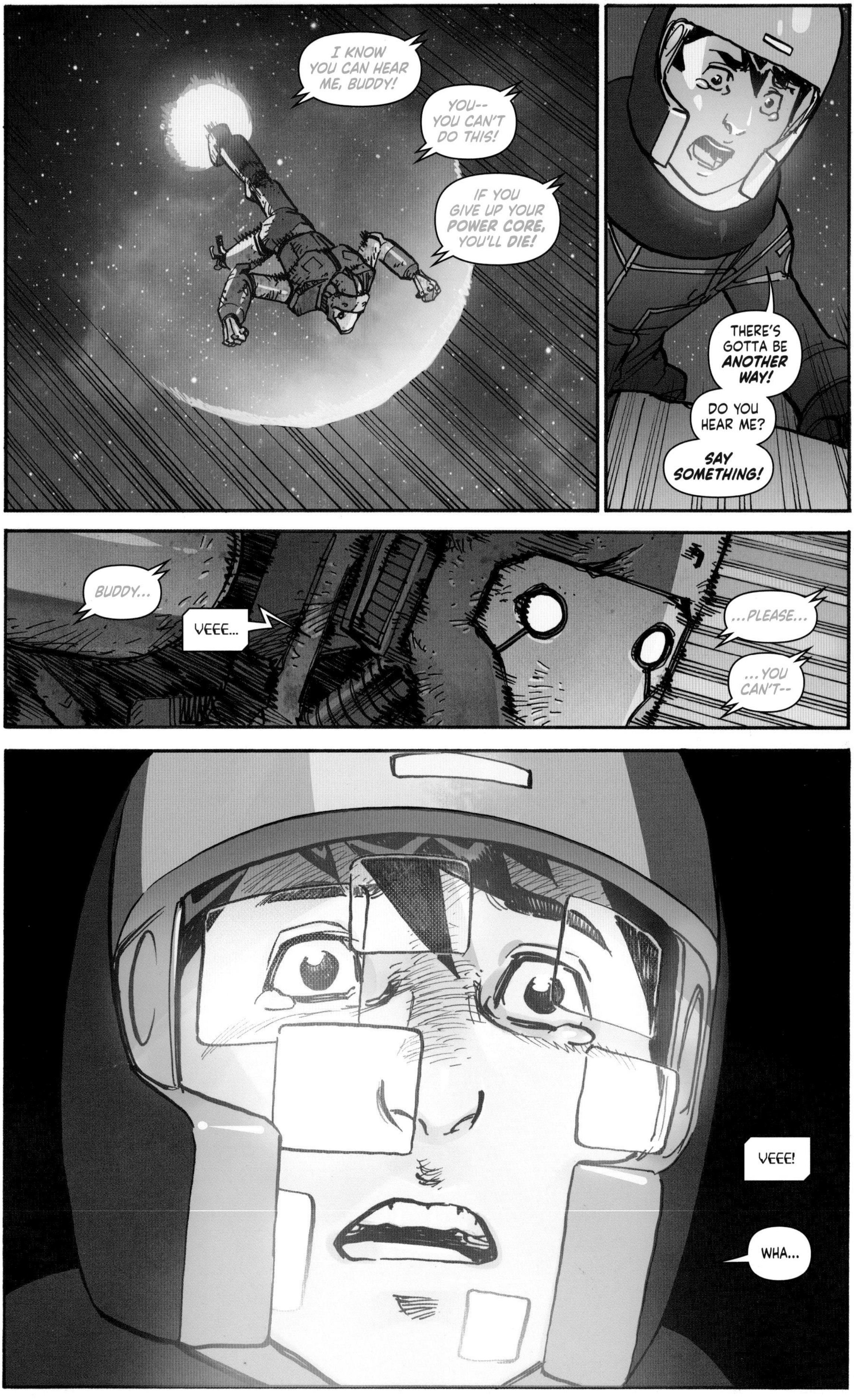
I KNOW YOU CAN HEAR ME, BUDDY!
YOU-- YOU CAN'T DO THIS!
IF YOU GIVE UP YOUR POWER CORE, YOU'LL DIE!
THERE'S GOTTA BE ANOTHER WAY!
DO YOU HEAR ME?
SAY SOMETHING!
BUDDY...
VEEE...
...PLEASE...
...YOU CAN'T--
VEEE!
WHA...

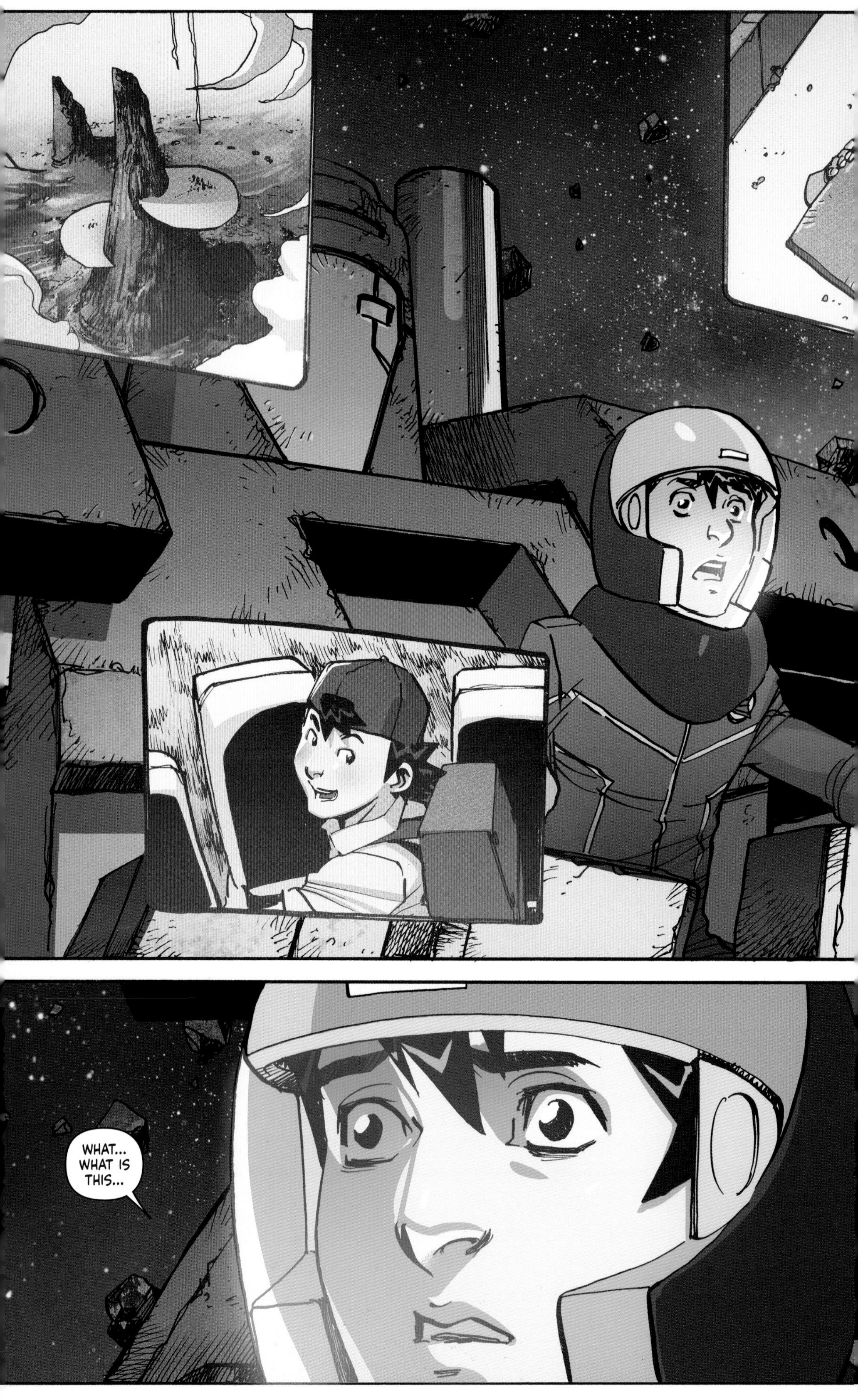
WHAT... WHAT IS THIS...

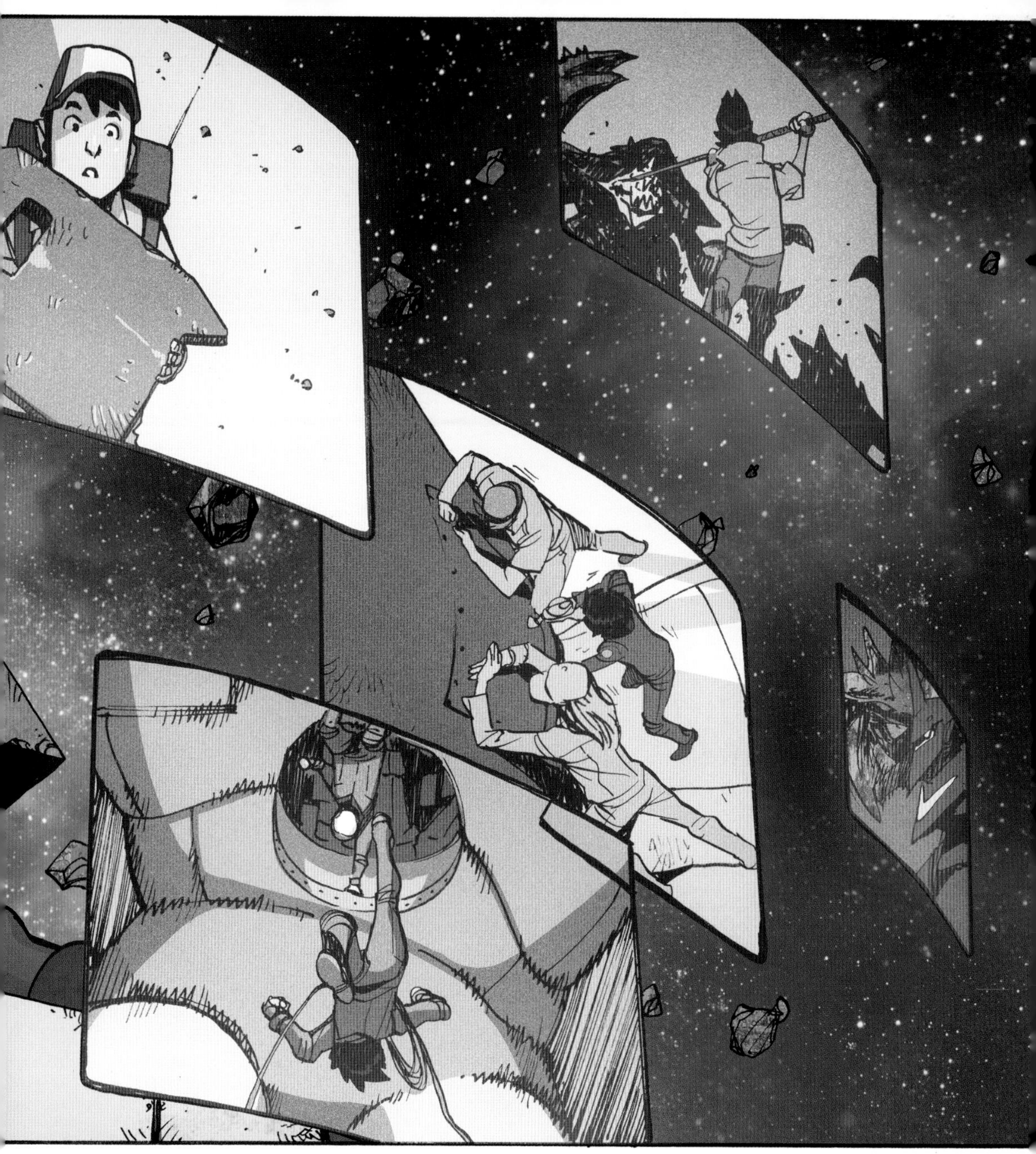

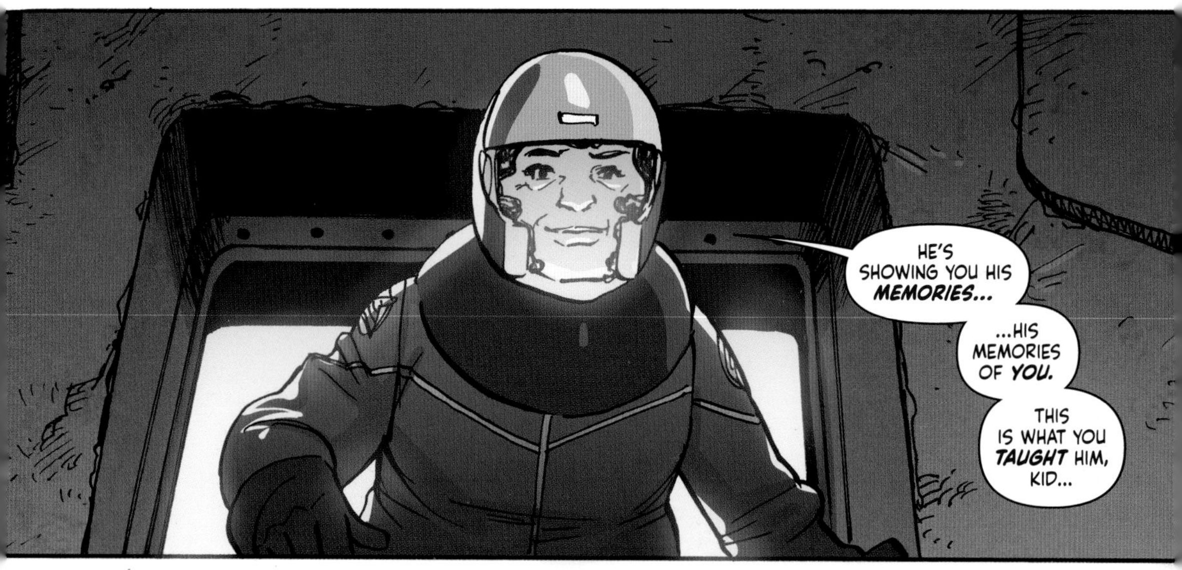
HE'S SHOWING YOU HIS MEMORIES...
...HIS MEMORIES OF YOU.
THIS IS WHAT YOU TAUGHT HIM, KID...

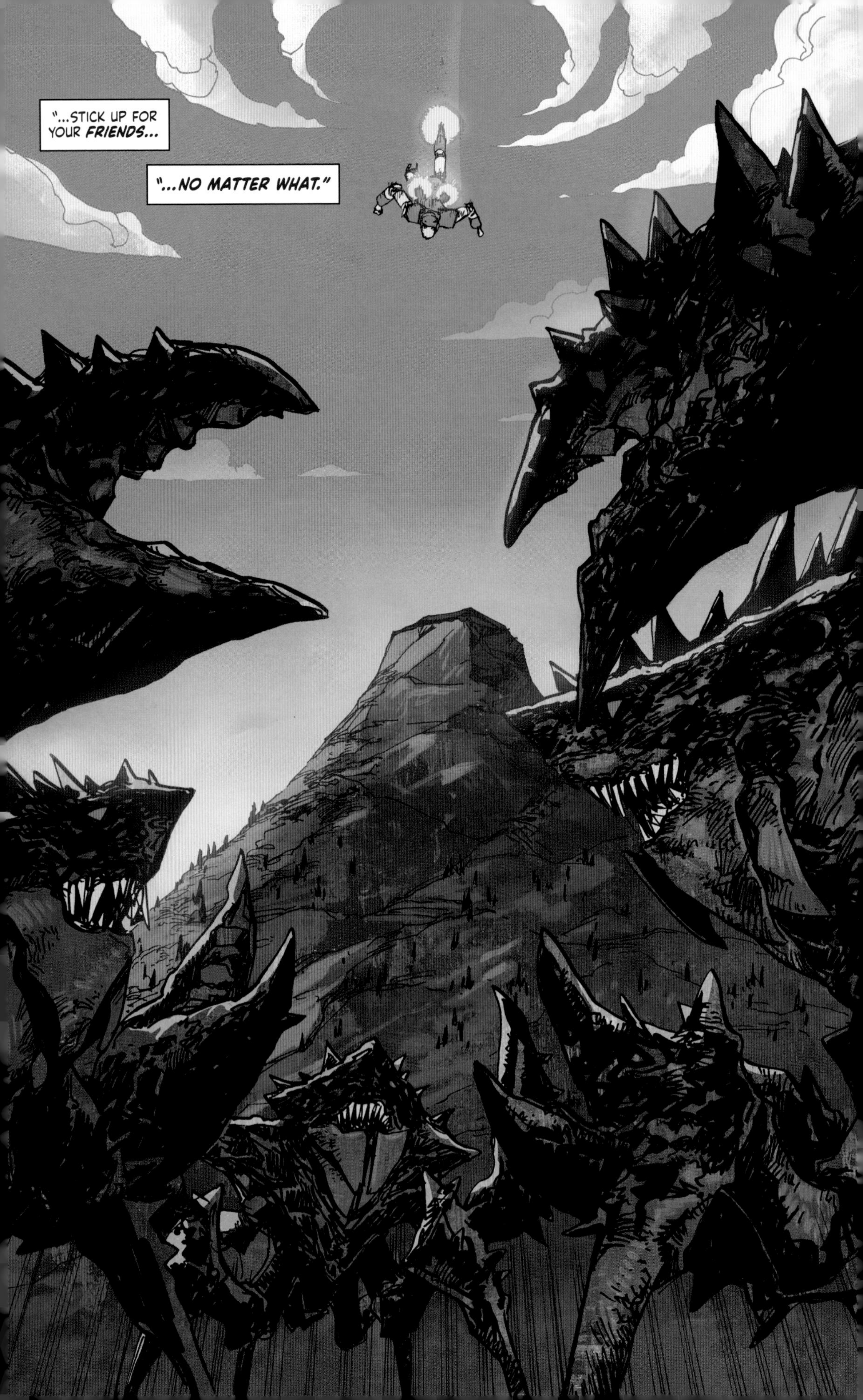
"...STICK UP FOR YOUR FRIENDS...
"...NO MATTER WHAT."

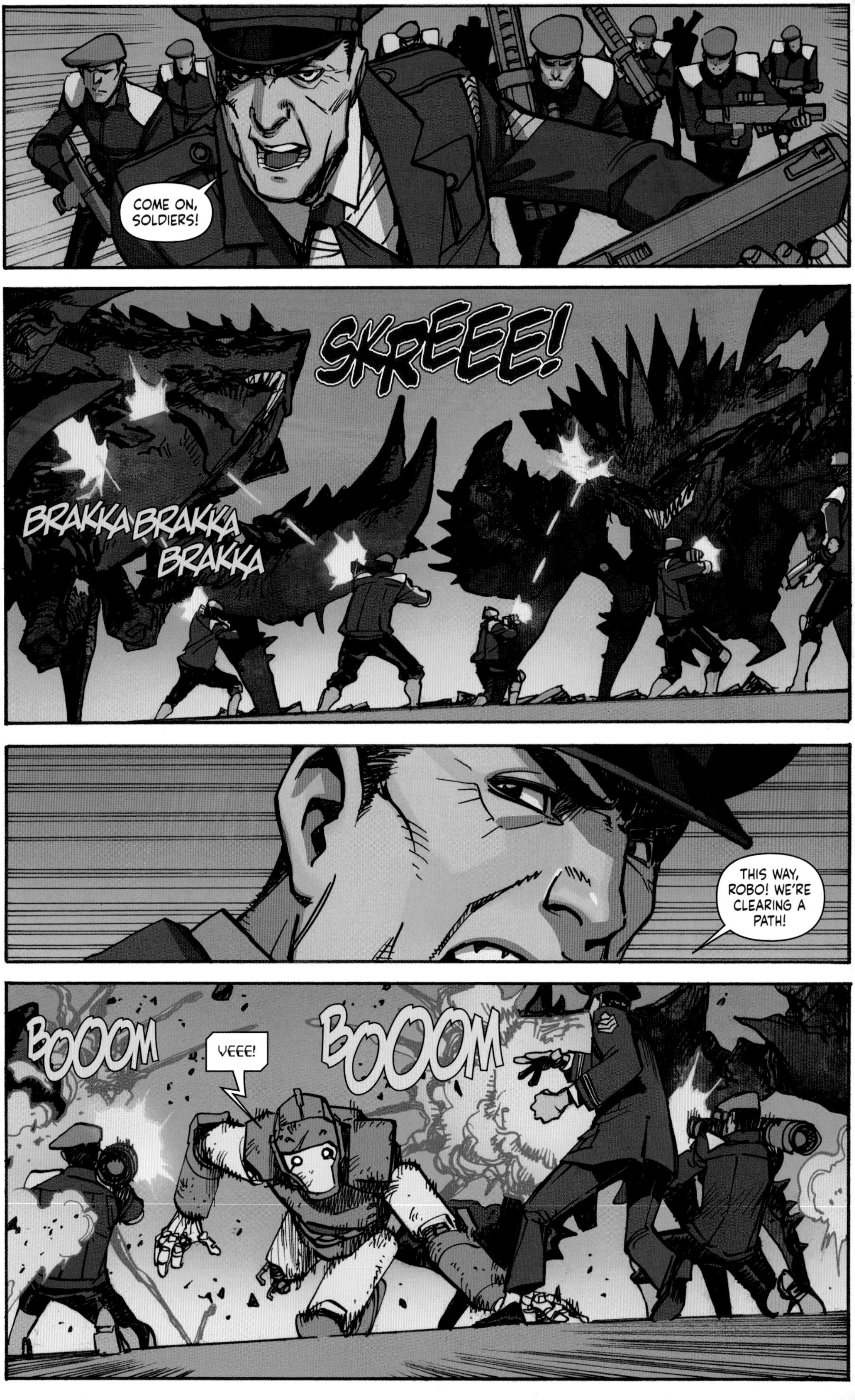
COME ON, SOLDIERS!
SKREEEE!
BRAKKA BRAKKA BRAKKA
THIS WAY, ROBO! WE'RE CLEARING A PATH!
BOOOM
VEEE!
BOOOM

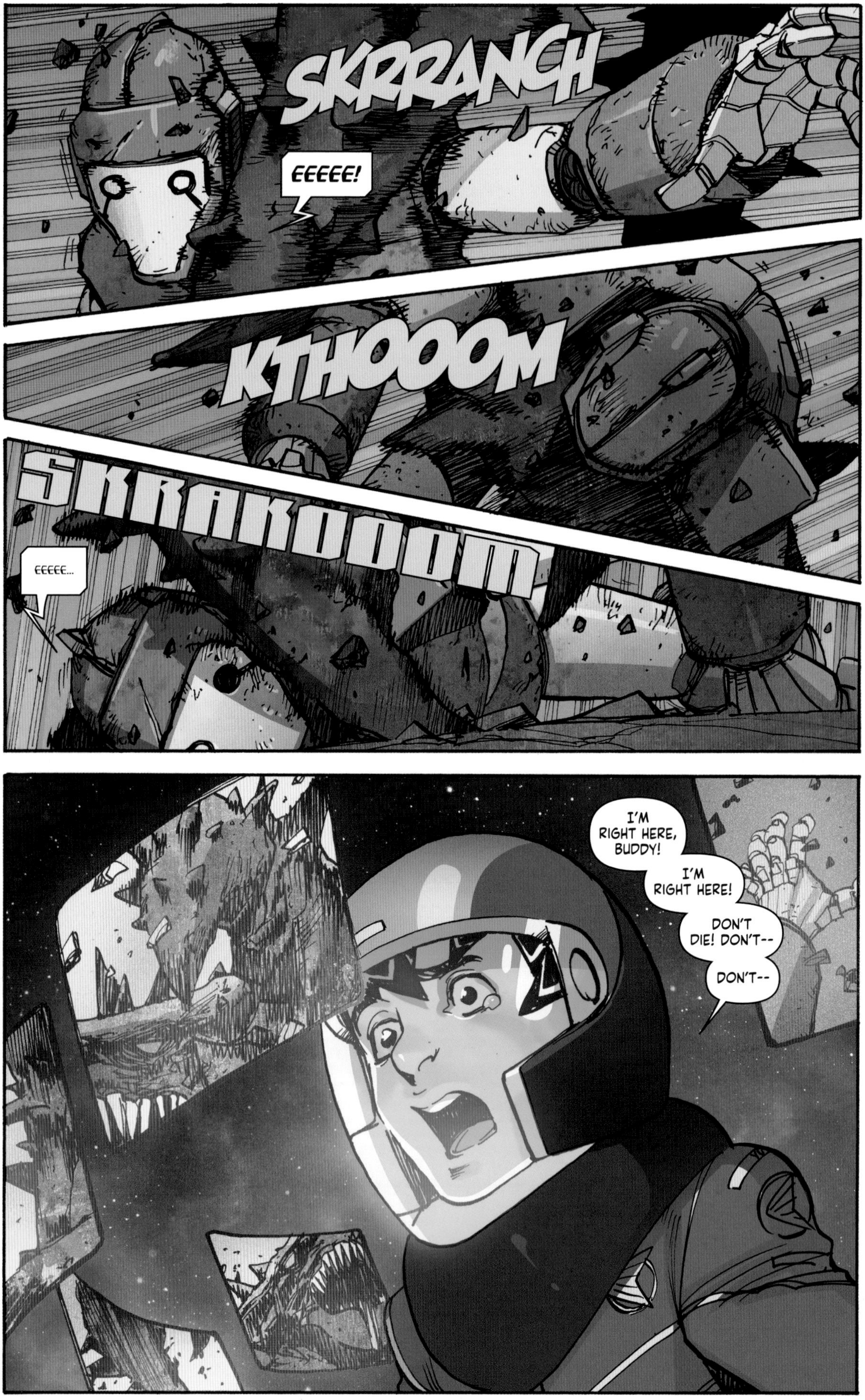
SKRRANCH
EEEEE!
KTHOOOM
SKRAKOOOM
EEEEE...
I'M RIGHT HERE, BUDDY!
I'M RIGHT HERE!
DON'T DIE! DON'T--
DON'T--

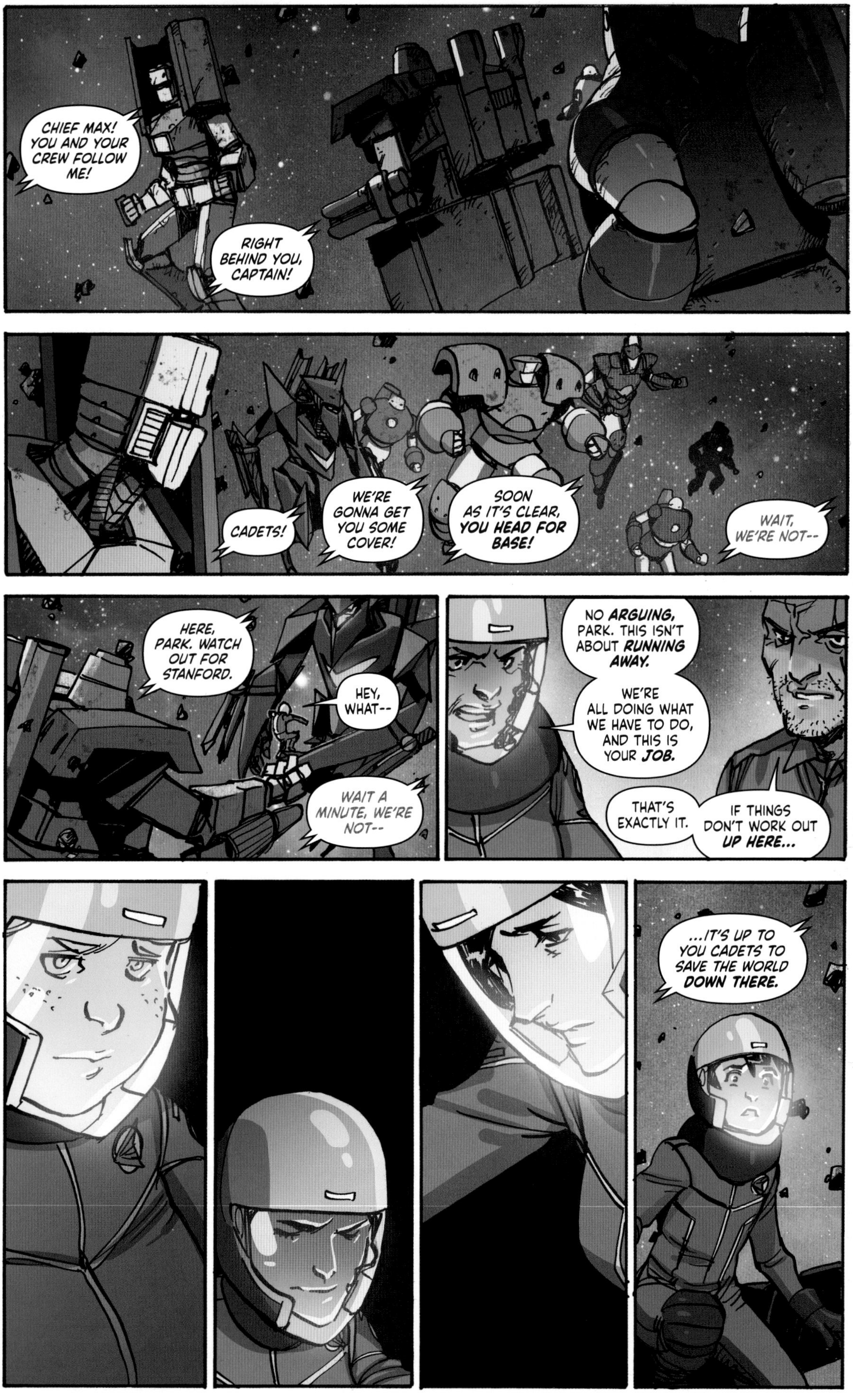
CHIEF MAX! YOU AND YOUR CREW FOLLOW ME!
RIGHT BEHIND YOU, CAPTAIN!
CADETS!
WE'RE GONNA GET YOU SOME COVER!
SOON AS IT'S CLEAR, YOU HEAD FOR BASE!
WAIT, WE'RE NOT--
HERE, PARK. WATCH OUT FOR STANFORD.
HEY, WHAT--
WAIT A MINUTE, WE'RE NOT--
NO ARGUING, PARK. THIS ISN'T ABOUT RUNNING AWAY.
WE'RE ALL DOING WHAT WE HAVE TO DO, AND THIS IS YOUR JOB.
THAT'S EXACTLY IT.
IF THINGS DON'T WORK OUT UP HERE...
...IT'S UP TO YOU CADETS TO SAVE THE WORLD DOWN THERE.

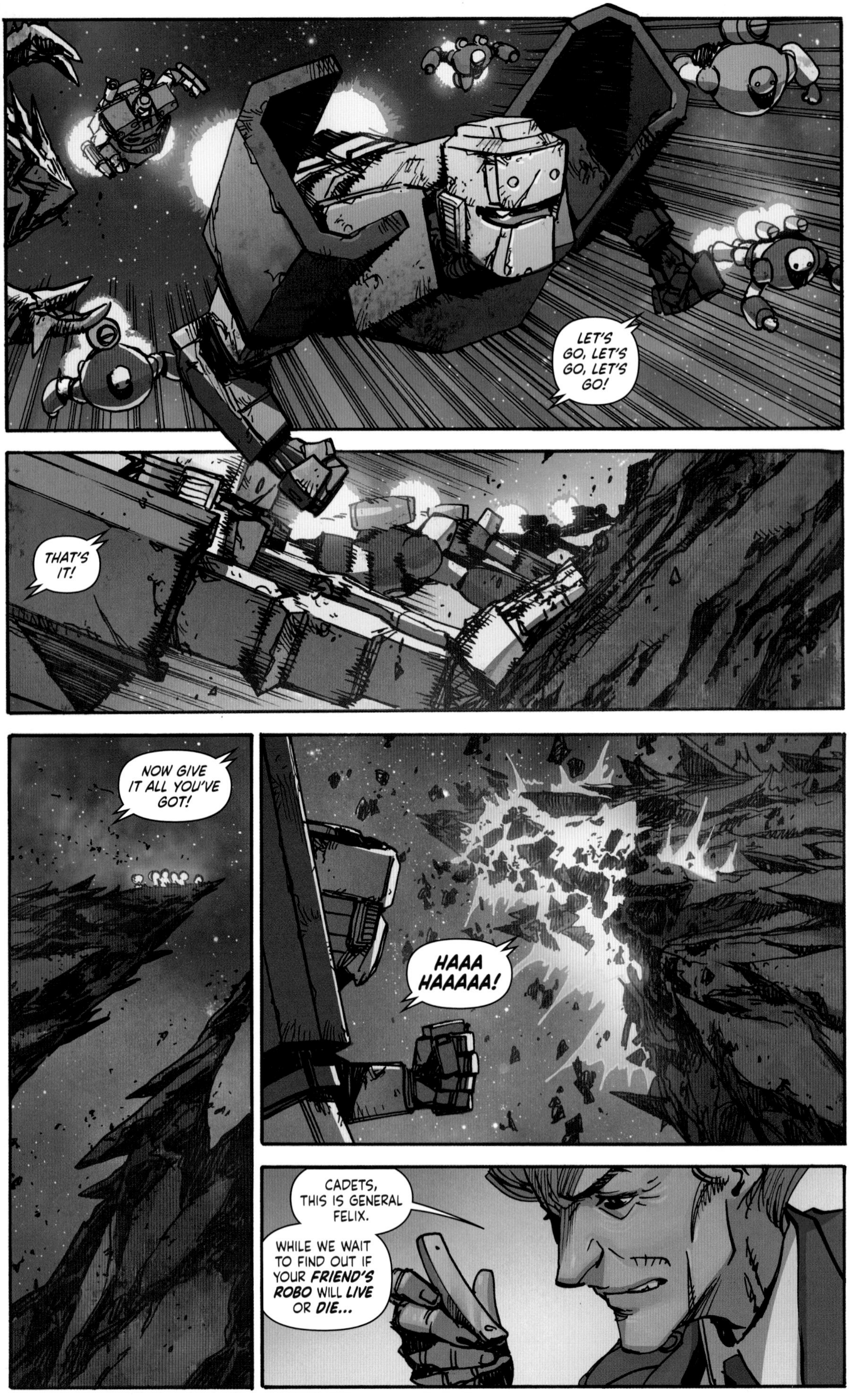
LET'S GO, LET'S GO, LET'S GO!
THAT'S IT!
NOW GIVE IT ALL YOU'VE GOT!
HAAA HAAAAA!
CADETS, THIS IS GENERAL FELIX.
WHILE WE WAIT TO FIND OUT IF YOUR FRIEND'S ROBO WILL LIVE OR DIE...

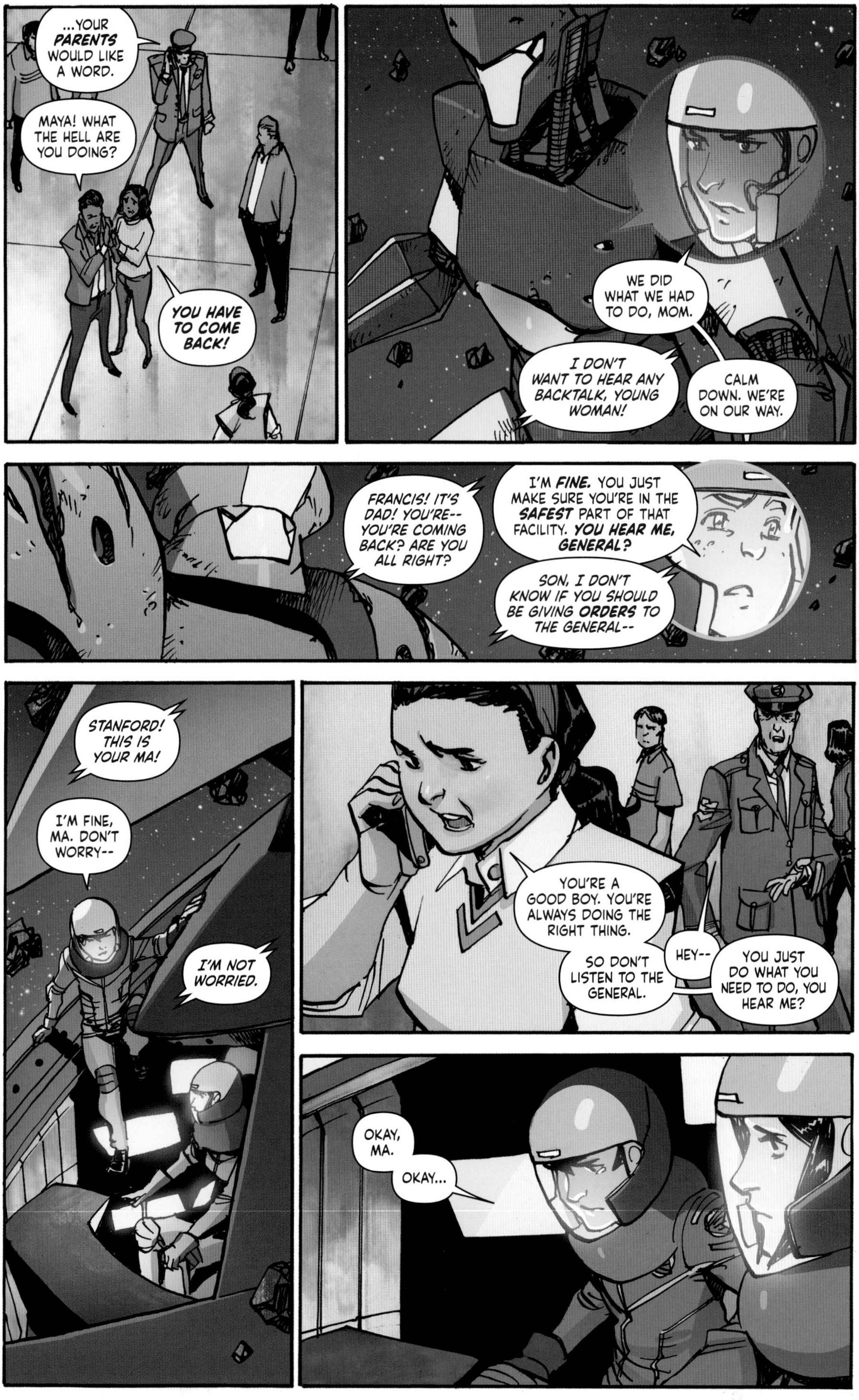
...YOUR PARENTS WOULD LIKE A WORD.
MAYA! WHAT THE HELL ARE YOU DOING?
YOU HAVE TO COME BACK!
WE DID WHAT WE HAD TO DO, MOM.
I DON'T WANT TO HEAR ANY BACKTALK, YOUNG WOMAN!
CALM DOWN. WE'RE ON OUR WAY.
FRANCIS! IT'S DAD! YOU'RE-- YOU'RE COMING BACK? ARE YOU ALL RIGHT?
I'M FINE. YOU JUST MAKE SURE YOU'RE IN THE SAFEST PART OF THAT FACILITY. YOU HEAR ME, GENERAL?
SON, I DON'T KNOW IF YOU SHOULD BE GIVING ORDERS TO THE GENERAL--
STANFORD! THIS IS YOUR MA!
I'M FINE, MA. DON'T WORRY--
I'M NOT WORRIED.
YOU'RE A GOOD BOY. YOU'RE ALWAYS DOING THE RIGHT THING.
SO DON'T LISTEN TO THE GENERAL.
HEY--
YOU JUST DO WHAT YOU NEED TO DO, YOU HEAR ME?
OKAY, MA.
OKAY...

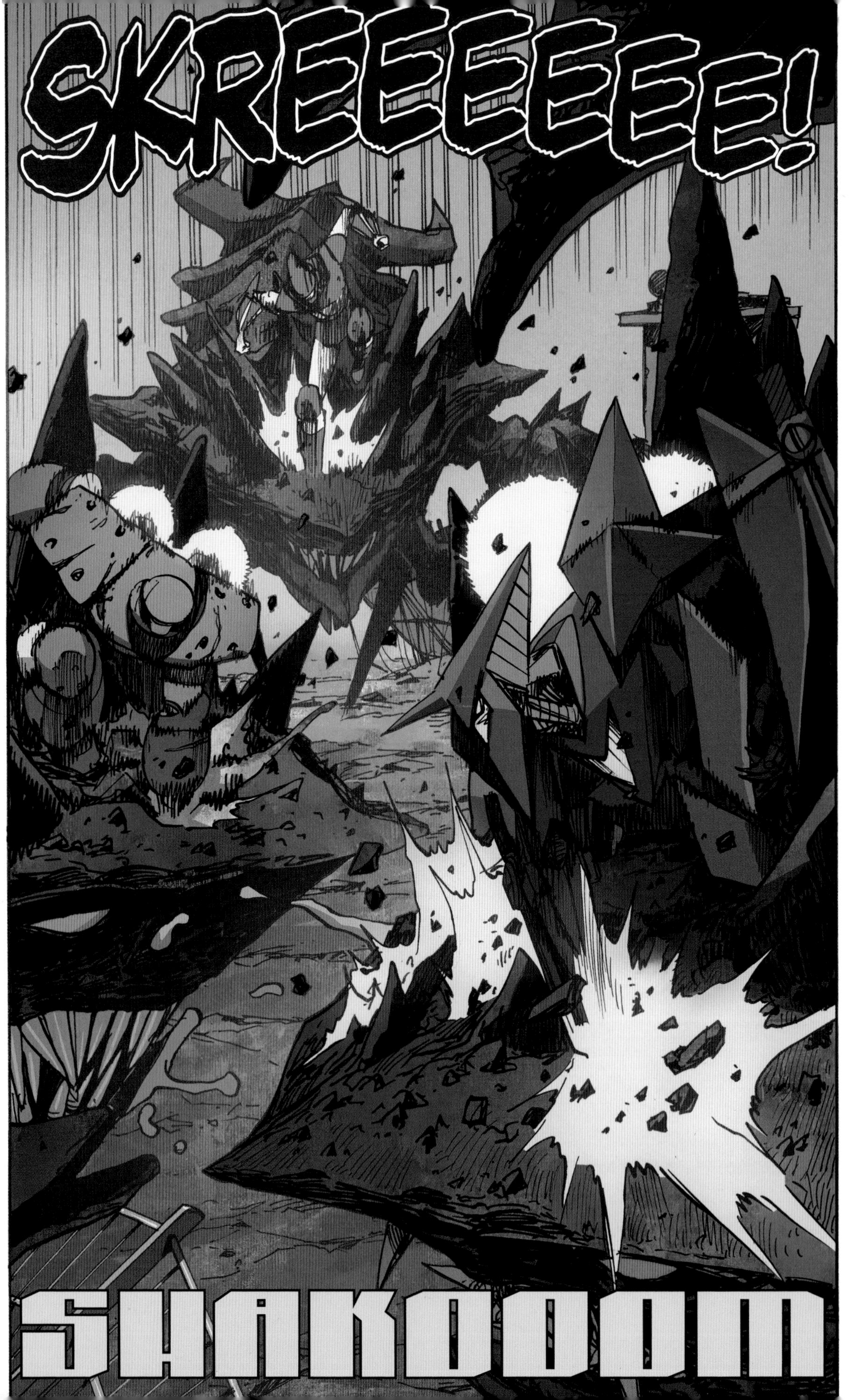
SKREEEEEEE!
SHAKOOOM

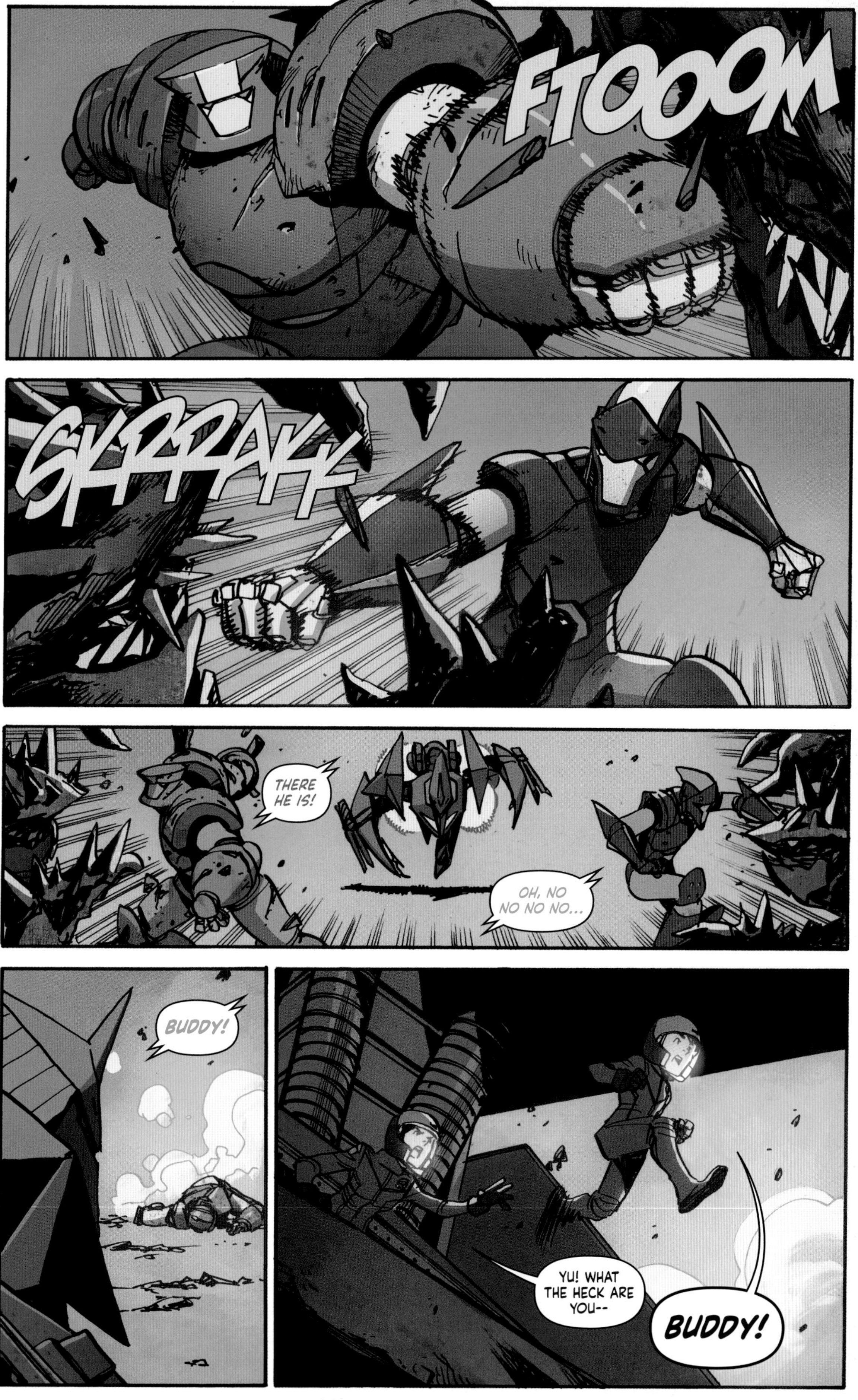
FTOOOM
SKRRAKK
THERE HE IS!
OH, NO NO NO NO...
BUDDY!
YU! WHAT THE HECK ARE YOU--
BUDDY!

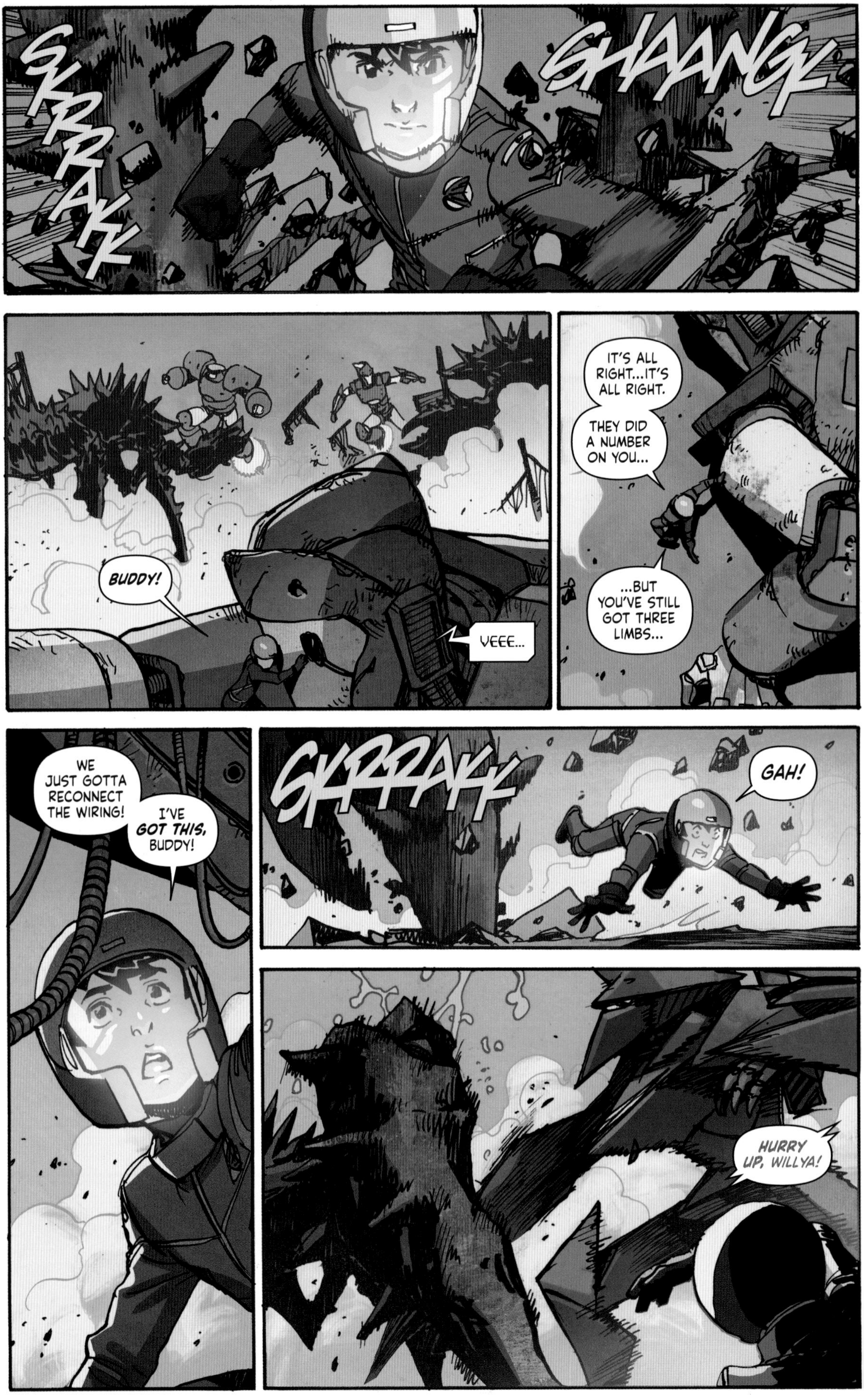
SKRRAKK
SHAANGK
BUDDY!
VEEE...
IT'S ALL RIGHT...IT'S ALL RIGHT.
THEY DID A NUMBER ON YOU...
...BUT YOU'VE STILL GOT THREE LIMBS...
WE JUST GOTTA RECONNECT THE WIRING!
I'VE GOT THIS, BUDDY!
SKRRAKK
GAH!
HURRY UP, WILLYA!

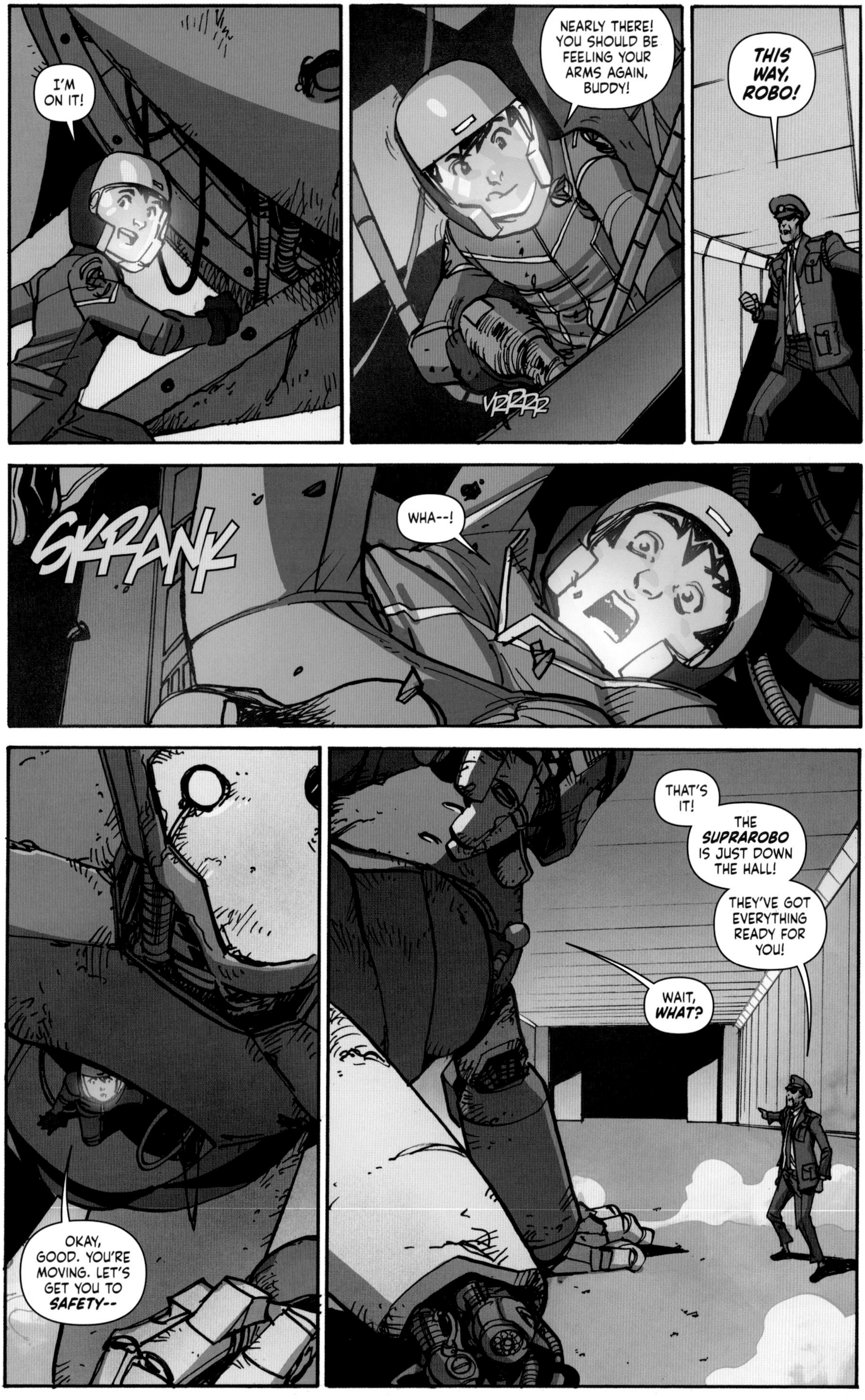
I'M ON IT!
NEARLY THERE! YOU SHOULD BE FEELING YOUR ARMS AGAIN, BUDDY!
VRRRRR
THIS WAY, ROBO!
SKRANK
WHA--!
OKAY, GOOD. YOU'RE MOVING. LET'S GET YOU TO SAFETY--
THAT'S IT!
THE SUPRAROBO IS JUST DOWN THE HALL!
THEY'VE GOT EVERYTHING READY FOR YOU!
WAIT, WHAT?

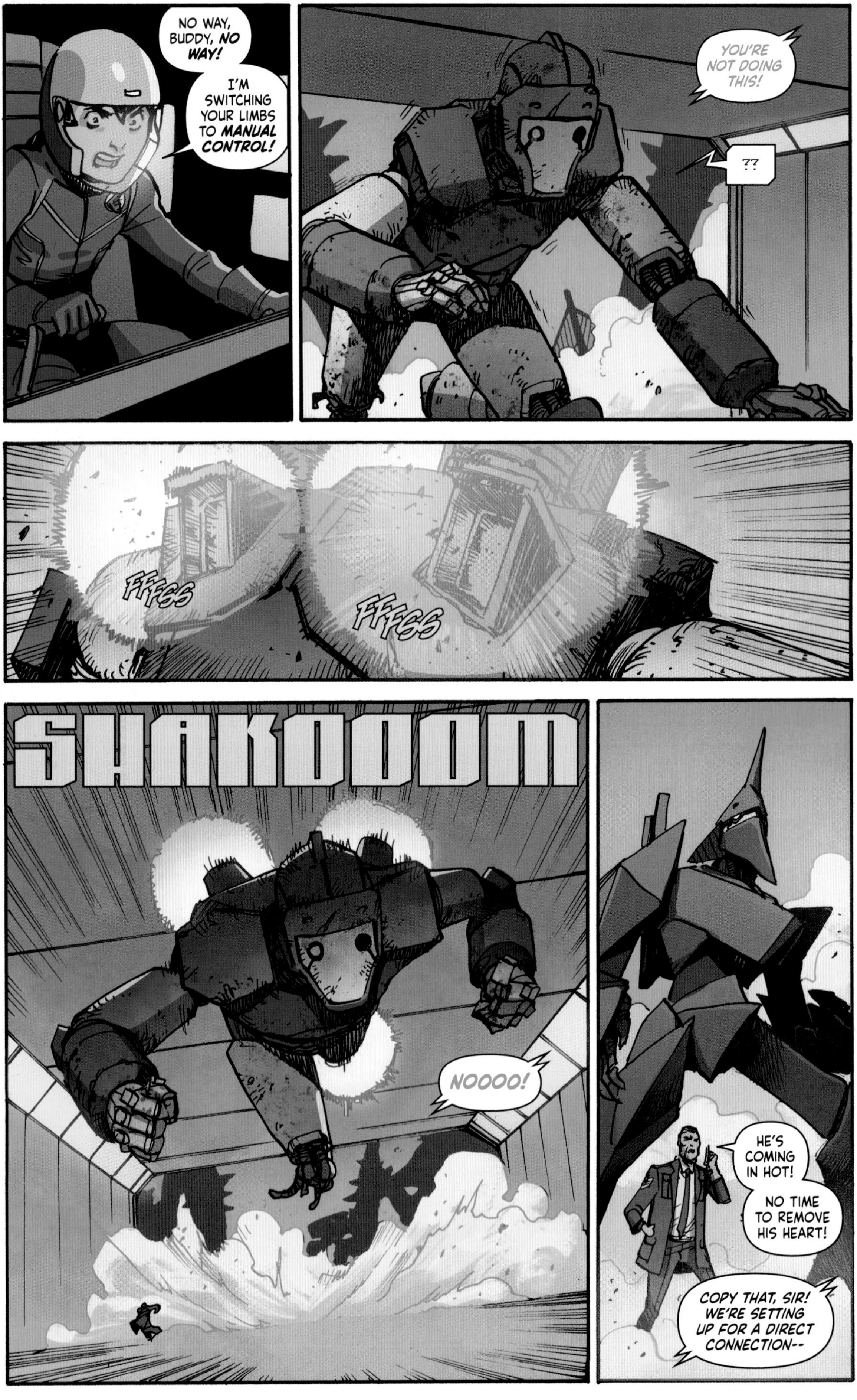
NO WAY, BUDDY, NO WAY!
I'M SWITCHING YOUR LIMBS TO MANUAL CONTROL!
YOU'RE NOT DOING THIS!
??
FFFSS
FFFSS
SHAKOOOM
NOOOO!
HE'S COMING IN HOT!
NO TIME TO REMOVE HIS HEART!
COPY THAT, SIR! WE'RE SETTING UP FOR A DIRECT CONNECTION--

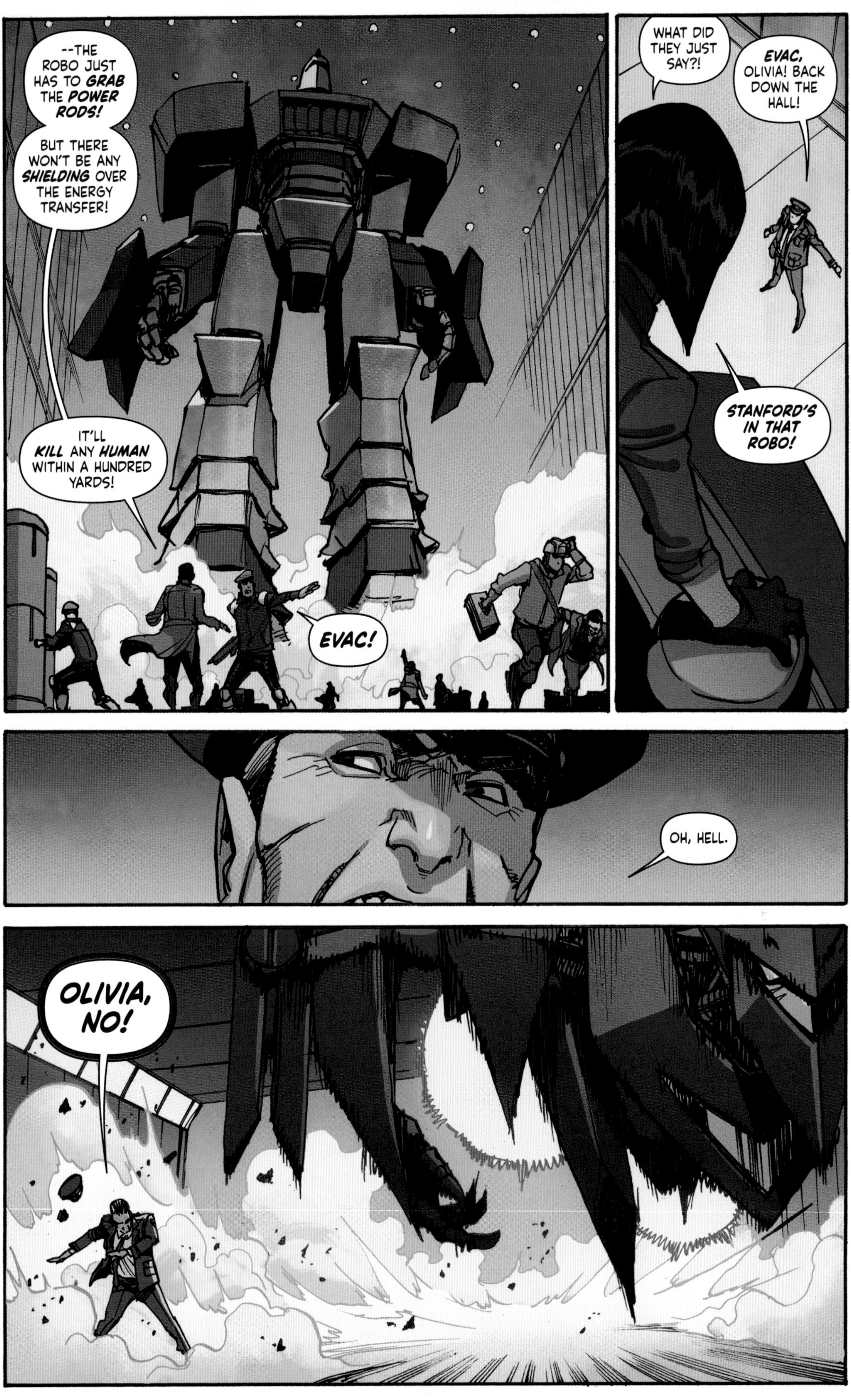
--THE ROBO JUST HAS TO GRAB THE POWER RODS!
BUT THERE WON'T BE ANY SHIELDING OVER THE ENERGY TRANSFER!
IT'LL KILL ANY HUMAN WITHIN A HUNDRED YARDS!
EVAC!
WHAT DID THEY JUST SAY?!
EVAC, OLIVIA! BACK DOWN THE HALL!
STANFORD'S IN THAT ROBO!
OH, HELL.
OLIVIA, NO!

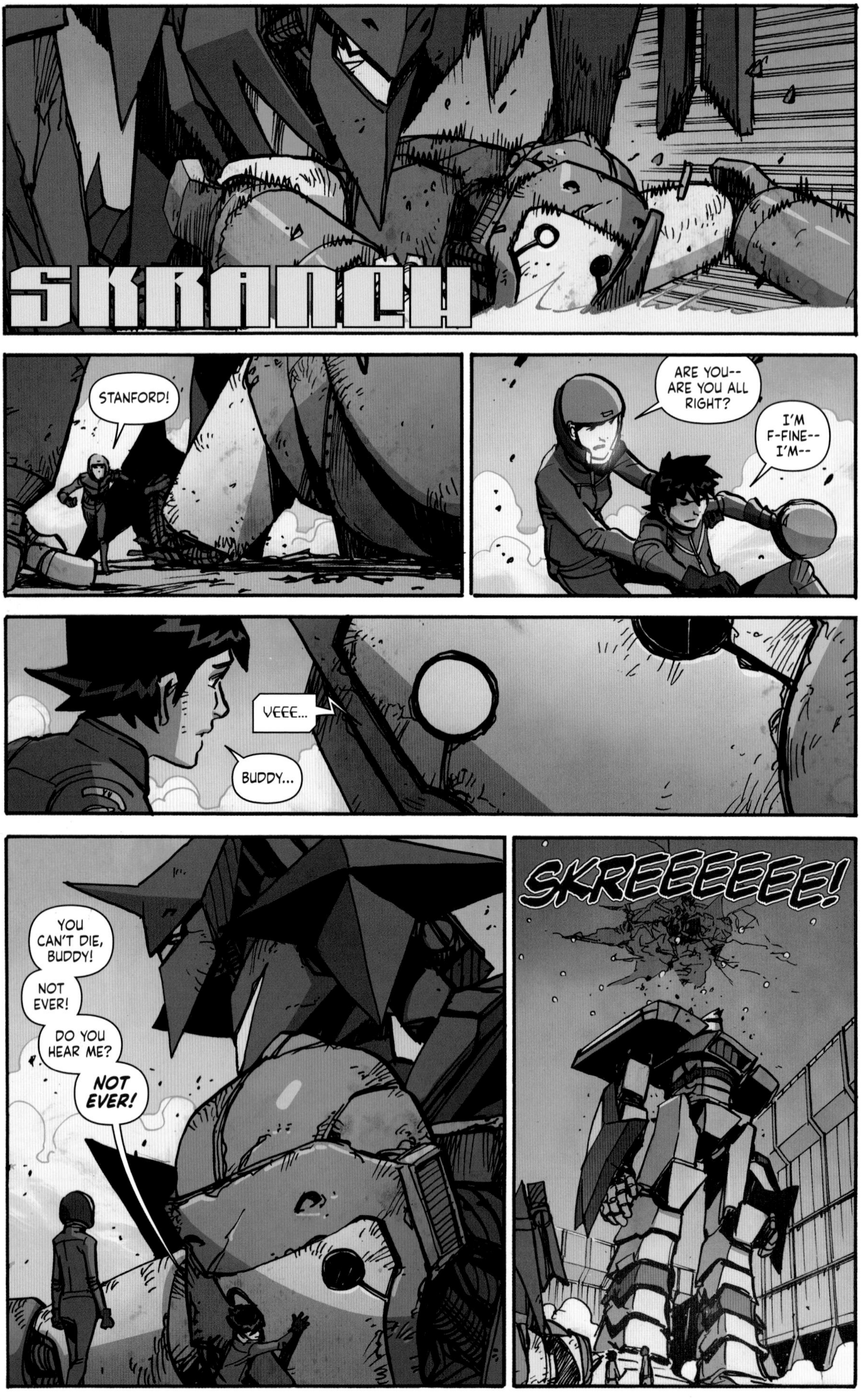
SKRANCH
STANFORD!
ARE YOU-- ARE YOU ALL RIGHT?
I'M F-FINE-- I'M--
VEEE...
BUDDY...
YOU CAN'T DIE, BUDDY!
NOT EVER!
DO YOU HEAR ME?
NOT EVER!
SKREEEEEEE!

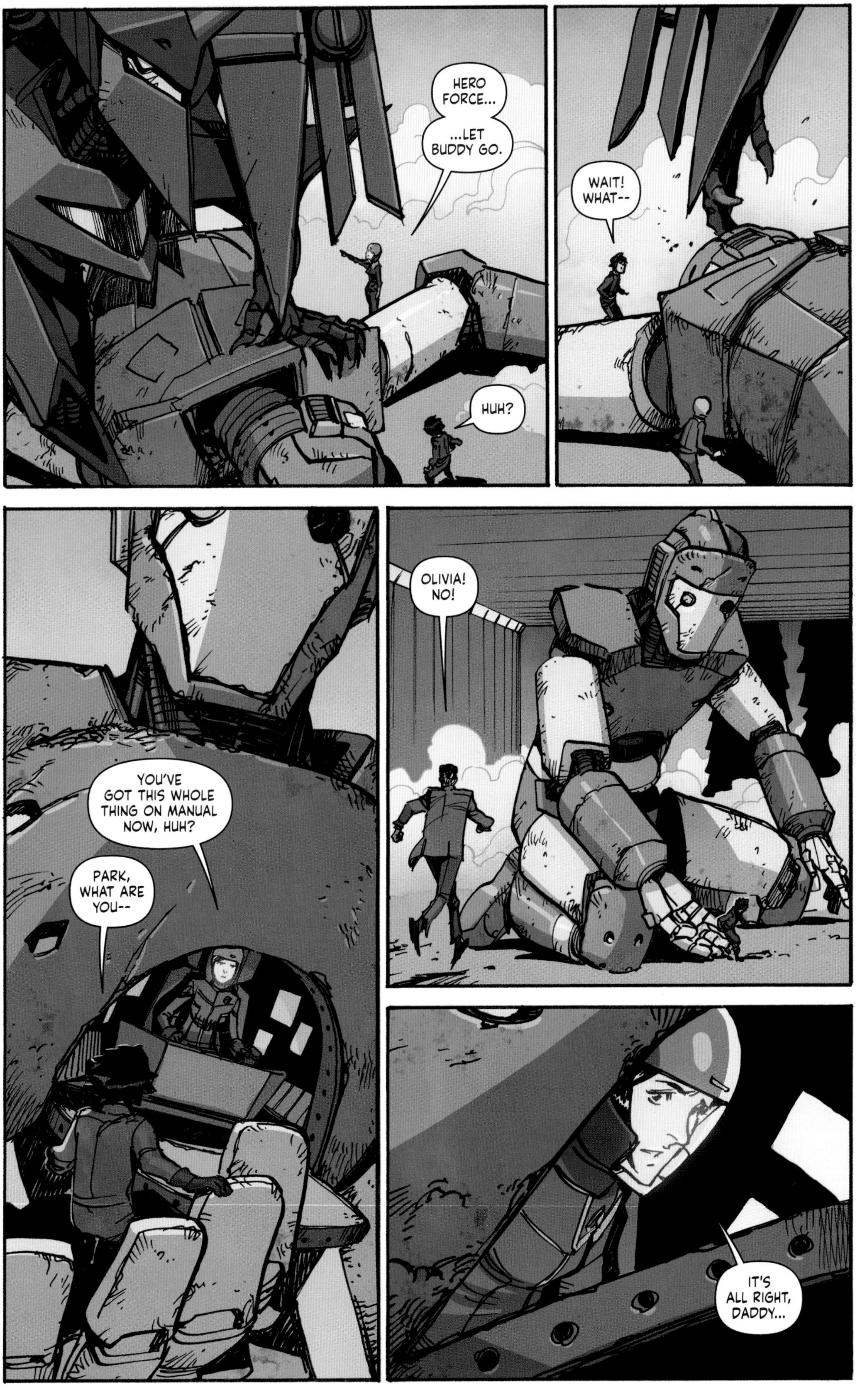
HERO FORCE...
...LET BUDDY GO.
HUH?
WAIT! WHAT--
YOU'VE GOT THIS WHOLE THING ON MANUAL NOW, HUH?
PARK, WHAT ARE YOU--
OLIVIA! NO!
IT'S ALL RIGHT, DADDY...

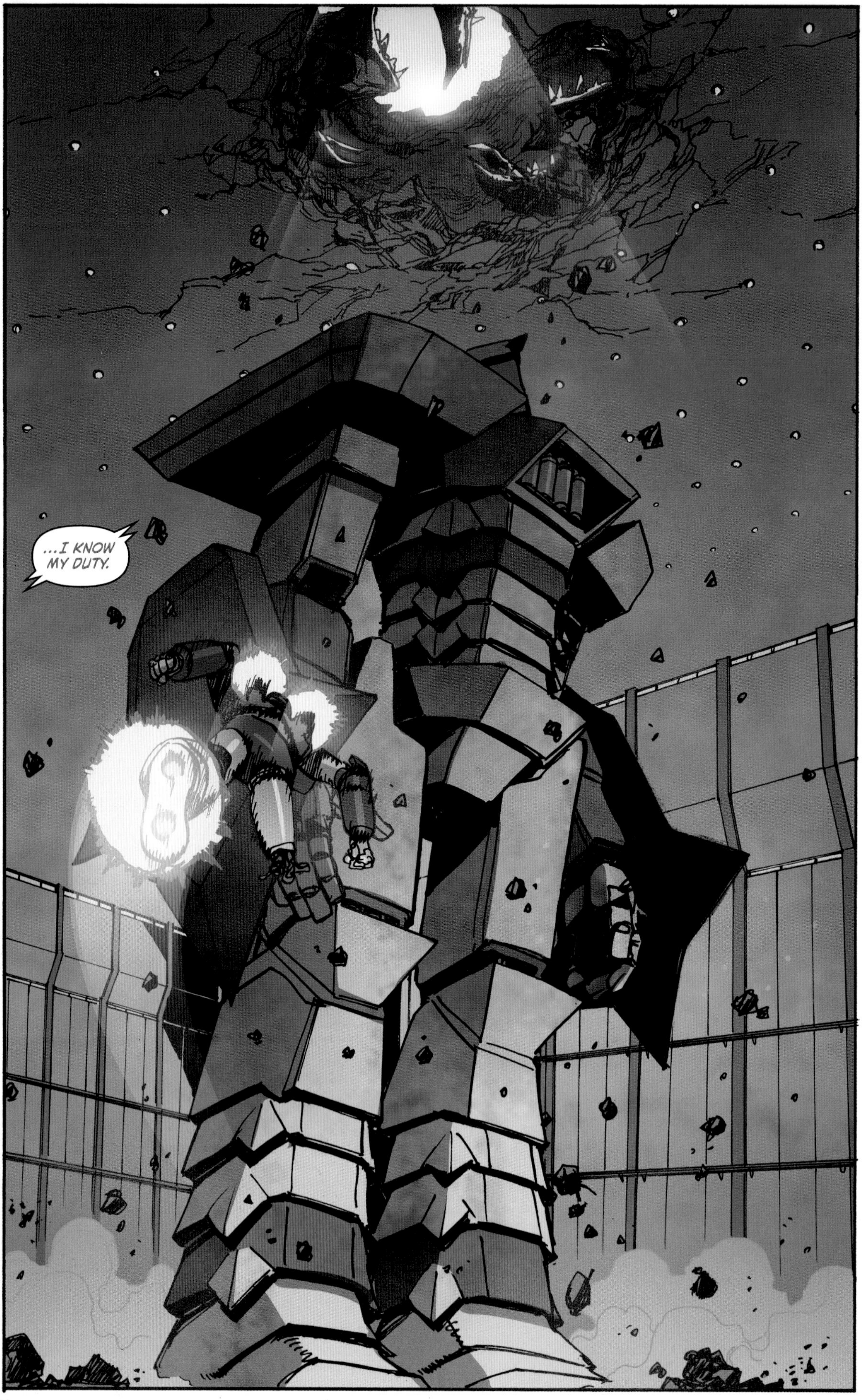
...I KNOW MY DUTY.

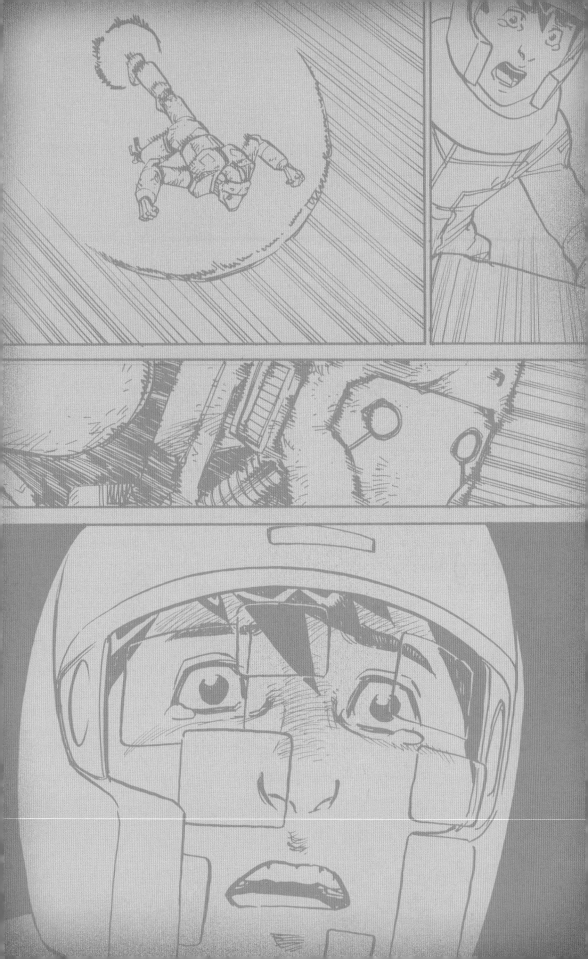

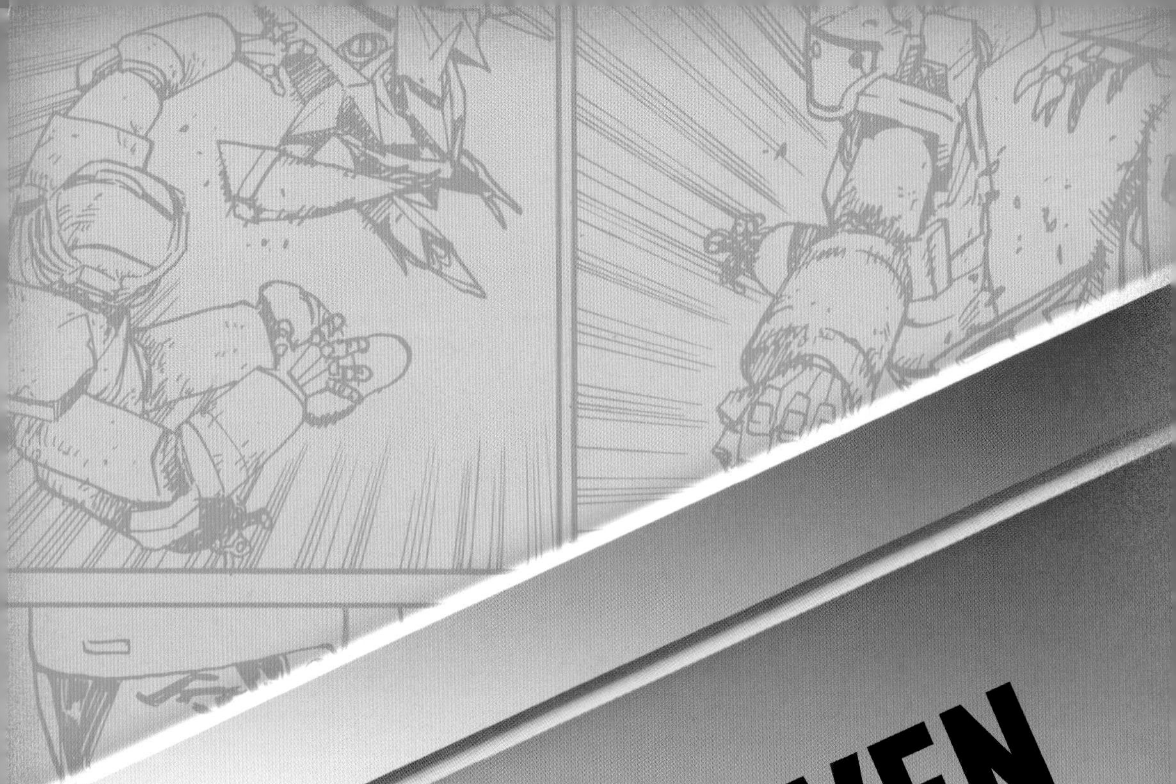

CHAPTER ELEVEN

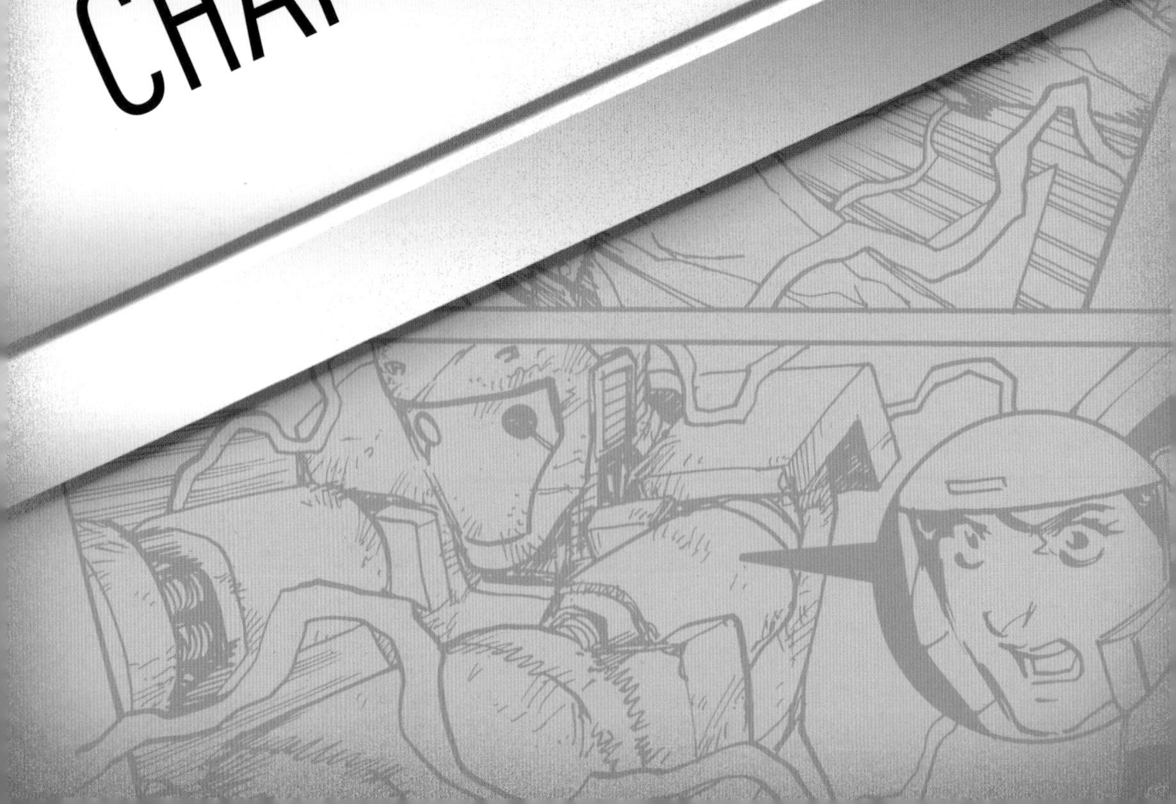

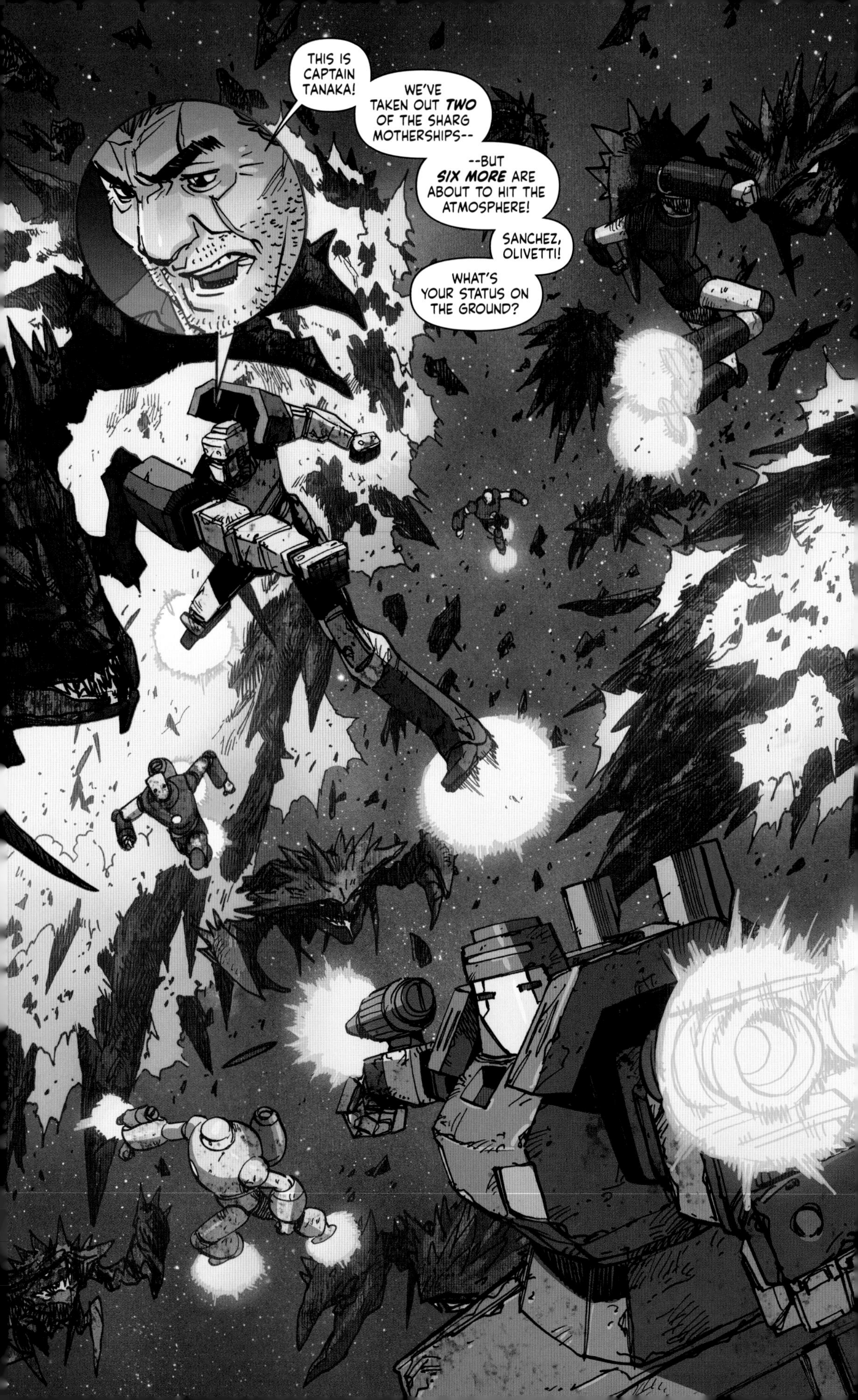
THIS IS CAPTAIN TANAKA!
WE'VE TAKEN OUT TWO OF THE SHARG MOTHERSHIPS--
--BUT SIX MORE ARE ABOUT TO HIT THE ATMOSPHERE!
SANCHEZ, OLIVETTI!
WHAT'S YOUR STATUS ON THE GROUND?

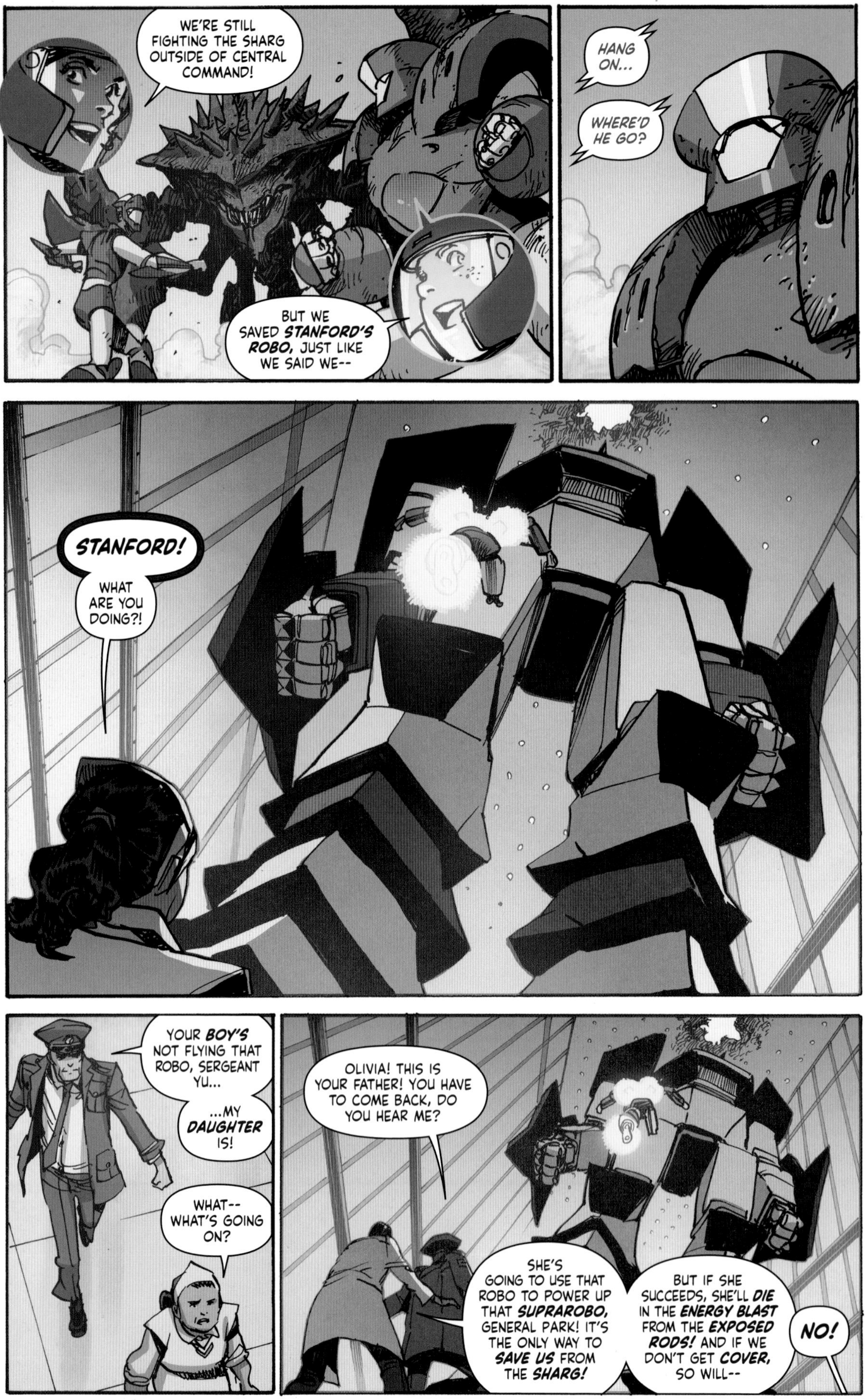
WE'RE STILL FIGHTING THE SHARG OUTSIDE OF CENTRAL COMMAND!
BUT WE SAVED STANFORD'S ROBO, JUST LIKE WE SAID WE--
HANG ON...
WHERE'D HE GO?
STANFORD!
WHAT ARE YOU DOING?!
YOUR BOY'S NOT FLYING THAT ROBO, SERGEANT YU...
...MY DAUGHTER IS!
WHAT-- WHAT'S GOING ON?
OLIVIA! THIS IS YOUR FATHER! YOU HAVE TO COME BACK, DO YOU HEAR ME?
SHE'S GOING TO USE THAT ROBO TO POWER UP THAT SUPRAROBO, GENERAL PARK! IT'S THE ONLY WAY TO SAVE US FROM THE SHARG!
BUT IF SHE SUCCEEDS, SHE'LL DIE IN THE ENERGY BLAST FROM THE EXPOSED RODS! AND IF WE DON'T GET COVER, SO WILL--
NO!

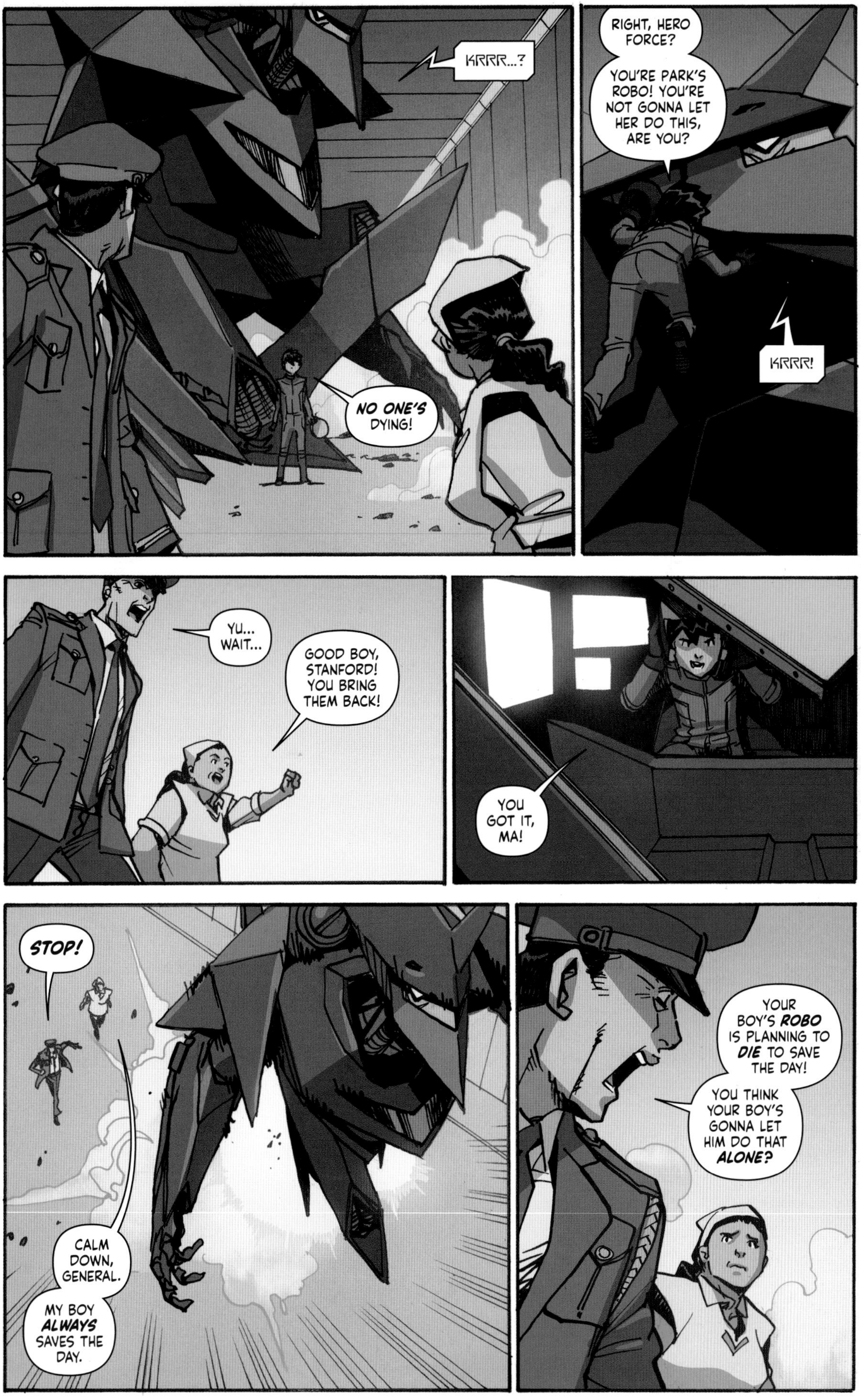
KRRR...?
NO ONE'S DYING!
RIGHT, HERO FORCE?
YOU'RE PARK'S ROBO! YOU'RE NOT GONNA LET HER DO THIS, ARE YOU?
KRRR!
YU... WAIT...
GOOD BOY, STANFORD! YOU BRING THEM BACK!
YOU GOT IT, MA!
STOP!
CALM DOWN, GENERAL.
MY BOY ALWAYS SAVES THE DAY.
YOUR BOY'S ROBO IS PLANNING TO DIE TO SAVE THE DAY!
YOU THINK YOUR BOY'S GONNA LET HIM DO THAT ALONE?

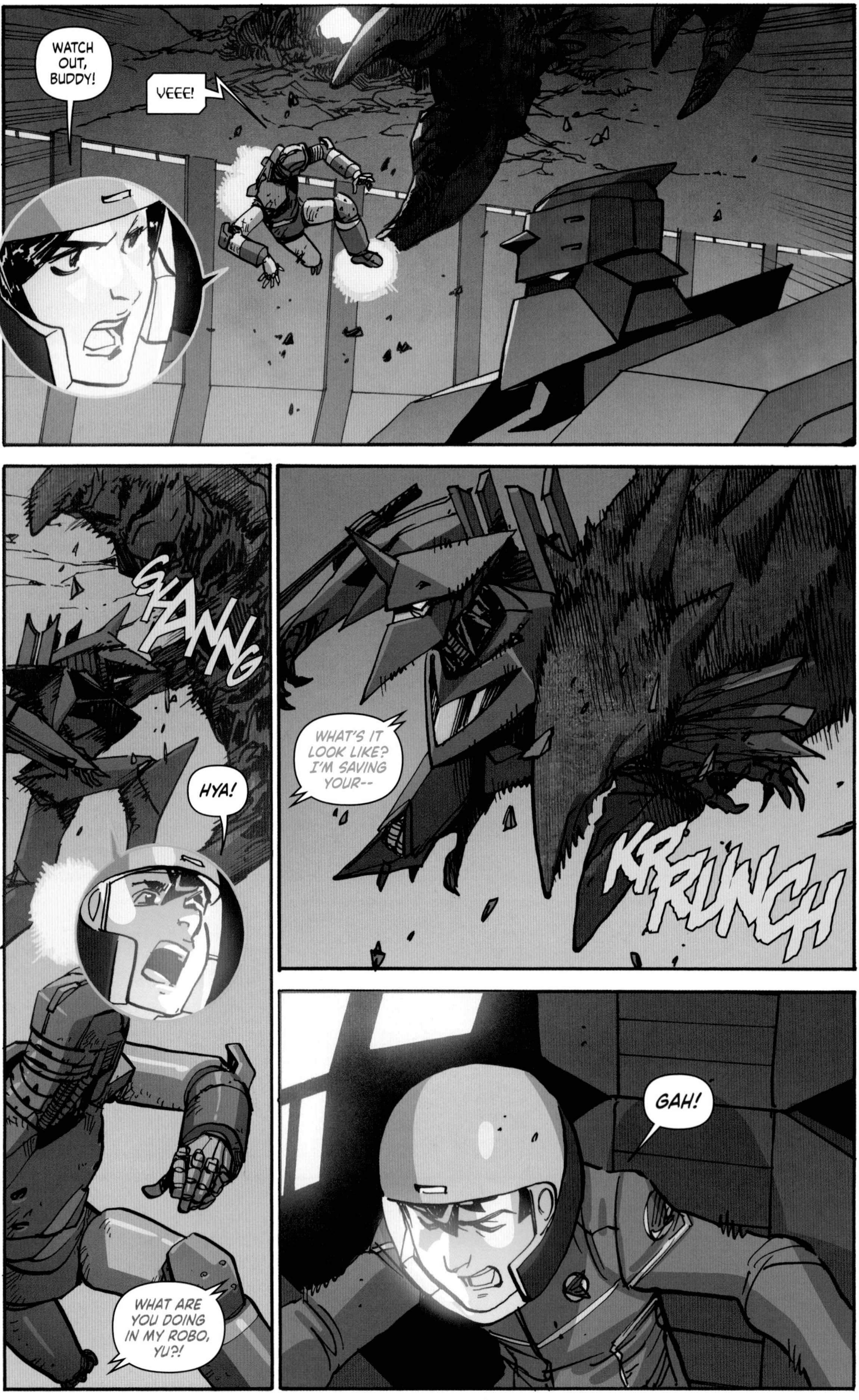
WATCH OUT, BUDDY!
VEEE!
SKANNG
HYA!
WHAT ARE YOU DOING IN MY ROBO, YU?!
WHAT'S IT LOOK LIKE? I'M SAVING YOUR--
KRRUNCH
GAH!

KRRAAA!

WHAT ARE YOU *DOING*, HERO FORCE? YOU STAY OUT OF *TROUBLE*, NOW, ALL RIGHT?

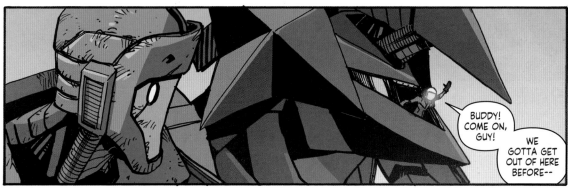

BUDDY! COME ON, GUY!

WE GOTTA GET OUT OF HERE BEFORE--

VEEE...

BUDDY?

DANGIT!

SKRAKOOSH!

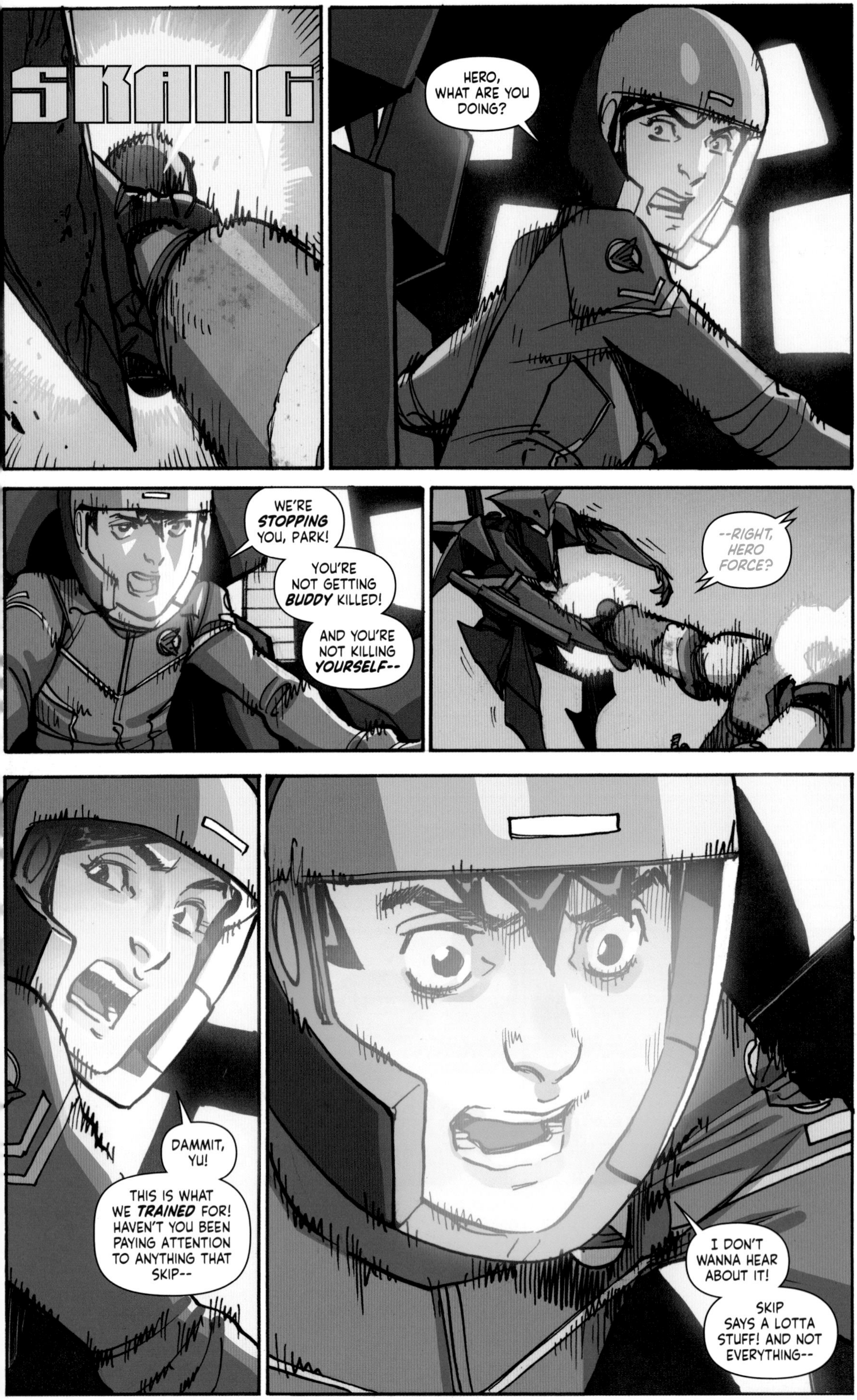
SKANG
HERO, WHAT ARE YOU DOING?
WE'RE STOPPING YOU, PARK!
YOU'RE NOT GETTING BUDDY KILLED!
AND YOU'RE NOT KILLING YOURSELF--
--RIGHT, HERO FORCE?
DAMMIT, YU!
THIS IS WHAT WE TRAINED FOR! HAVEN'T YOU BEEN PAYING ATTENTION TO ANYTHING THAT SKIP--
I DON'T WANNA HEAR ABOUT IT!
SKIP SAYS A LOTTA STUFF! AND NOT EVERYTHING--

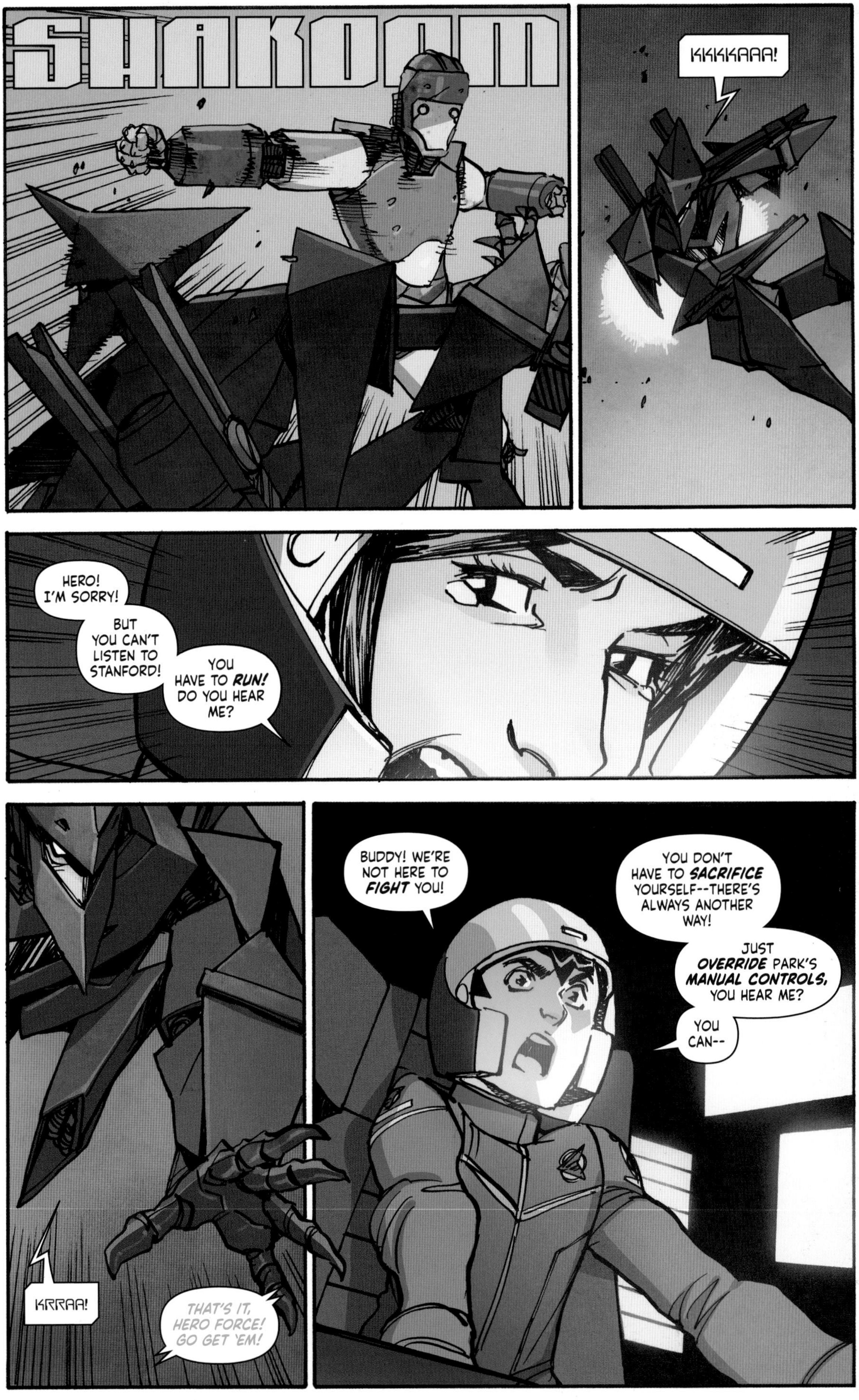
SHAKOOM
KKKKAAA!
HERO! I'M SORRY!
BUT YOU CAN'T LISTEN TO STANFORD!
YOU HAVE TO **RUN!** DO YOU HEAR ME?
KRRAA!
THAT'S IT, HERO FORCE! GO GET 'EM!
BUDDY! WE'RE NOT HERE TO **FIGHT** YOU!
YOU DON'T HAVE TO **SACRIFICE** YOURSELF--THERE'S ALWAYS ANOTHER WAY!
JUST **OVERRIDE** PARK'S **MANUAL CONTROLS,** YOU HEAR ME?
YOU CAN--

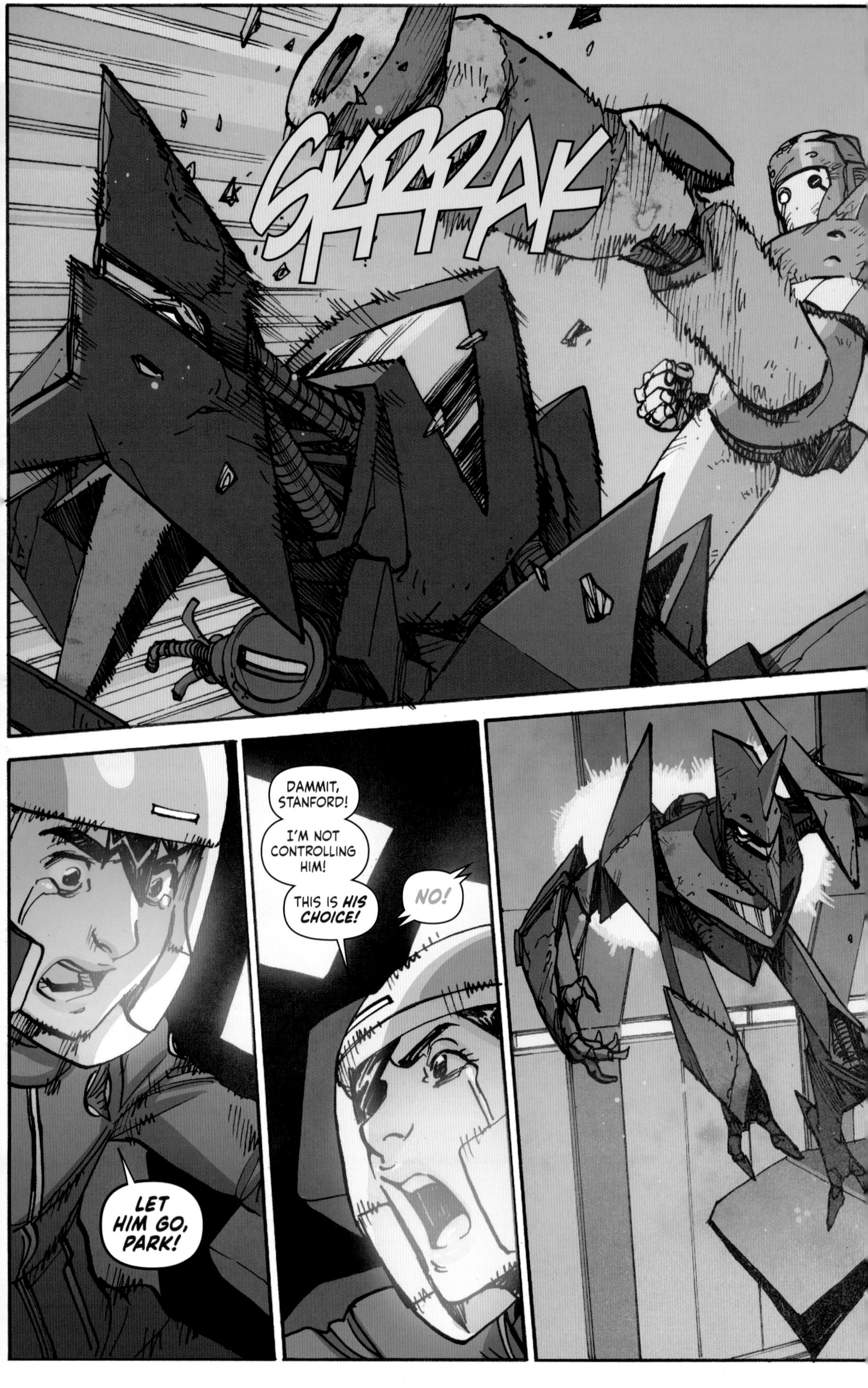
SKRRAK
LET HIM GO, PARK!
DAMMIT, STANFORD!
I'M NOT CONTROLLING HIM!
THIS IS HIS CHOICE!
NO!

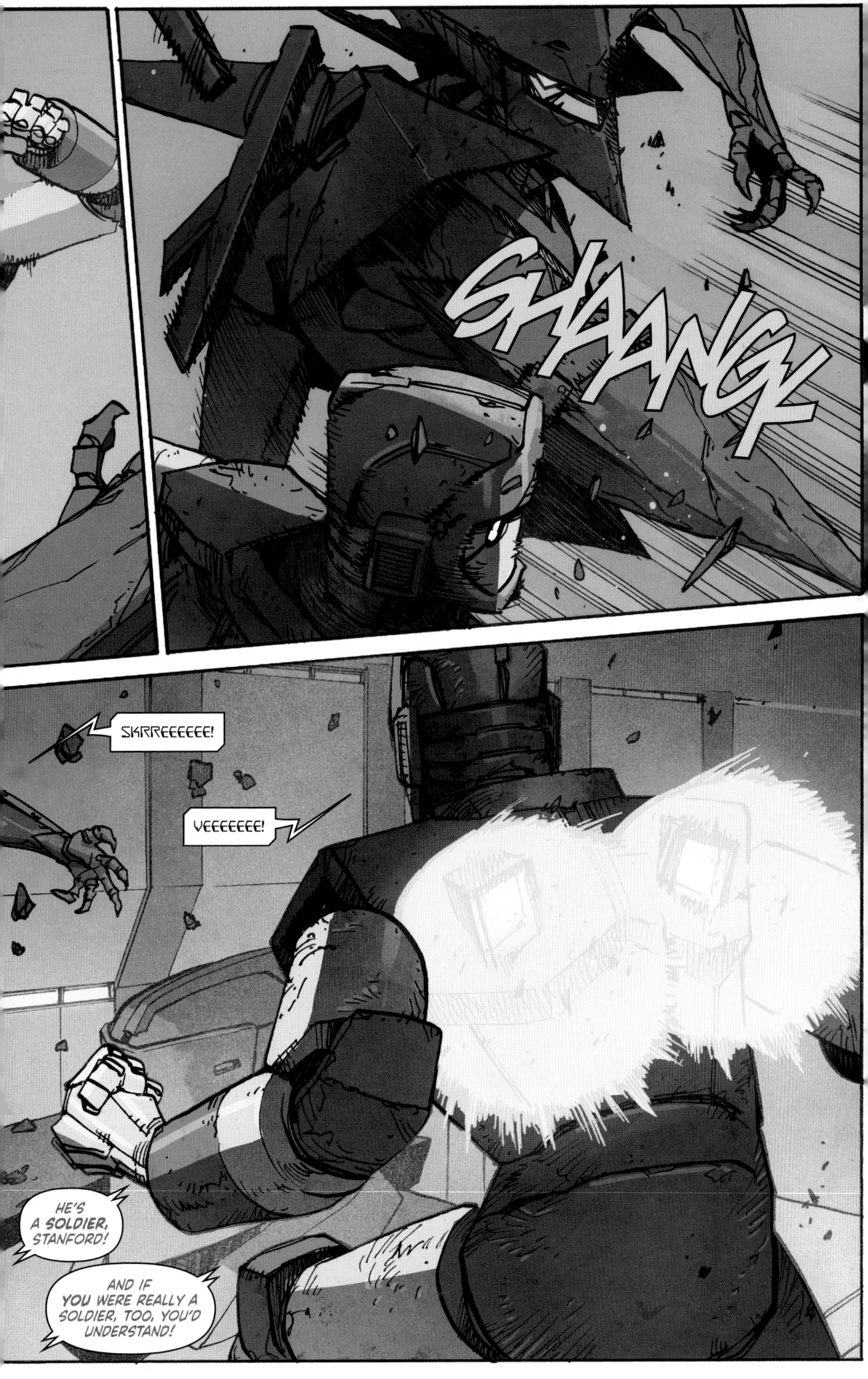
SHAANGK
SKRREEEEEE!
VEEEEEEE!
HE'S A SOLDIER, STANFORD!
AND IF YOU WERE REALLY A SOLDIER, TOO, YOU'D UNDERSTAND!

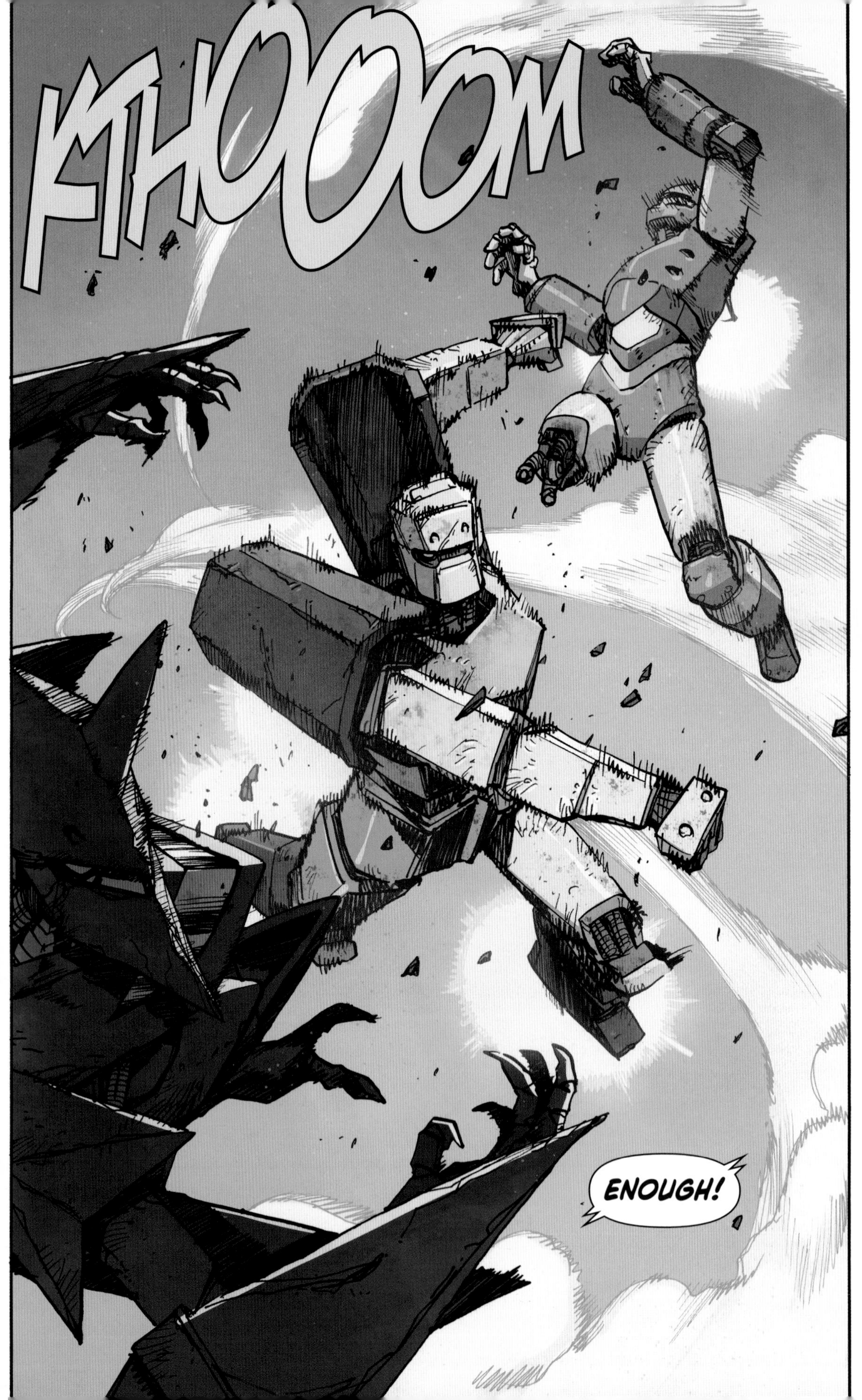
KTHOOOOM
ENOUGH!

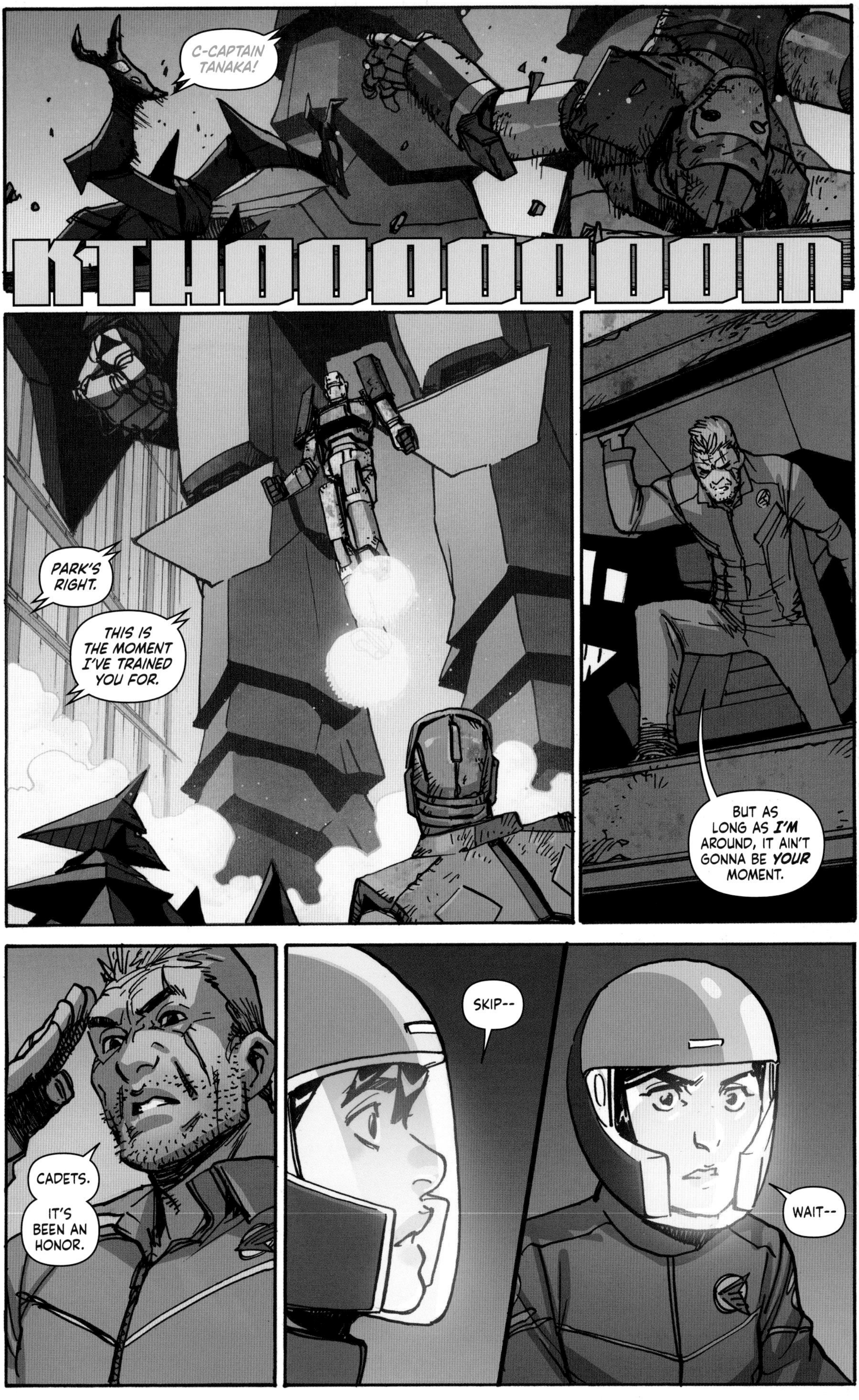
C-CAPTAIN TANAKA!
KTHOOOOOOOOM
PARK'S RIGHT.
THIS IS THE MOMENT I'VE TRAINED YOU FOR.
BUT AS LONG AS *I'M* AROUND, IT AIN'T GONNA BE *YOUR* MOMENT.
CADETS.
IT'S BEEN AN HONOR.
SKIP--
WAIT--

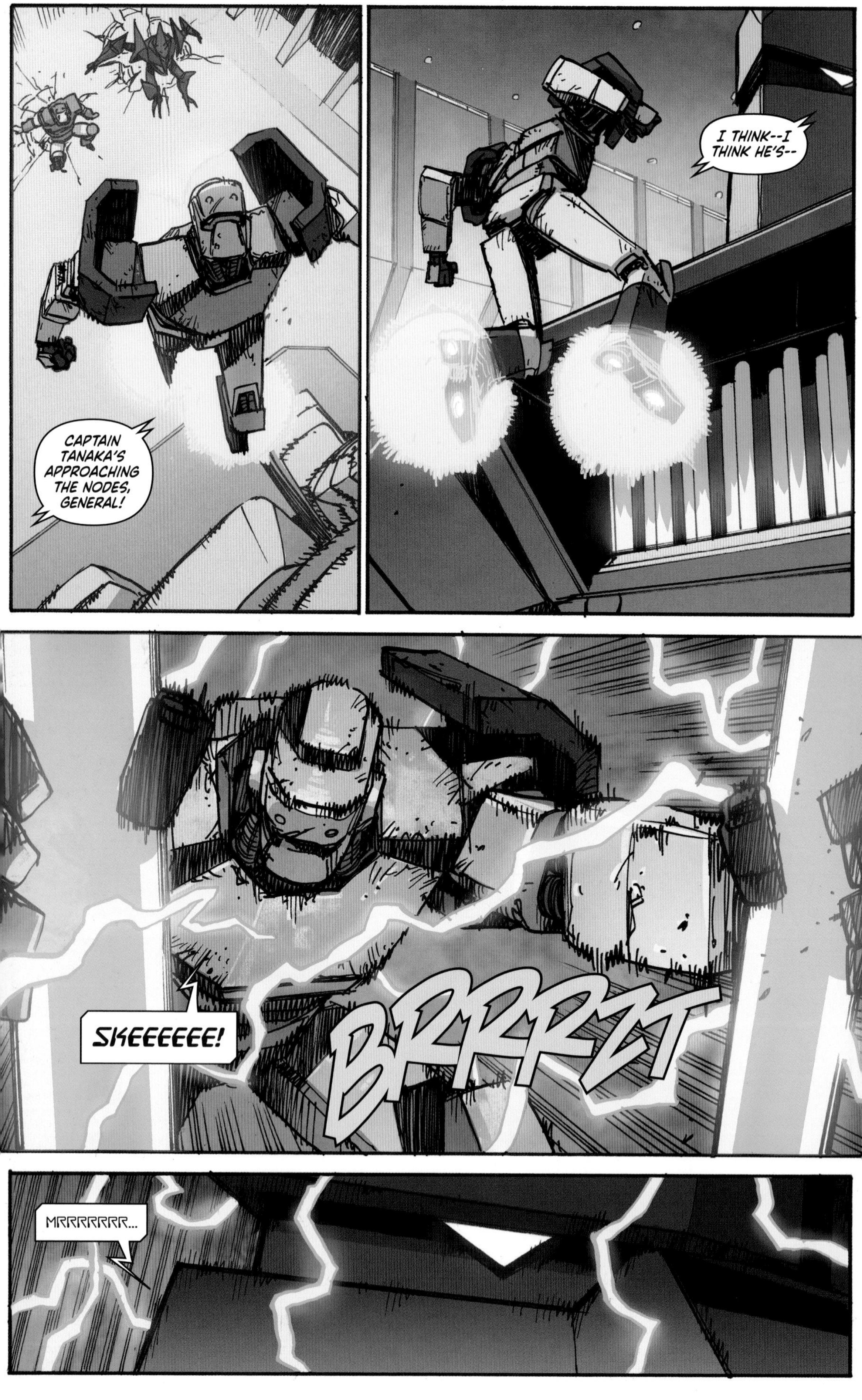
CAPTAIN TANAKA'S APPROACHING THE NODES, GENERAL!
I THINK--I THINK HE'S--
SKEEEEEEE!
BRRRZT
MRRRRRRRR...

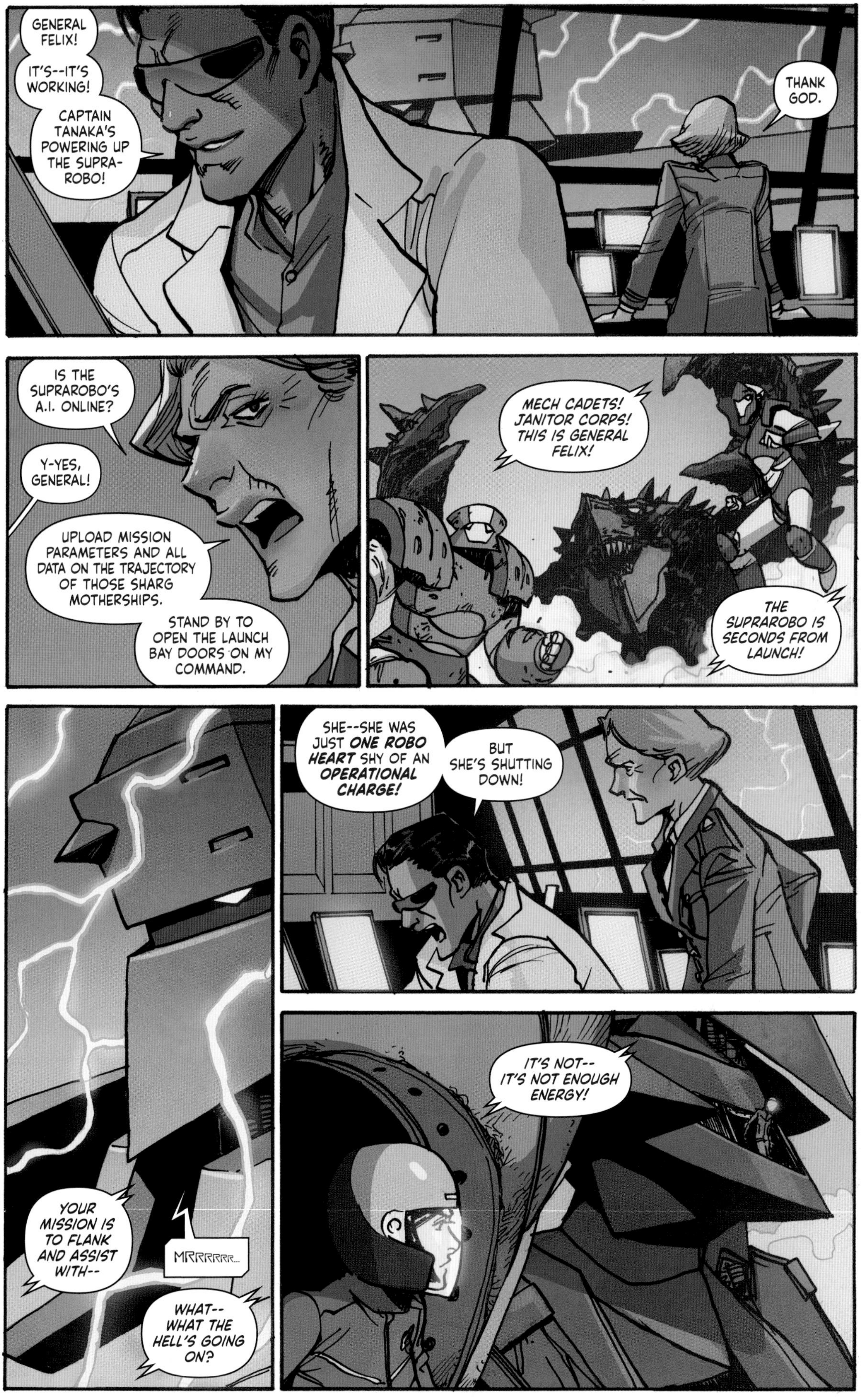
GENERAL FELIX!
IT'S--IT'S WORKING!
CAPTAIN TANAKA'S POWERING UP THE SUPRA-ROBO!
THANK GOD.
IS THE SUPRAROBO'S A.I. ONLINE?
Y-YES, GENERAL!
UPLOAD MISSION PARAMETERS AND ALL DATA ON THE TRAJECTORY OF THOSE SHARG MOTHERSHIPS.
STAND BY TO OPEN THE LAUNCH BAY DOORS ON MY COMMAND.
MECH CADETS! JANITOR CORPS! THIS IS GENERAL FELIX!
THE SUPRAROBO IS SECONDS FROM LAUNCH!
YOUR MISSION IS TO FLANK AND ASSIST WITH--
MRRRRRRR...
WHAT-- WHAT THE HELL'S GOING ON?
SHE--SHE WAS JUST ONE ROBO HEART SHY OF AN OPERATIONAL CHARGE!
BUT SHE'S SHUTTING DOWN!
IT'S NOT-- IT'S NOT ENOUGH ENERGY!

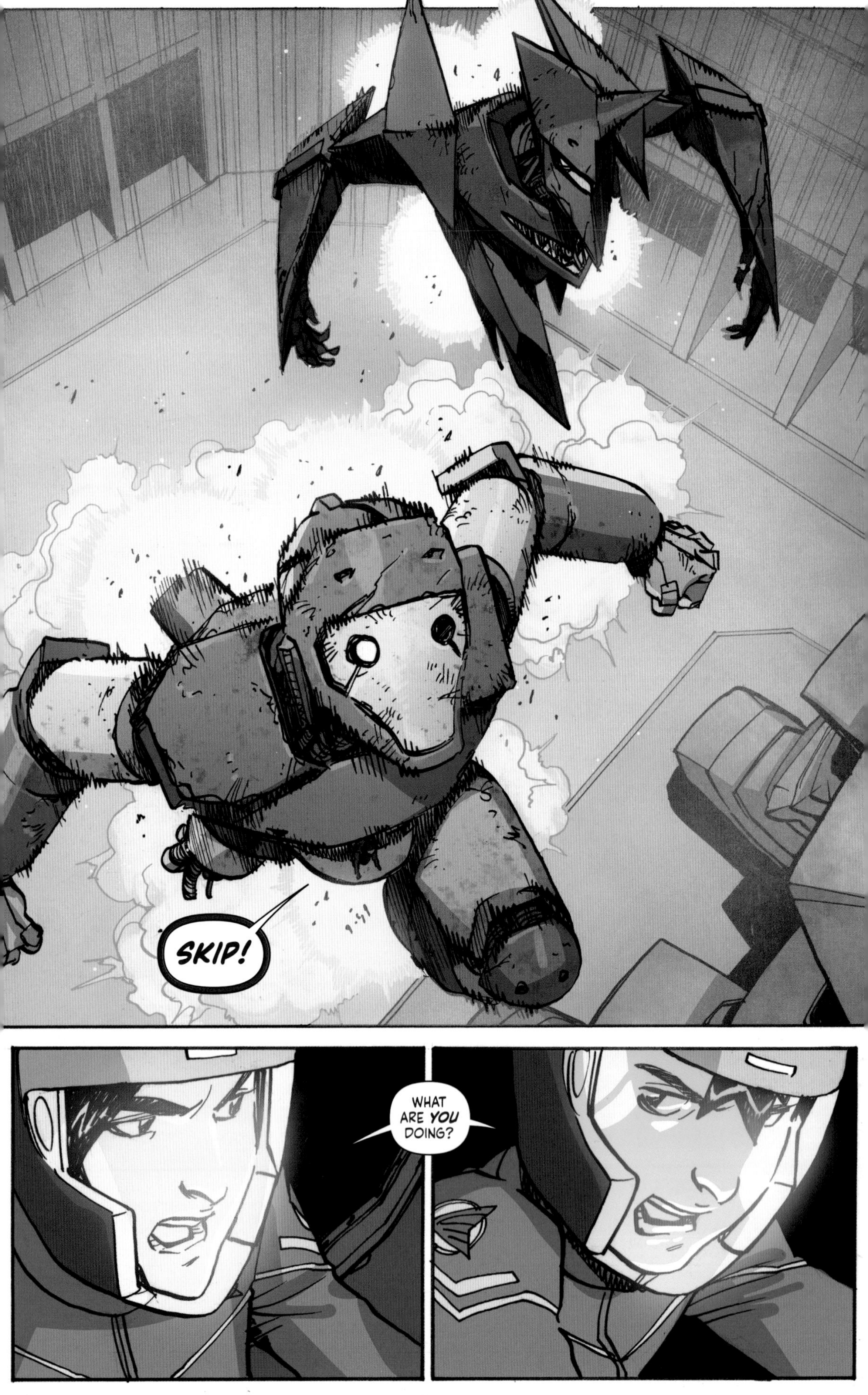
SKIP!
WHAT ARE YOU DOING?

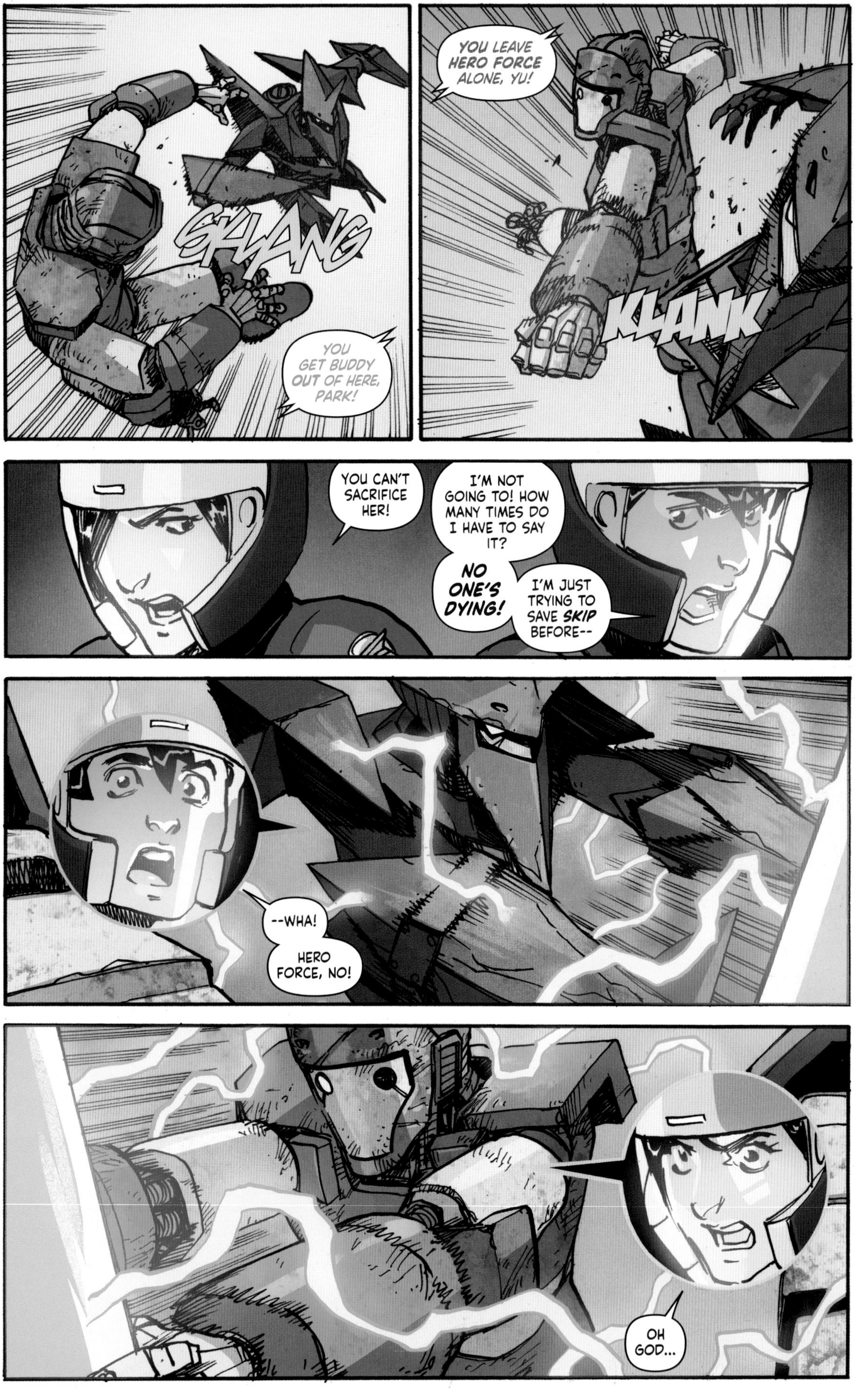
SKWANG
YOU GET BUDDY OUT OF HERE, PARK!
YOU LEAVE HERO FORCE ALONE, YU!
KLANK
YOU CAN'T SACRIFICE HER!
I'M NOT GOING TO! HOW MANY TIMES DO I HAVE TO SAY IT?
NO ONE'S DYING!
I'M JUST TRYING TO SAVE SKIP BEFORE--
--WHA!
HERO FORCE, NO!
OH GOD...

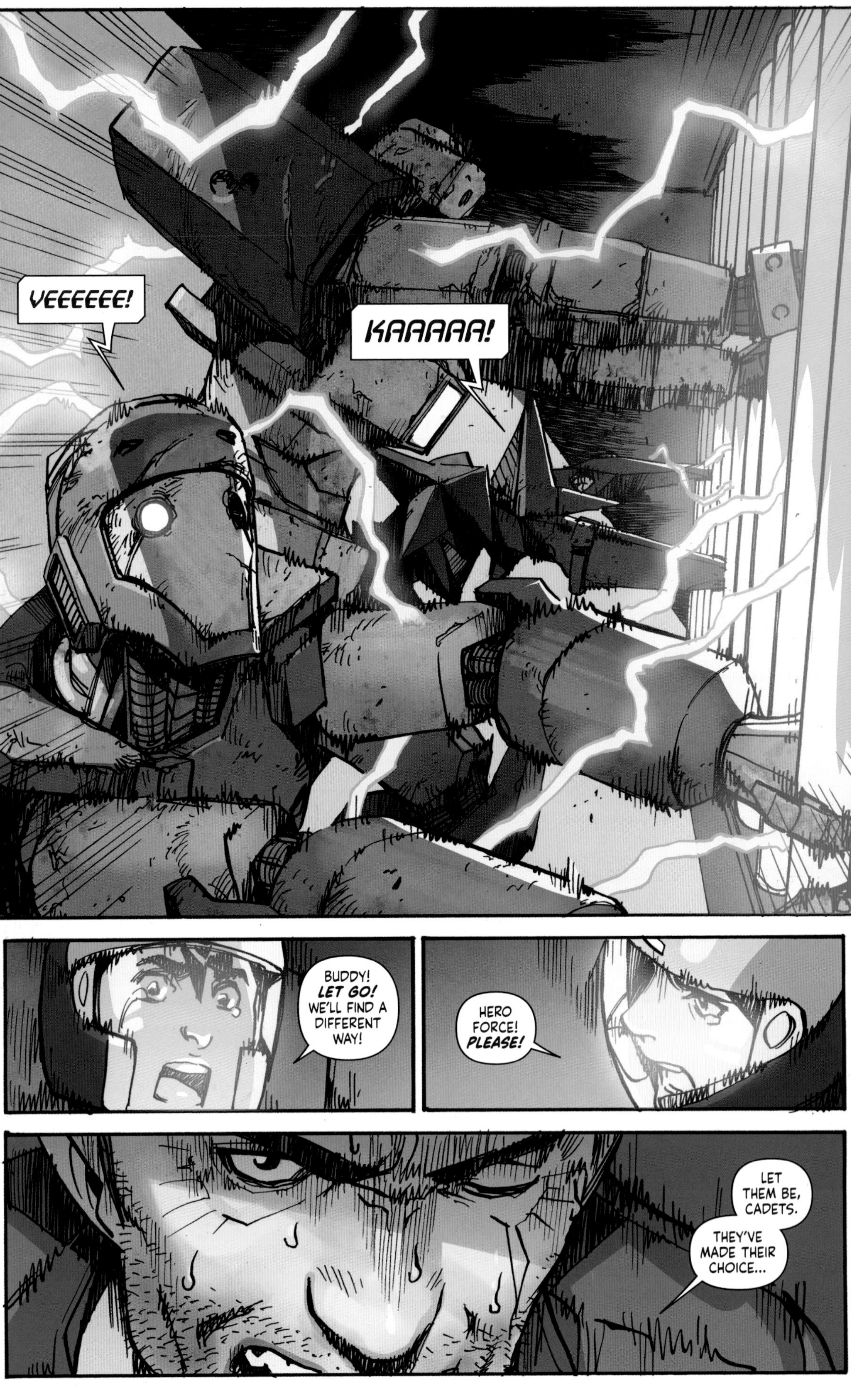
VEEEEEE!
KAAAAA!
BUDDY! LET GO! WE'LL FIND A DIFFERENT WAY!
HERO FORCE! PLEASE!
LET THEM BE, CADETS.
THEY'VE MADE THEIR CHOICE...

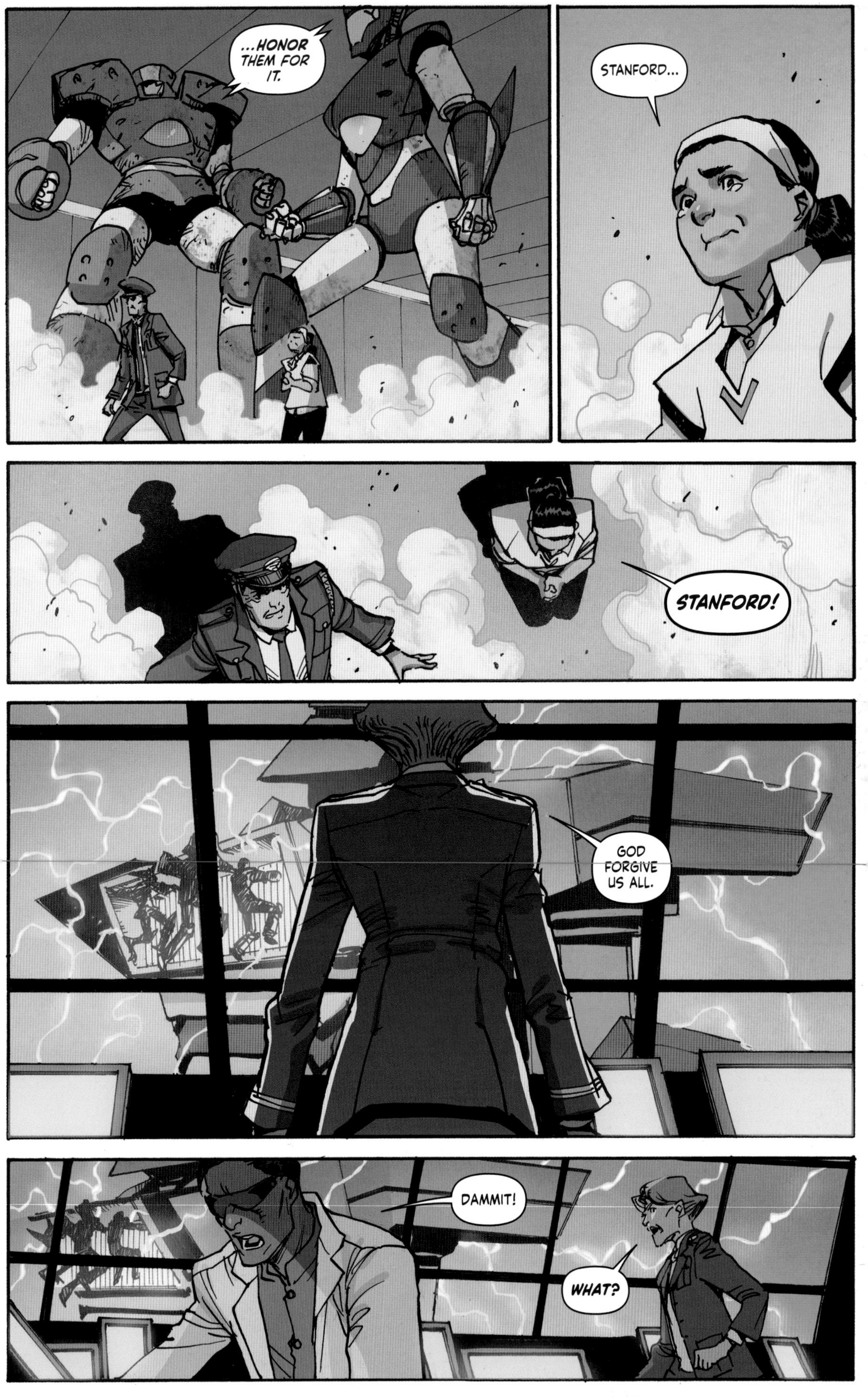
...HONOR THEM FOR IT.
STANFORD...
STANFORD!
GOD FORGIVE US ALL.
DAMMIT!
WHAT?

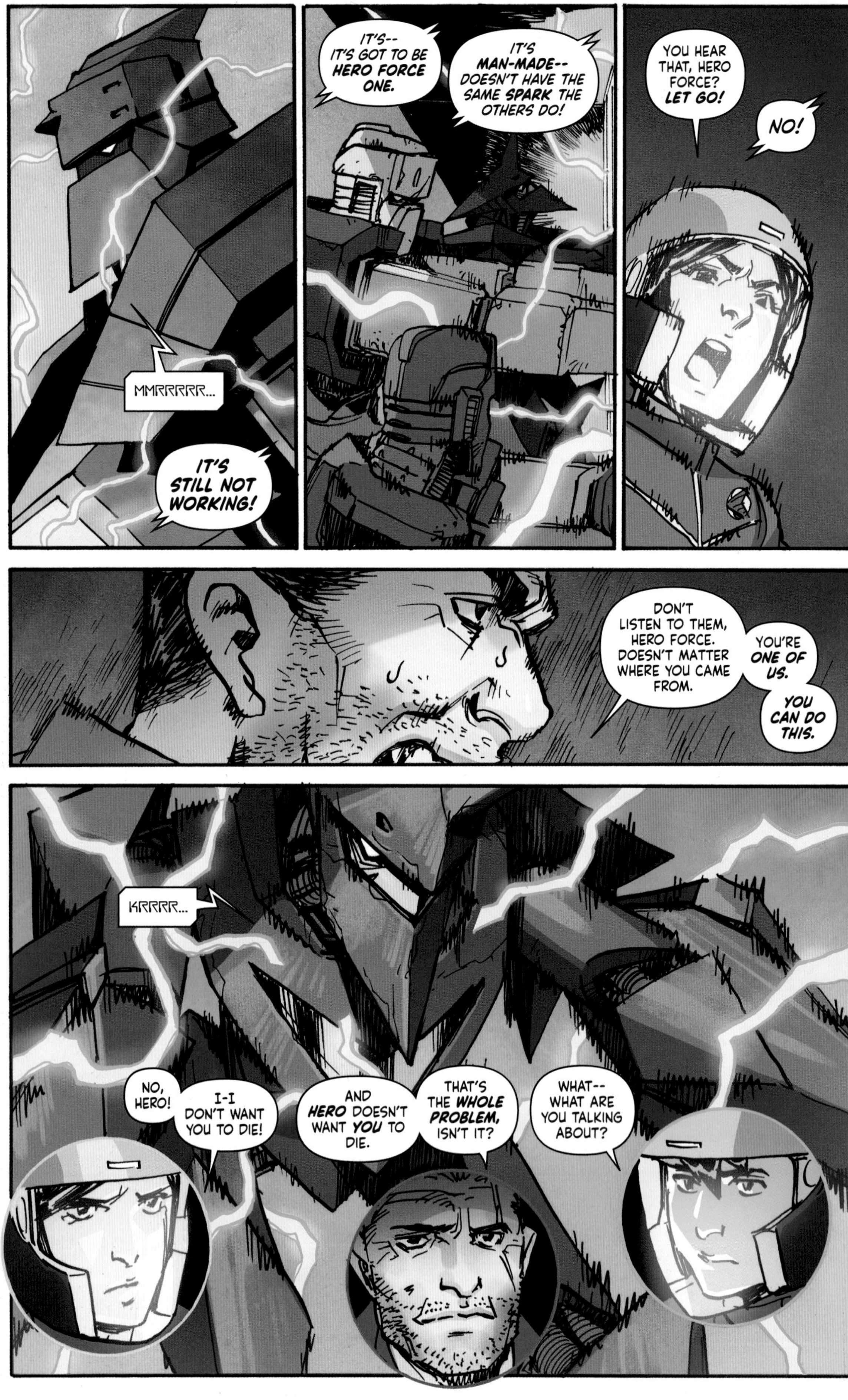
MMRRRRRR...
IT'S STILL NOT WORKING!
IT'S-- IT'S GOT TO BE HERO FORCE ONE.
IT'S MAN-MADE-- DOESN'T HAVE THE SAME SPARK THE OTHERS DO!
YOU HEAR THAT, HERO FORCE? LET GO!
NO!
DON'T LISTEN TO THEM, HERO FORCE. DOESN'T MATTER WHERE YOU CAME FROM.
YOU'RE ONE OF US.
YOU CAN DO THIS.
KRRRR...
NO, HERO!
I-I DON'T WANT YOU TO DIE!
AND HERO DOESN'T WANT YOU TO DIE.
THAT'S THE WHOLE PROBLEM, ISN'T IT?
WHAT-- WHAT ARE YOU TALKING ABOUT?

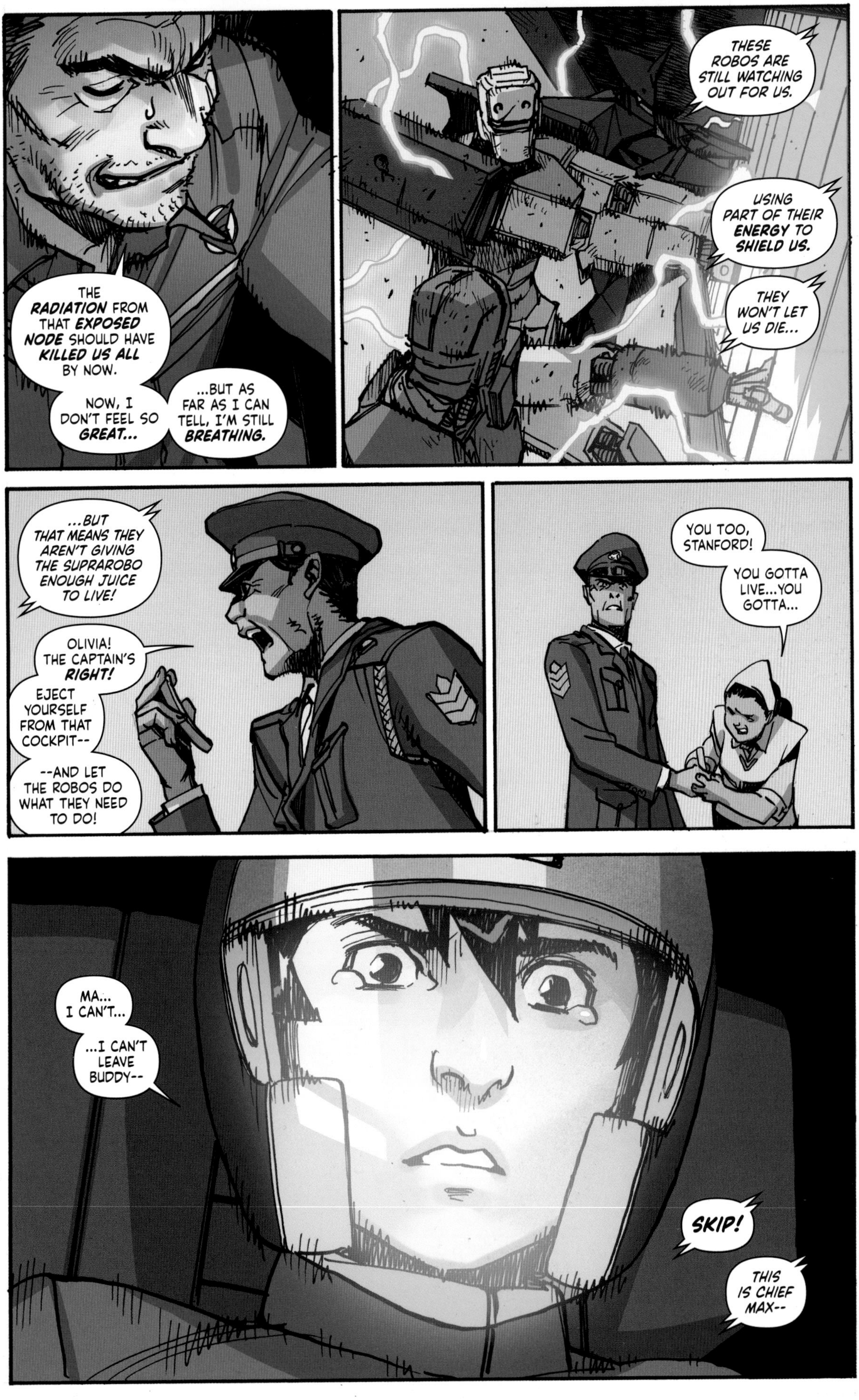
THE RADIATION FROM THAT EXPOSED NODE SHOULD HAVE KILLED US ALL BY NOW.
NOW, I DON'T FEEL SO GREAT...
...BUT AS FAR AS I CAN TELL, I'M STILL BREATHING.
THESE ROBOS ARE STILL WATCHING OUT FOR US.
USING PART OF THEIR ENERGY TO SHIELD US.
THEY WON'T LET US DIE...
...BUT THAT MEANS THEY AREN'T GIVING THE SUPRAROBO ENOUGH JUICE TO LIVE!
OLIVIA! THE CAPTAIN'S RIGHT!
EJECT YOURSELF FROM THAT COCKPIT--
--AND LET THE ROBOS DO WHAT THEY NEED TO DO!
YOU TOO, STANFORD!
YOU GOTTA LIVE...YOU GOTTA...
MA... I CAN'T...
...I CAN'T LEAVE BUDDY--
SKIP!
THIS IS CHIEF MAX--

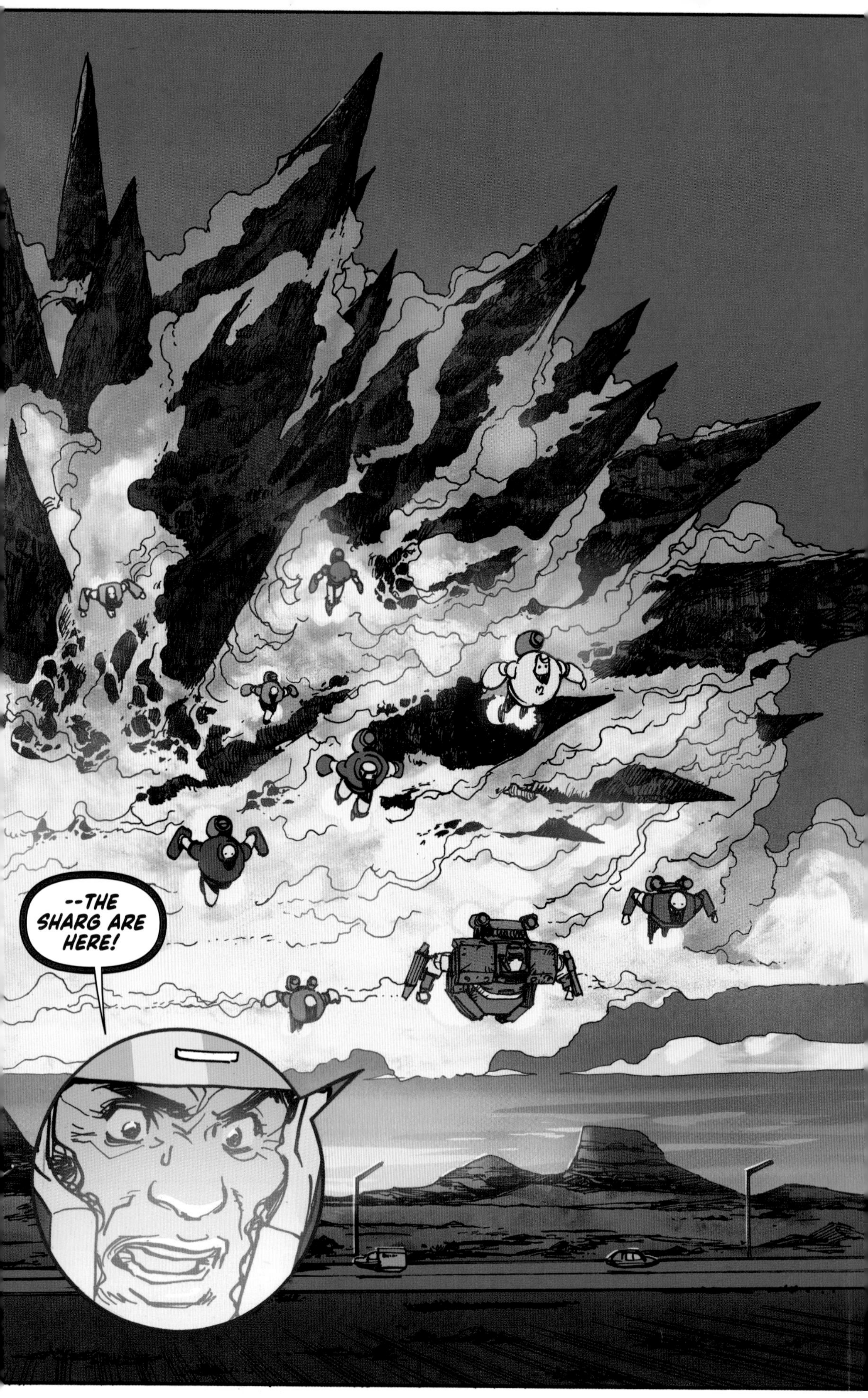
--THE SHARG ARE HERE!

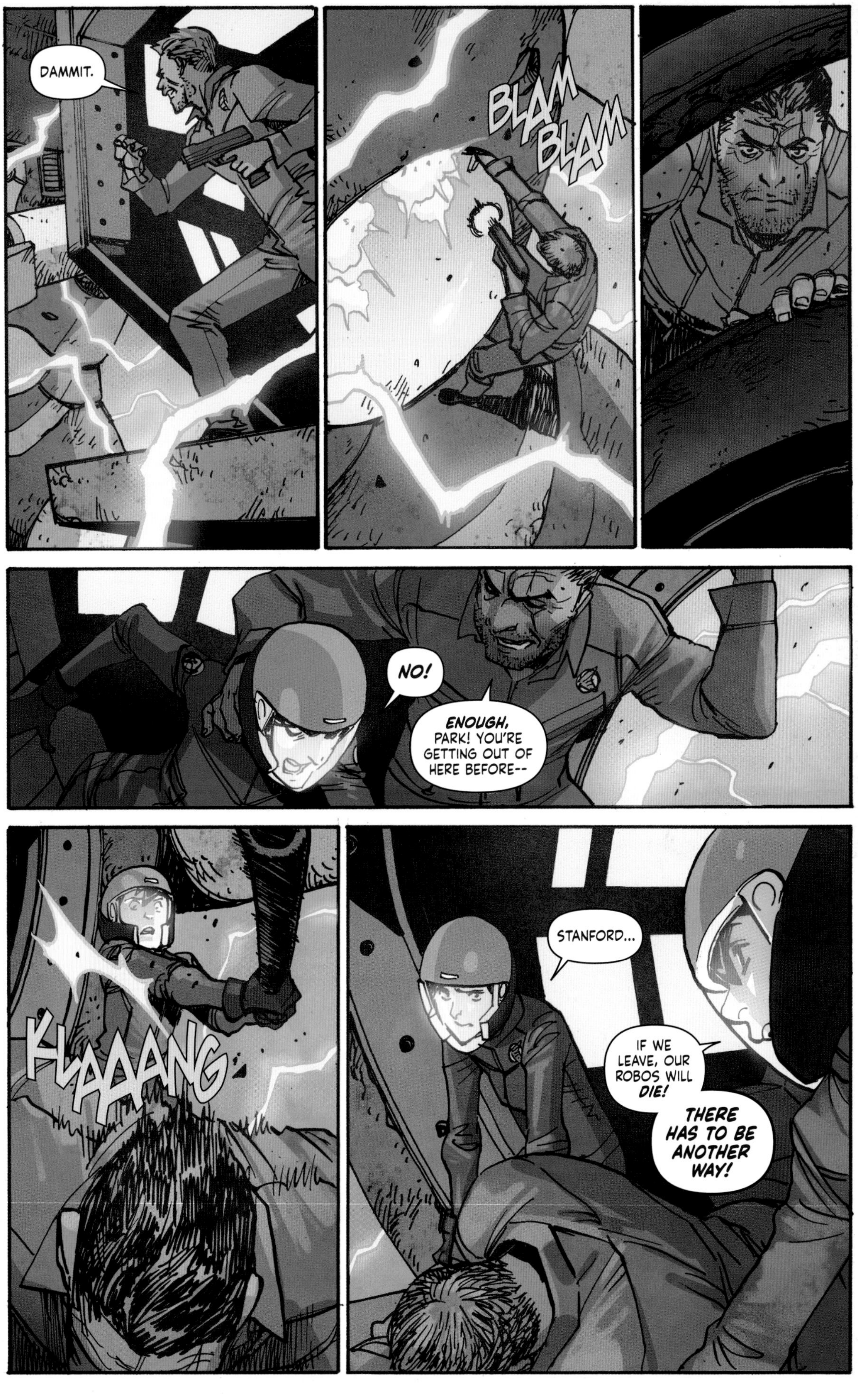
DAMMIT.
BLAM BLAM
NO!
ENOUGH, PARK! YOU'RE GETTING OUT OF HERE BEFORE--
KLAAANG
STANFORD...
IF WE LEAVE, OUR ROBOS WILL DIE!
THERE HAS TO BE ANOTHER WAY!

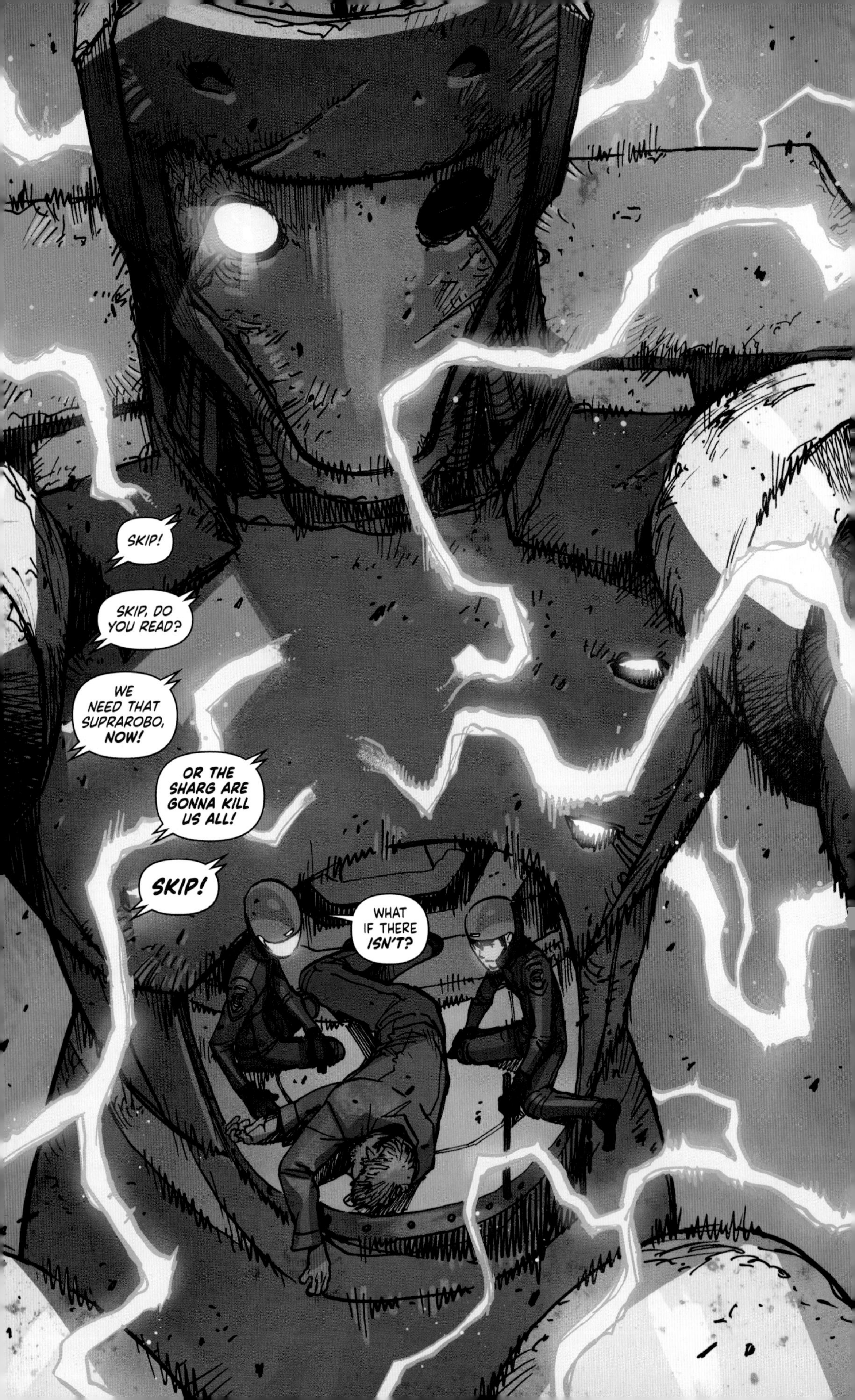
SKIP!
SKIP, DO YOU READ?
WE NEED THAT SUPRAROBO, NOW!
OR THE SHARG ARE GONNA KILL US ALL!
SKIP!
WHAT IF THERE ISN'T?

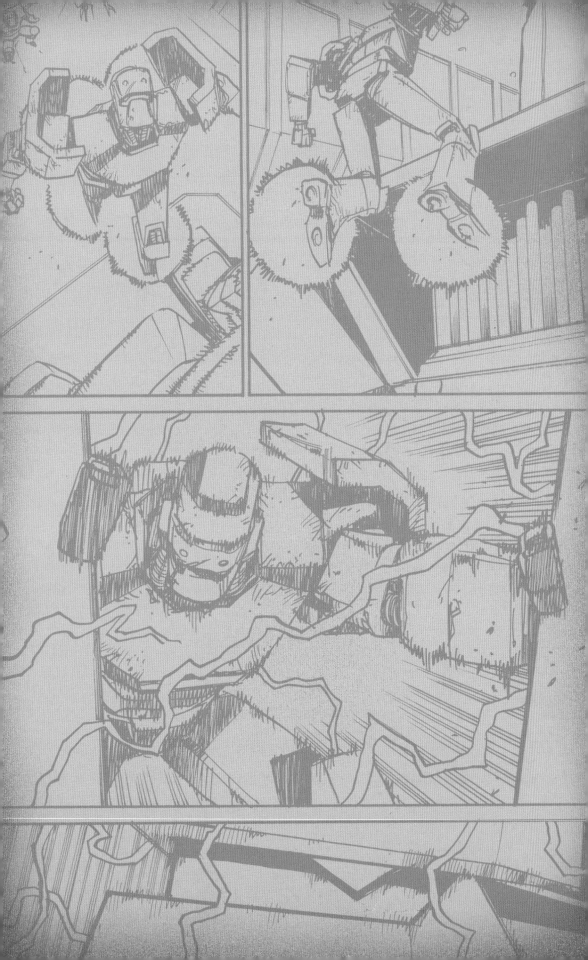

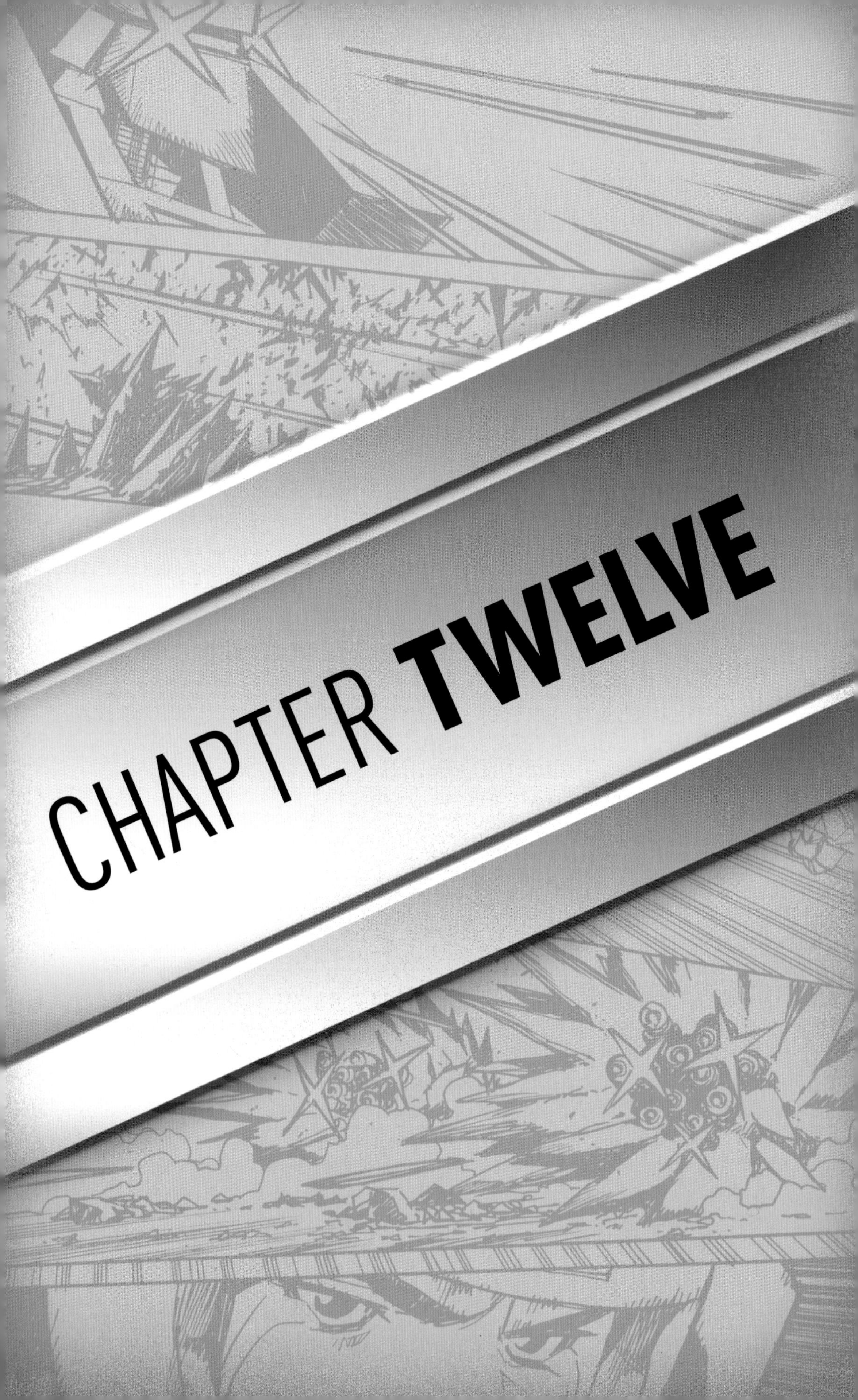

CHAPTER TWELVE

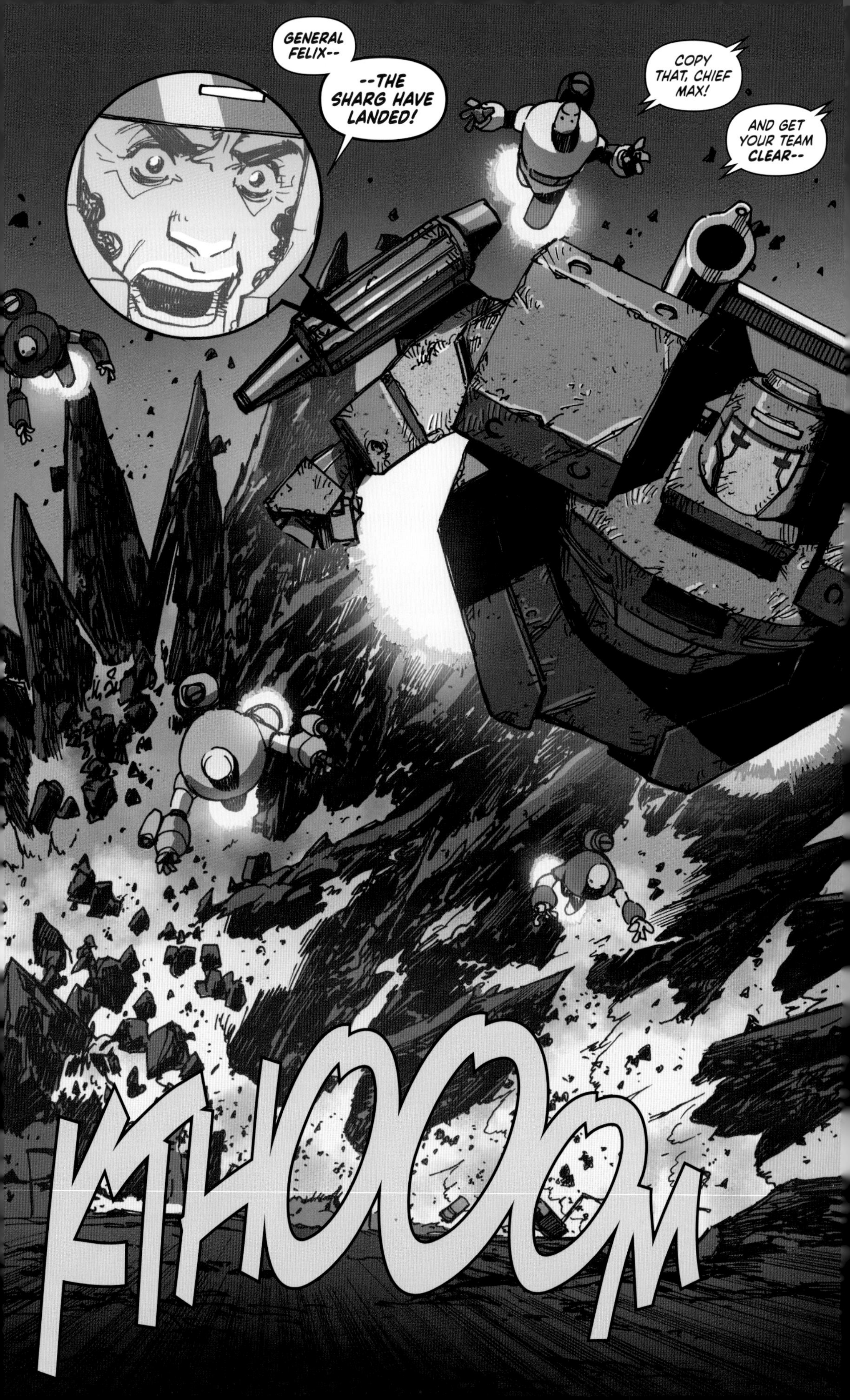
GENERAL FELIX--
--THE SHARG HAVE LANDED!
COPY THAT, CHIEF MAX!
AND GET YOUR TEAM CLEAR--
KHOOOM

--MISSILES INCOMING!

SKROOOW

SKROOOW

SKROOOW

BRAKOOOM

DANG IT! THE INDIVIDUAL SHARG ARE PROTECTING THEIR MOTHERSHIPS!

THIS IS IT, THEN.

LAST STAND, TRASH CANS!

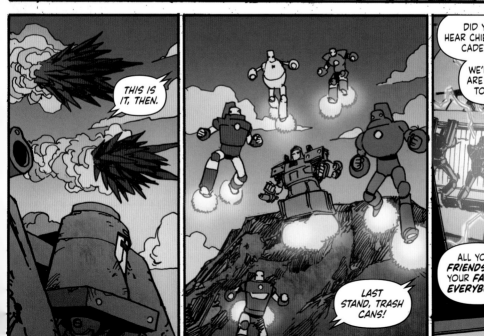

DID YOU HEAR CHIEF MAX, CADETS?

WE'RE ALL ARE ABOUT TO DIE!

ALL YOUR FRIENDS, ALL YOUR FAMILY, EVERYBODY!

WE NEED THAT SUPRAROBO, NOW!

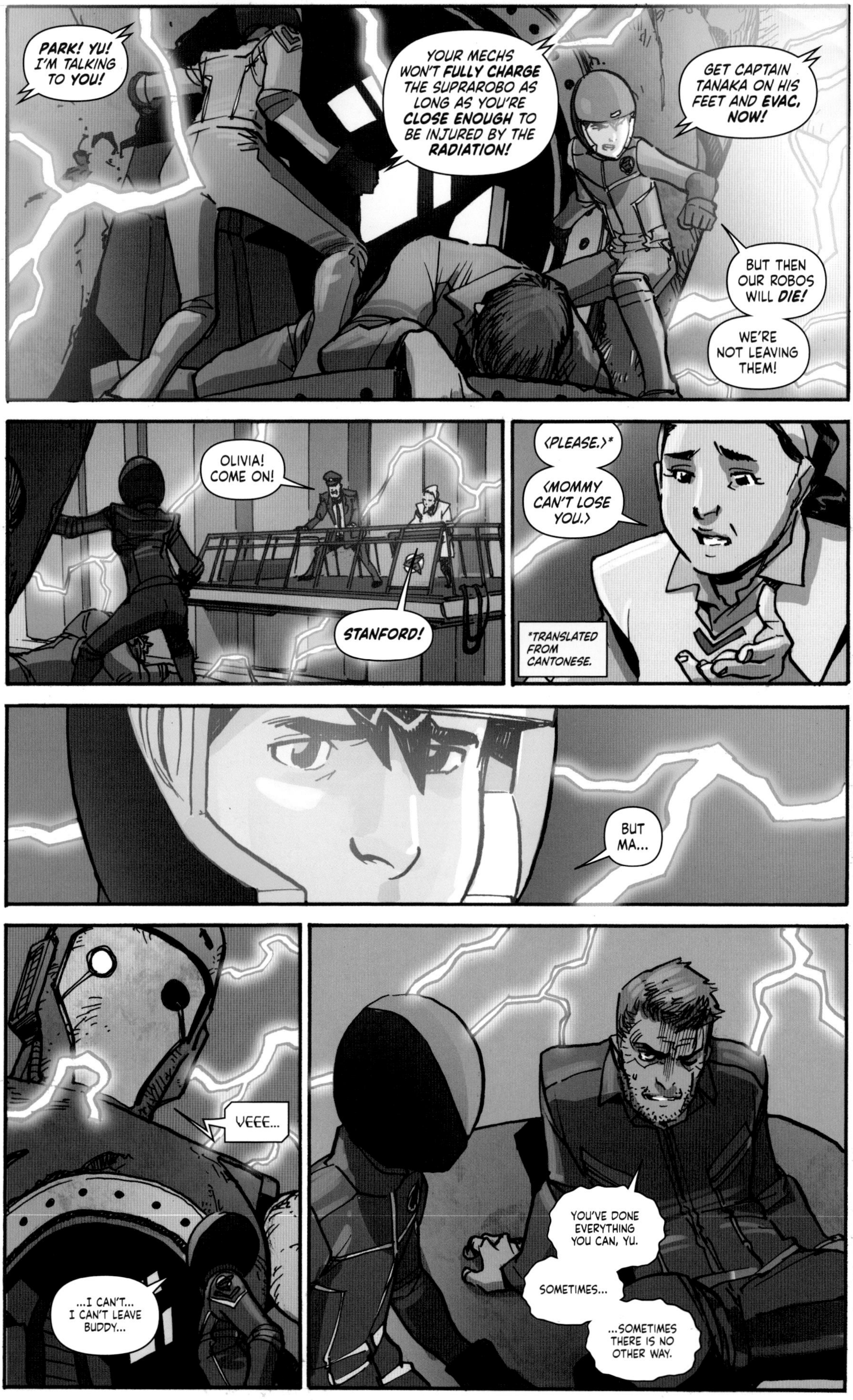
PARK! YU! I'M TALKING TO YOU!
YOUR MECHS WON'T FULLY CHARGE THE SUPRAROBO AS LONG AS YOU'RE CLOSE ENOUGH TO BE INJURED BY THE RADIATION!
GET CAPTAIN TANAKA ON HIS FEET AND EVAC, NOW!
BUT THEN OUR ROBOS WILL DIE!
WE'RE NOT LEAVING THEM!
OLIVIA! COME ON!
STANFORD!
⟨PLEASE.⟩*
⟨MOMMY CAN'T LOSE YOU.⟩
*TRANSLATED FROM CANTONESE.
BUT MA...
VEEE...
...I CAN'T... I CAN'T LEAVE BUDDY...
YOU'VE DONE EVERYTHING YOU CAN, YU.
SOMETIMES...
...SOMETIMES THERE IS NO OTHER WAY.

OLIVETTI! SANCHEZ! WHAT ARE YOU DOING--

PARDON ME, SERGEANT YU!

SORRY! COMING THROUGH!

WE JUST GOTTA FIGURE OUT WHERE TO PLUG IN...

KAAAA!

KACHUK KACHUK

AND THEN SOMETIMES THERE *IS!*

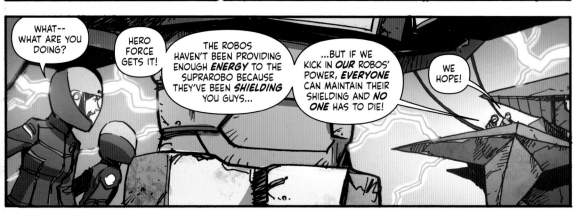

WHAT-- WHAT ARE YOU DOING?

HERO FORCE GETS IT!

THE ROBOS HAVEN'T BEEN PROVIDING ENOUGH *ENERGY* TO THE SUPRAROBO BECAUSE THEY'VE BEEN *SHIELDING* YOU GUYS...

...BUT IF WE KICK IN *OUR* ROBOS' POWER, *EVERYONE* CAN MAINTAIN THEIR SHIELDING AND *NO ONE* HAS TO DIE!

WE HOPE!

YOU GUYS...

YOU DID IT FOR *ME* ONCE, STANFORD.

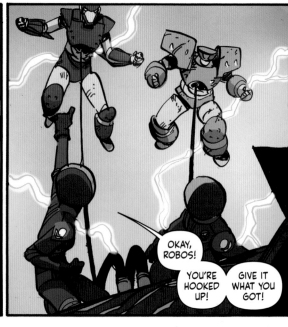

OKAY, ROBOS!

YOU'RE HOOKED UP!

GIVE IT WHAT YOU GOT!

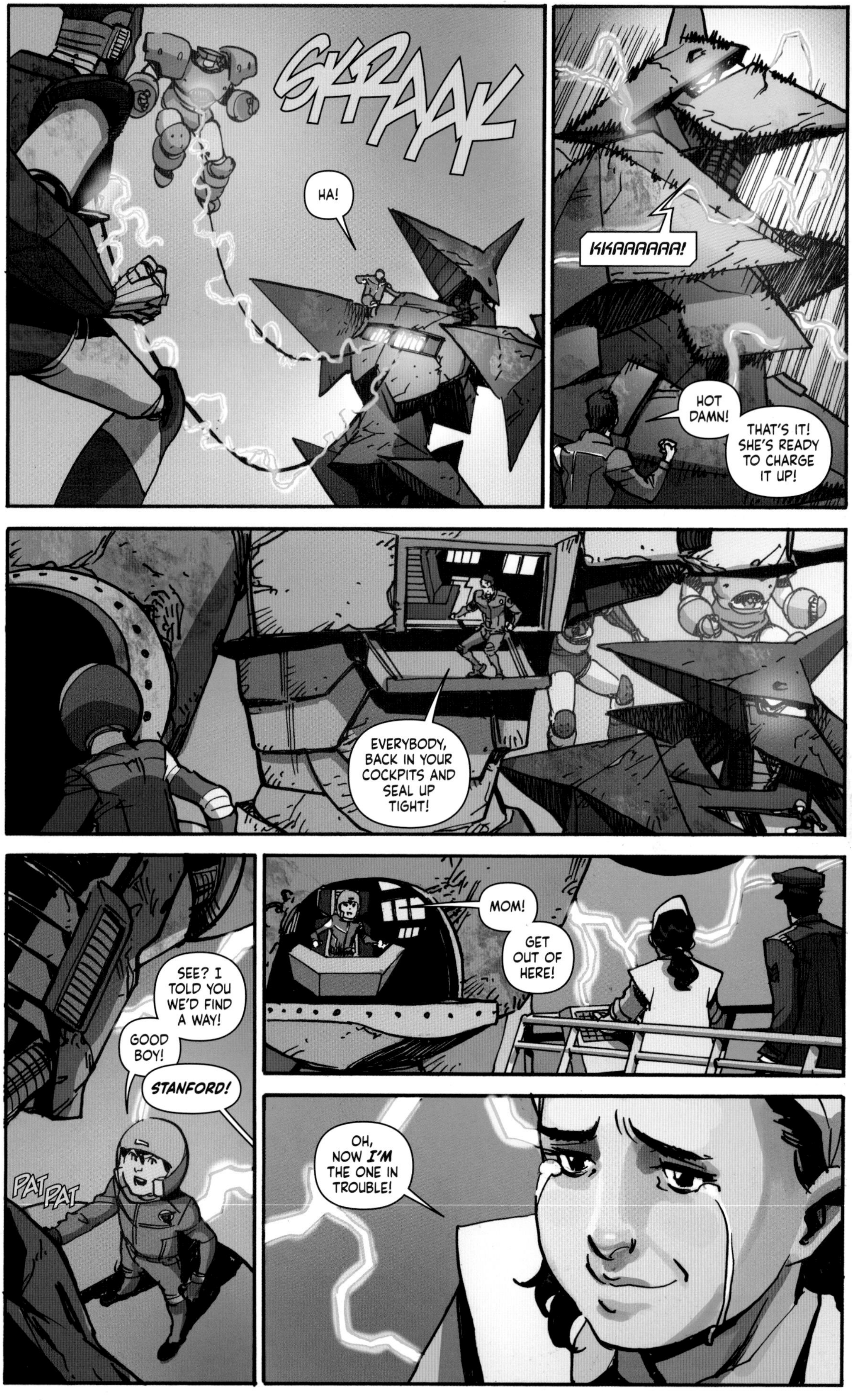
SKRAAK
HA!
KKAAAAAAA!
HOT DAMN!
THAT'S IT! SHE'S READY TO CHARGE IT UP!
EVERYBODY, BACK IN YOUR COCKPITS AND SEAL UP TIGHT!
SEE? I TOLD YOU WE'D FIND A WAY!
GOOD BOY!
STANFORD!
PAT PAT
MOM!
GET OUT OF HERE!
OH, NOW I'M THE ONE IN TROUBLE!

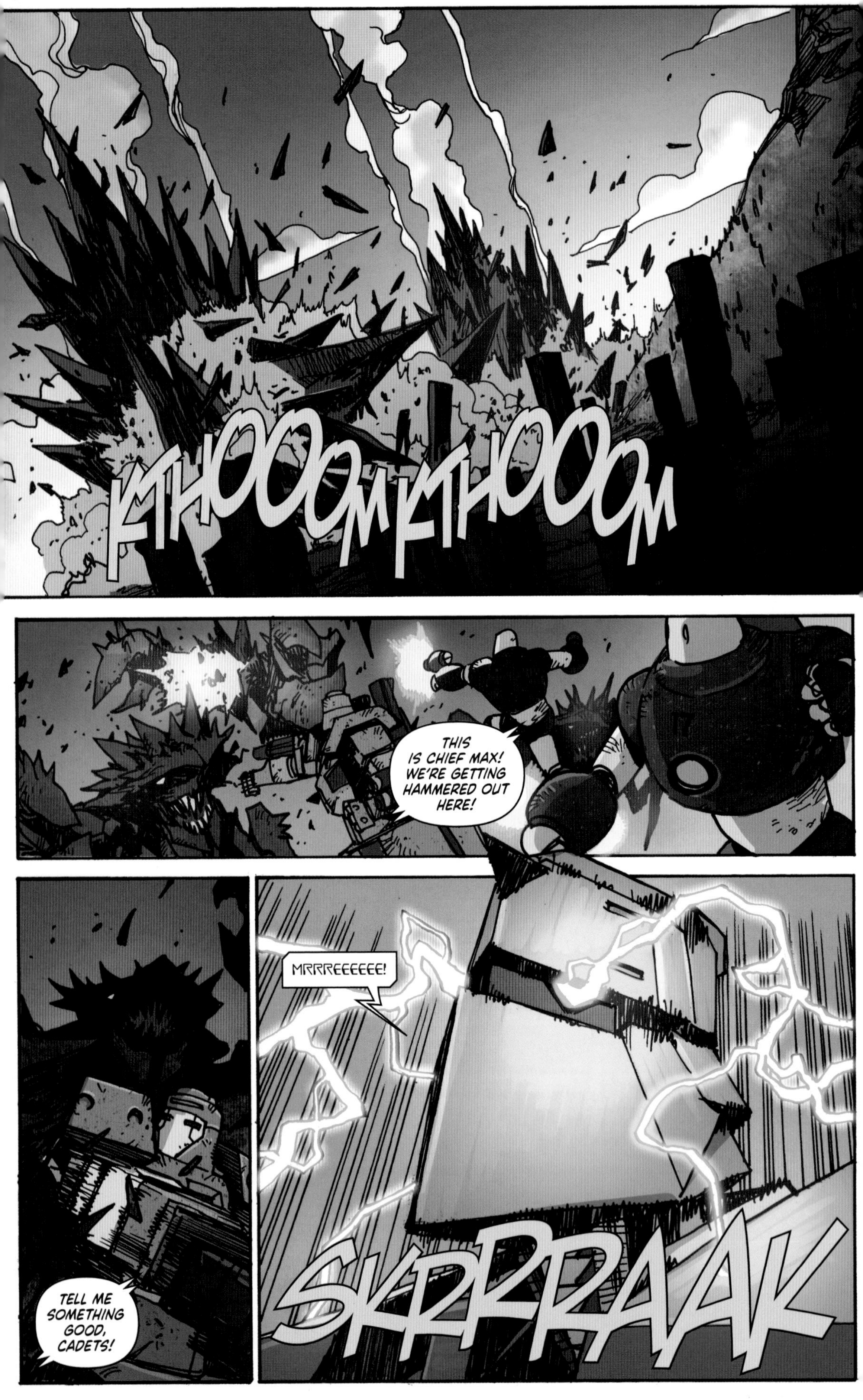
KTHOOOM KTHOOOM
THIS IS CHIEF MAX! WE'RE GETTING HAMMERED OUT HERE!
TELL ME SOMETHING GOOD, CADETS!
MRRREEEEEE!
SKRRRAAK

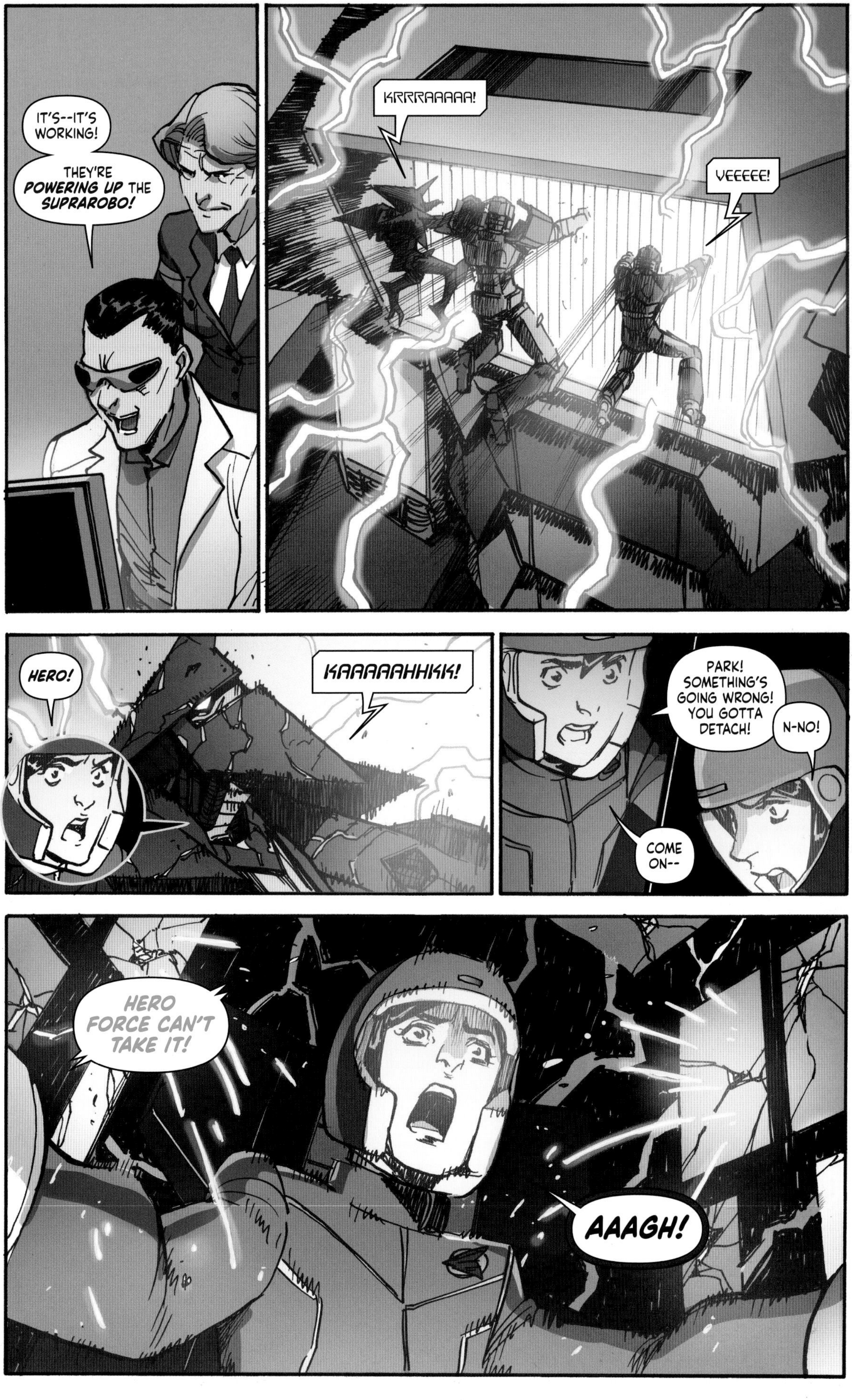
IT'S--IT'S WORKING!
THEY'RE *POWERING UP* THE *SUPRAROBO!*
KRRRAAAAA!
VEEEEE!
HERO!
KAAAAAHHKK!
PARK! SOMETHING'S GOING WRONG! YOU GOTTA DETACH!
N-NO!
COME ON--
HERO FORCE CAN'T TAKE IT!
AAAGH!

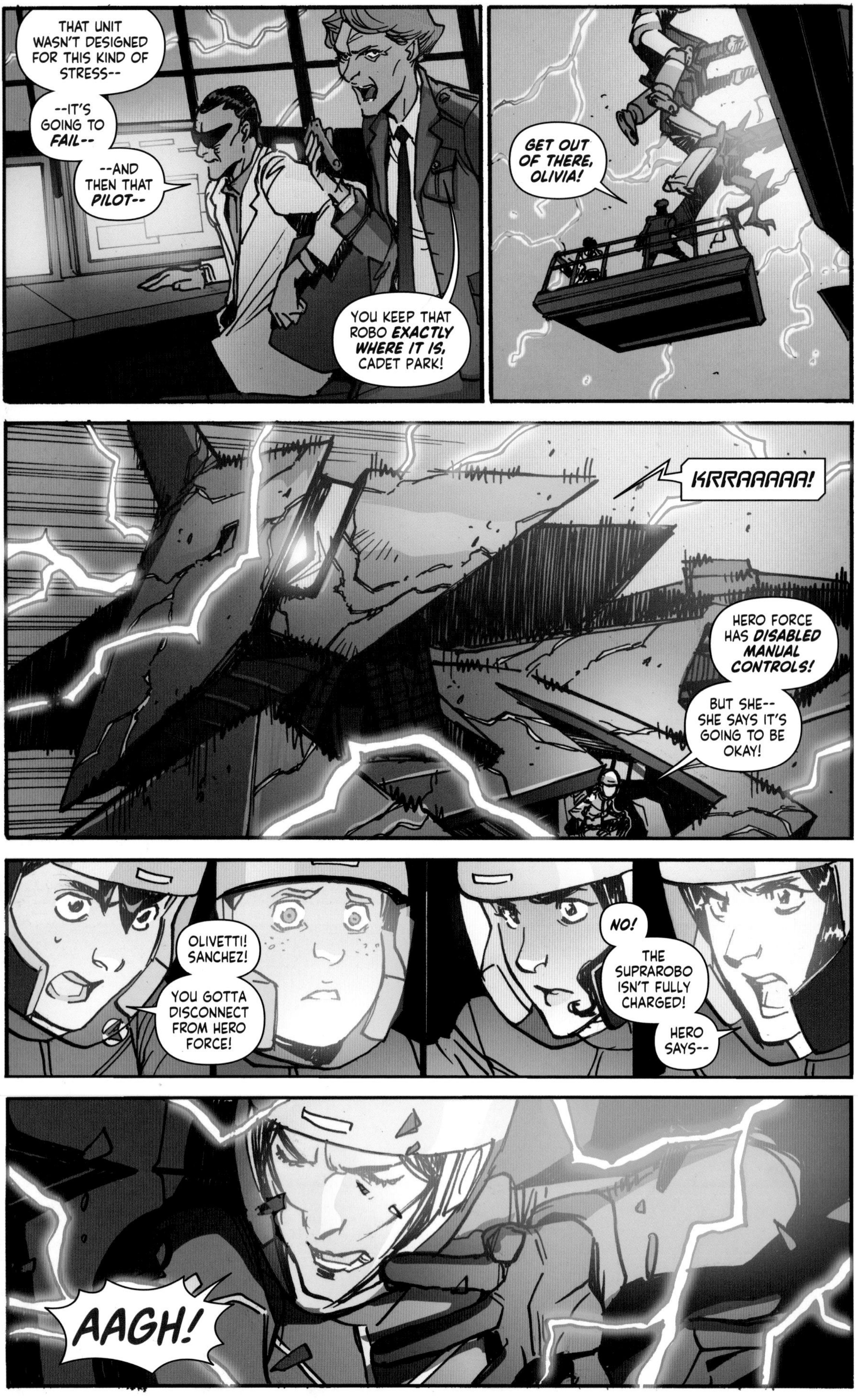
THAT UNIT WASN'T DESIGNED FOR THIS KIND OF STRESS--
--IT'S GOING TO *FAIL*--
--AND THEN THAT *PILOT*--
YOU KEEP THAT ROBO ***EXACTLY WHERE IT IS,*** CADET PARK!
GET OUT OF THERE, OLIVIA!
KRRAAAAA!
HERO FORCE HAS ***DISABLED MANUAL CONTROLS!***
BUT SHE-- SHE SAYS IT'S GOING TO BE OKAY!
OLIVETTI! SANCHEZ!
YOU GOTTA DISCONNECT FROM HERO FORCE!
NO!
THE SUPRAROBO ISN'T FULLY CHARGED!
HERO SAYS--
AAGH!

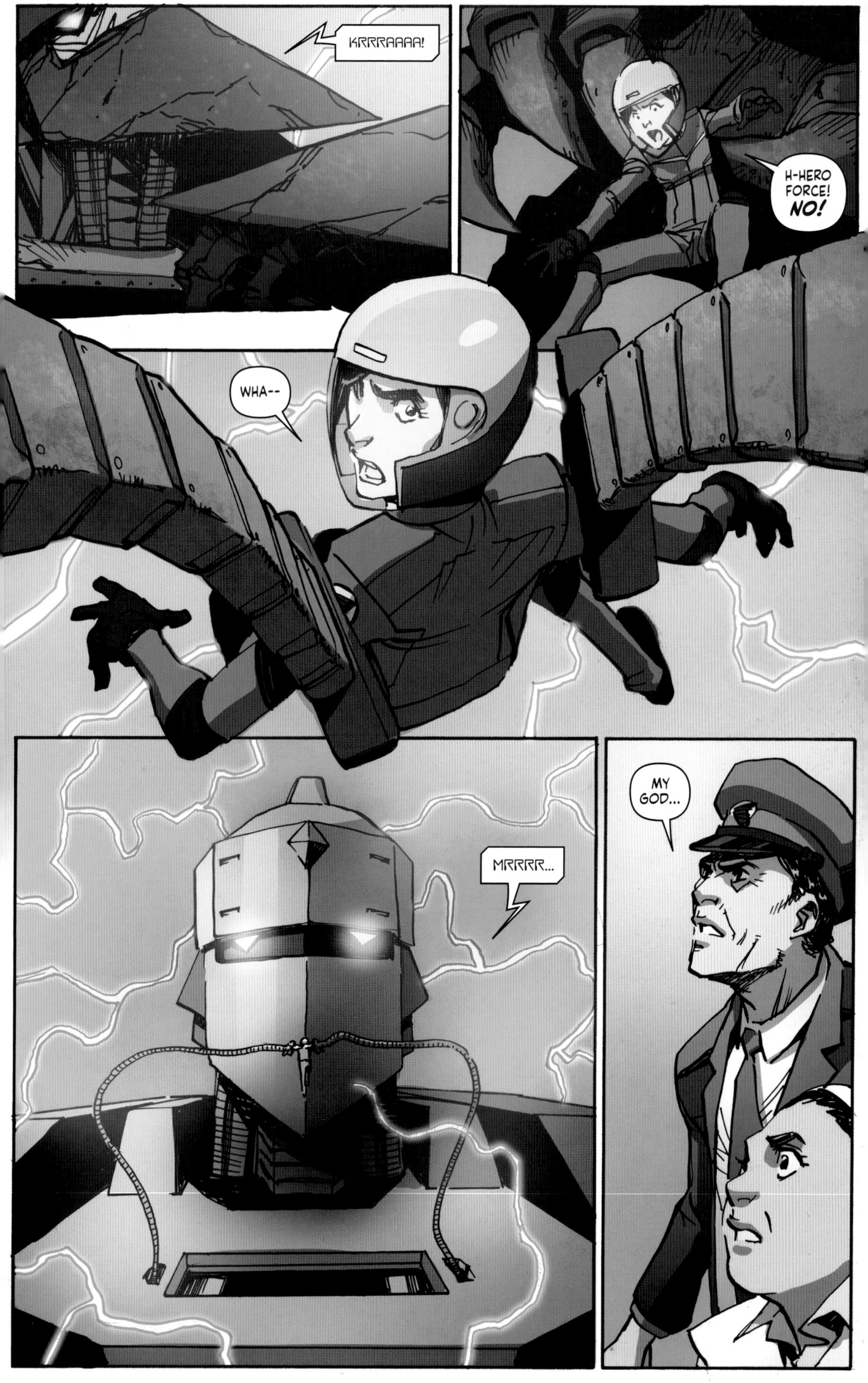
KRRRAAAA!
H-HERO FORCE! NO!
WHA--
MRRRR...
MY GOD...

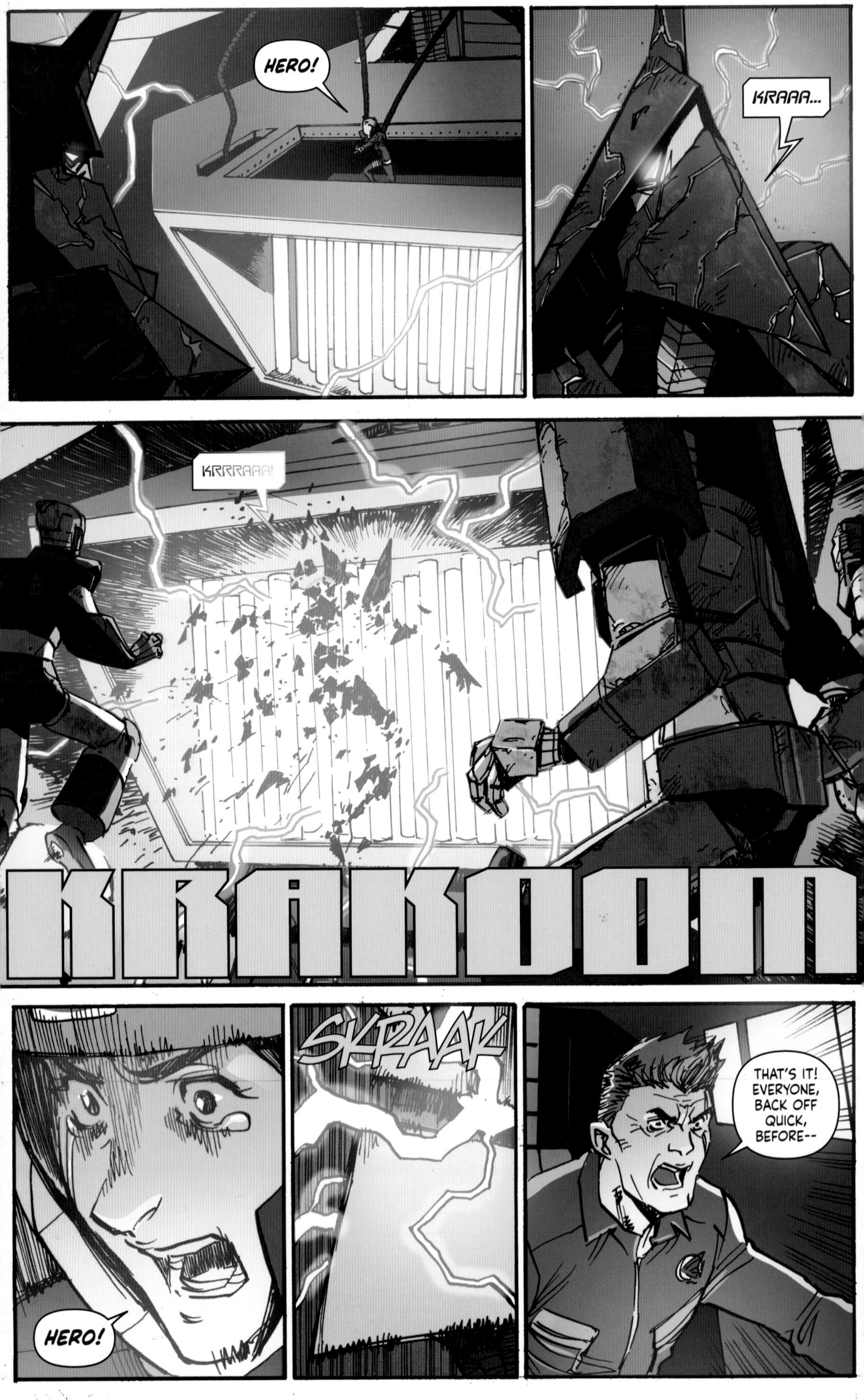
HERO!
KRAAA...
KRRRAAA!
KRAKOOM
HERO!
SKRAAK
THAT'S IT! EVERYONE, BACK OFF QUICK, BEFORE--

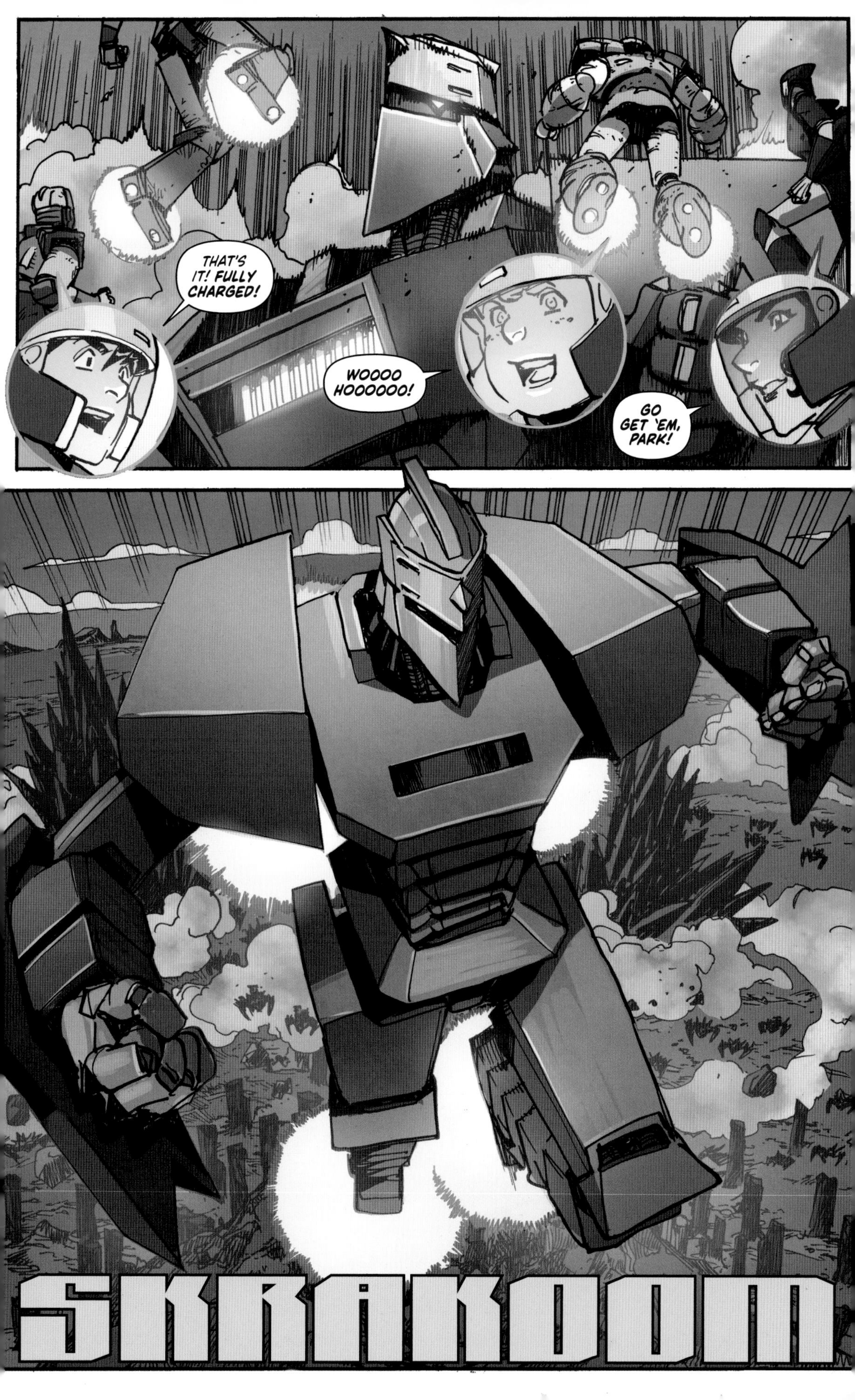
THAT'S IT! FULLY CHARGED!
WOOOO HOOOOOO!
GO GET 'EM, PARK!
SKRAKOOM

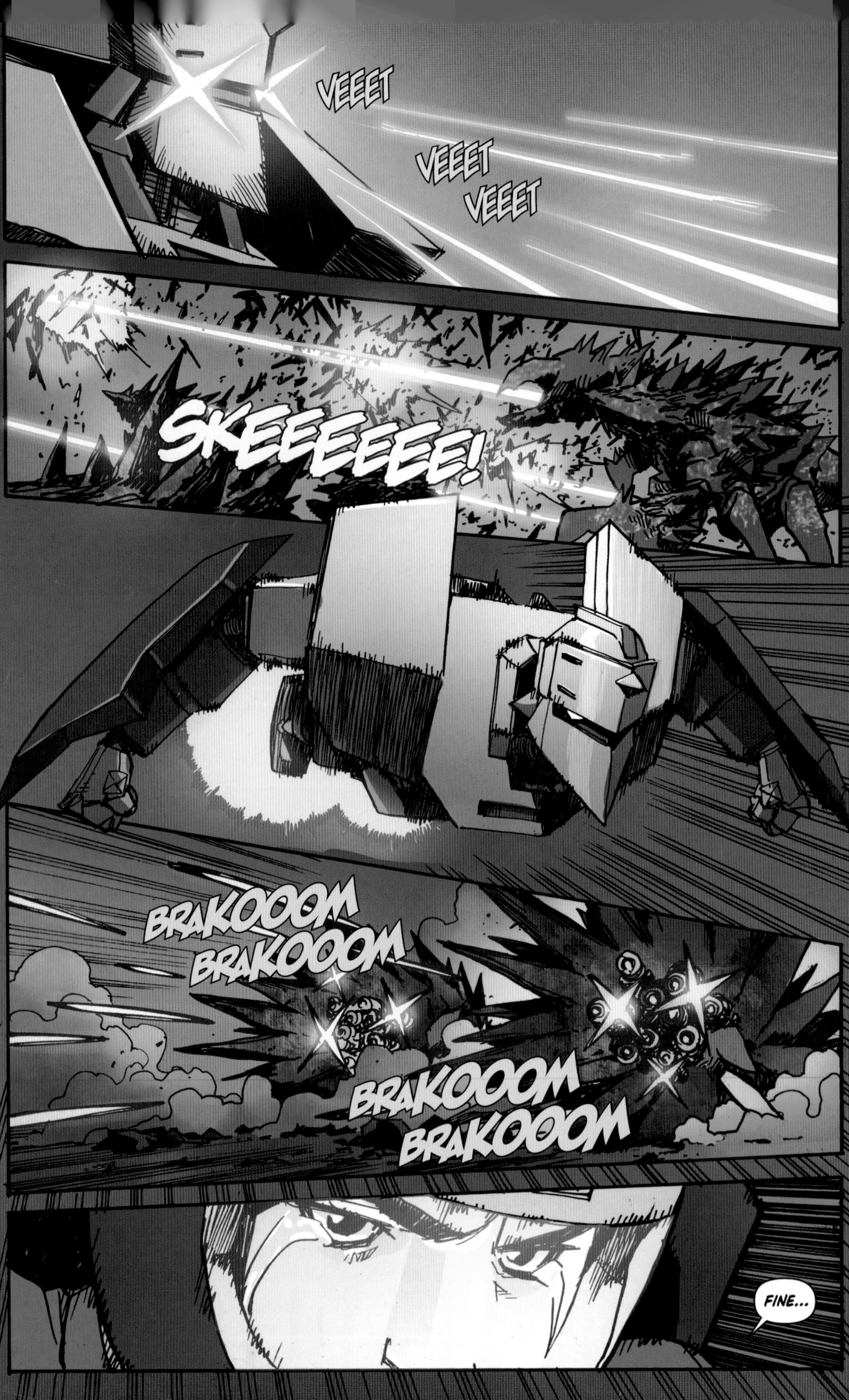
VEEET
VEEET
VEEET
SKEEEEEEEE!
BRAKOOOM
BRAKOOOM
BRAKOOOM
BRAKOOOM
FINE...

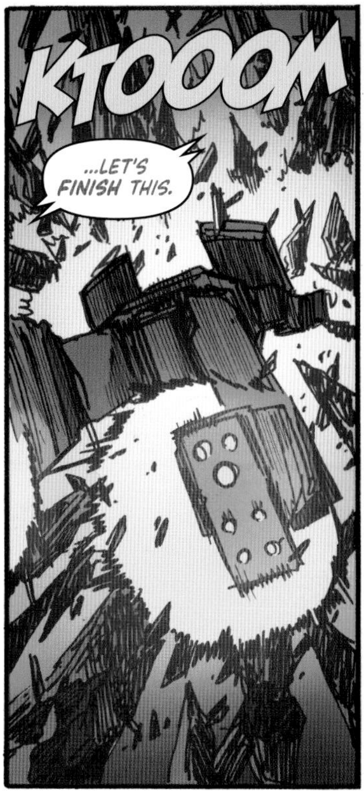
KTOOOM
...LET'S FINISH THIS.

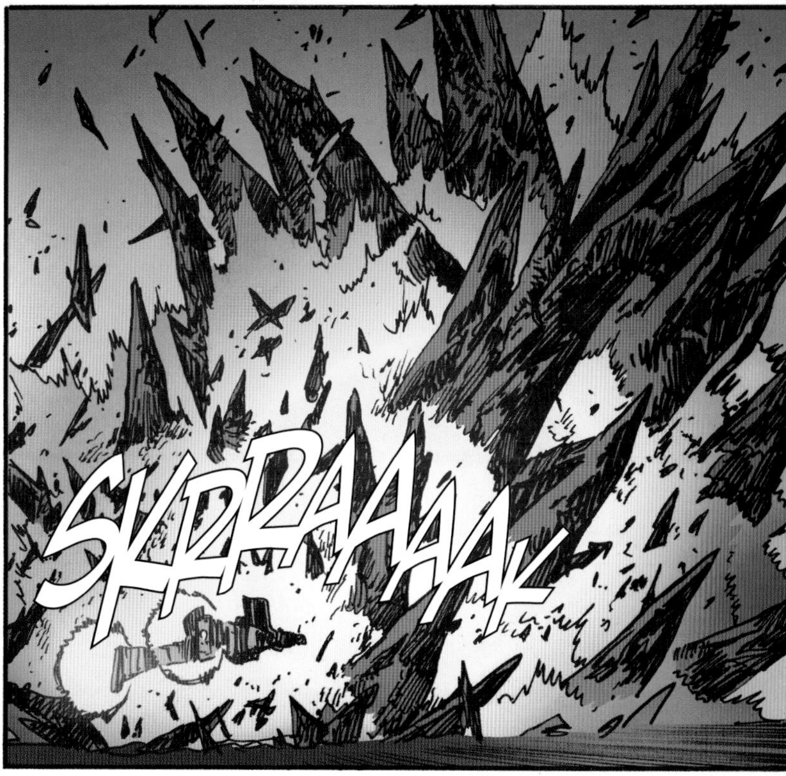
SKDRAAAAK

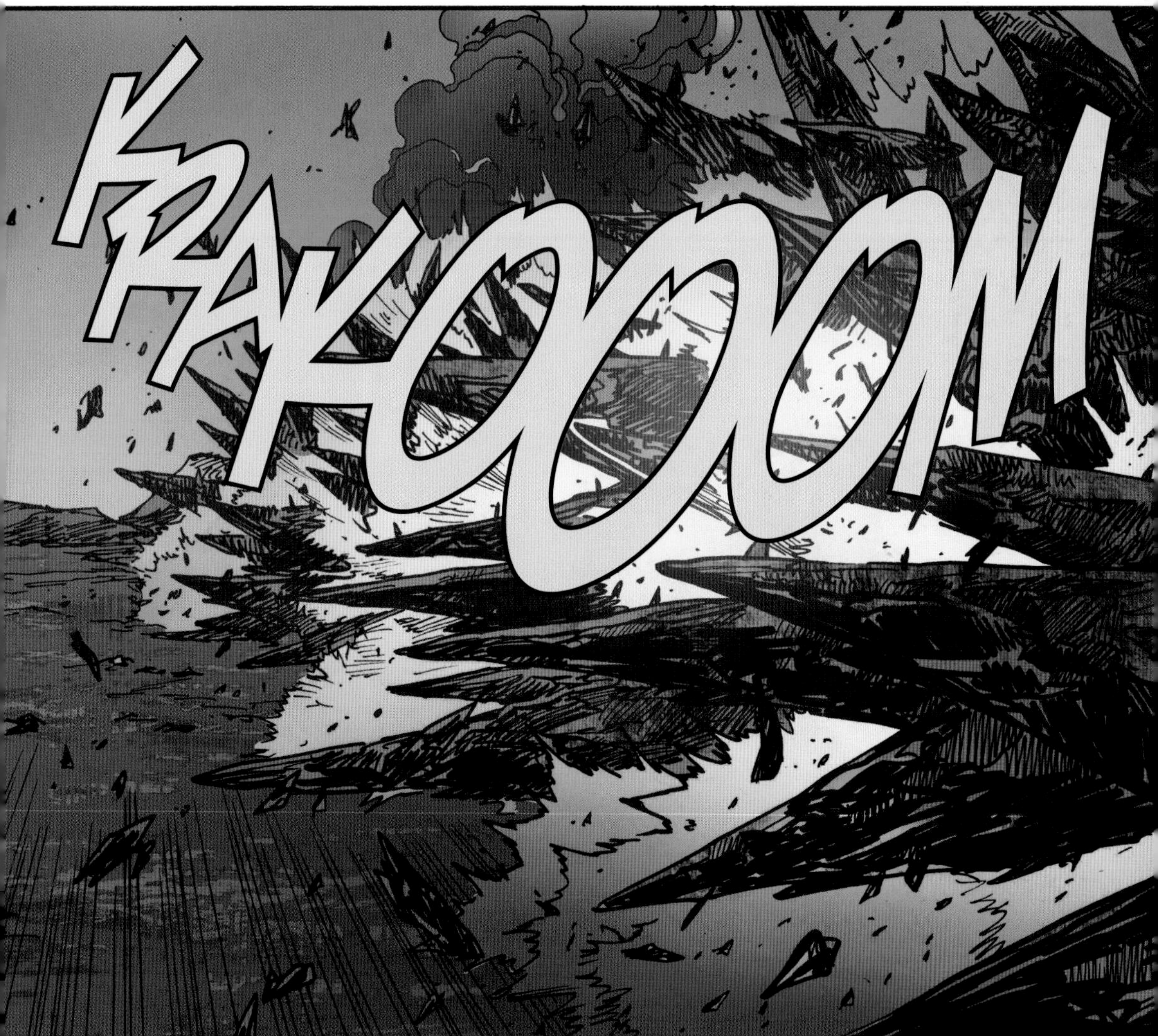
KRAKOOOM

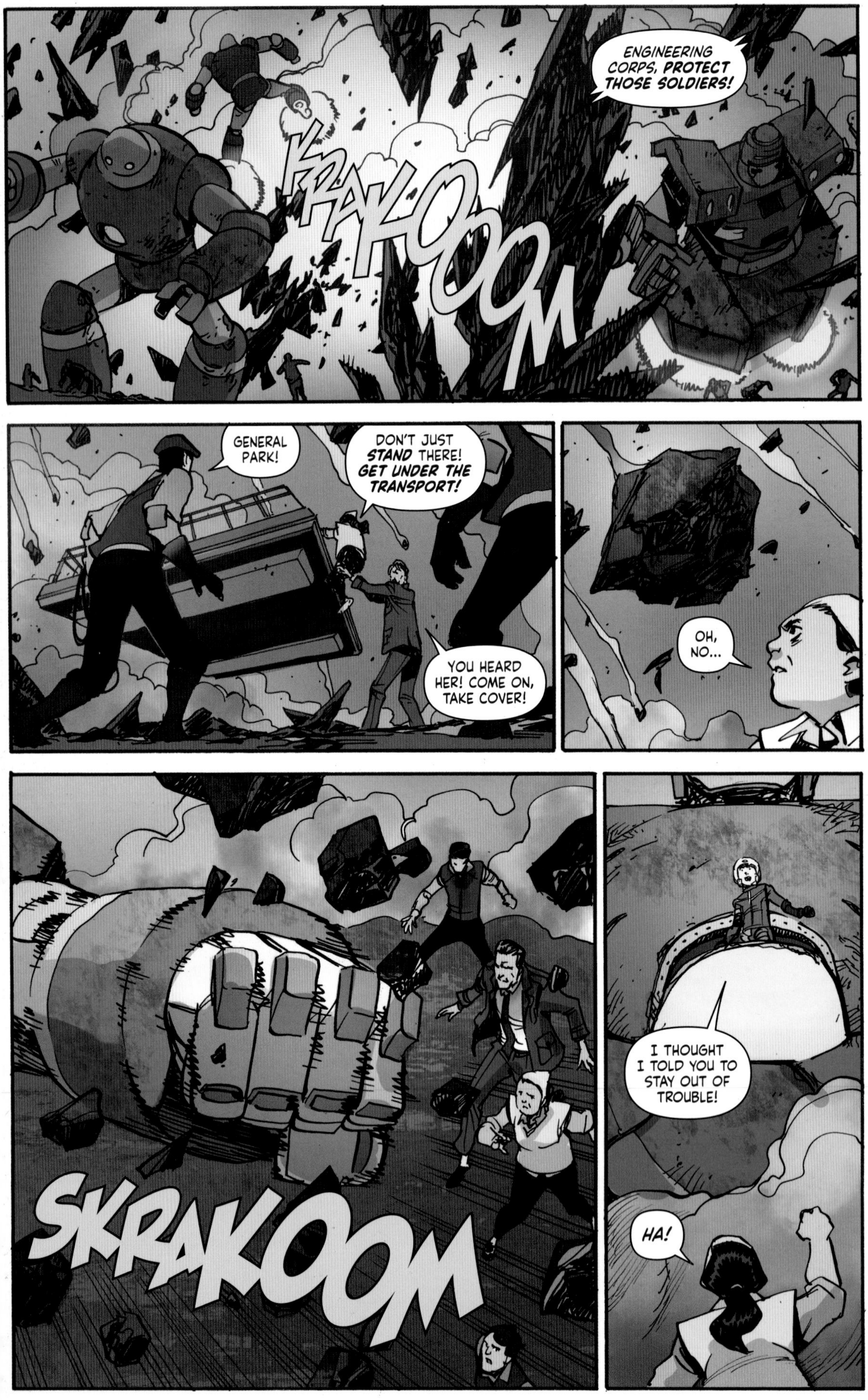
ENGINEERING CORPS, PROTECT THOSE SOLDIERS!
KRAKOOOM
GENERAL PARK!
DON'T JUST STAND THERE! GET UNDER THE TRANSPORT!
YOU HEARD HER! COME ON, TAKE COVER!
OH, NO...
SKRAKOOM
I THOUGHT I TOLD YOU TO STAY OUT OF TROUBLE!
HA!

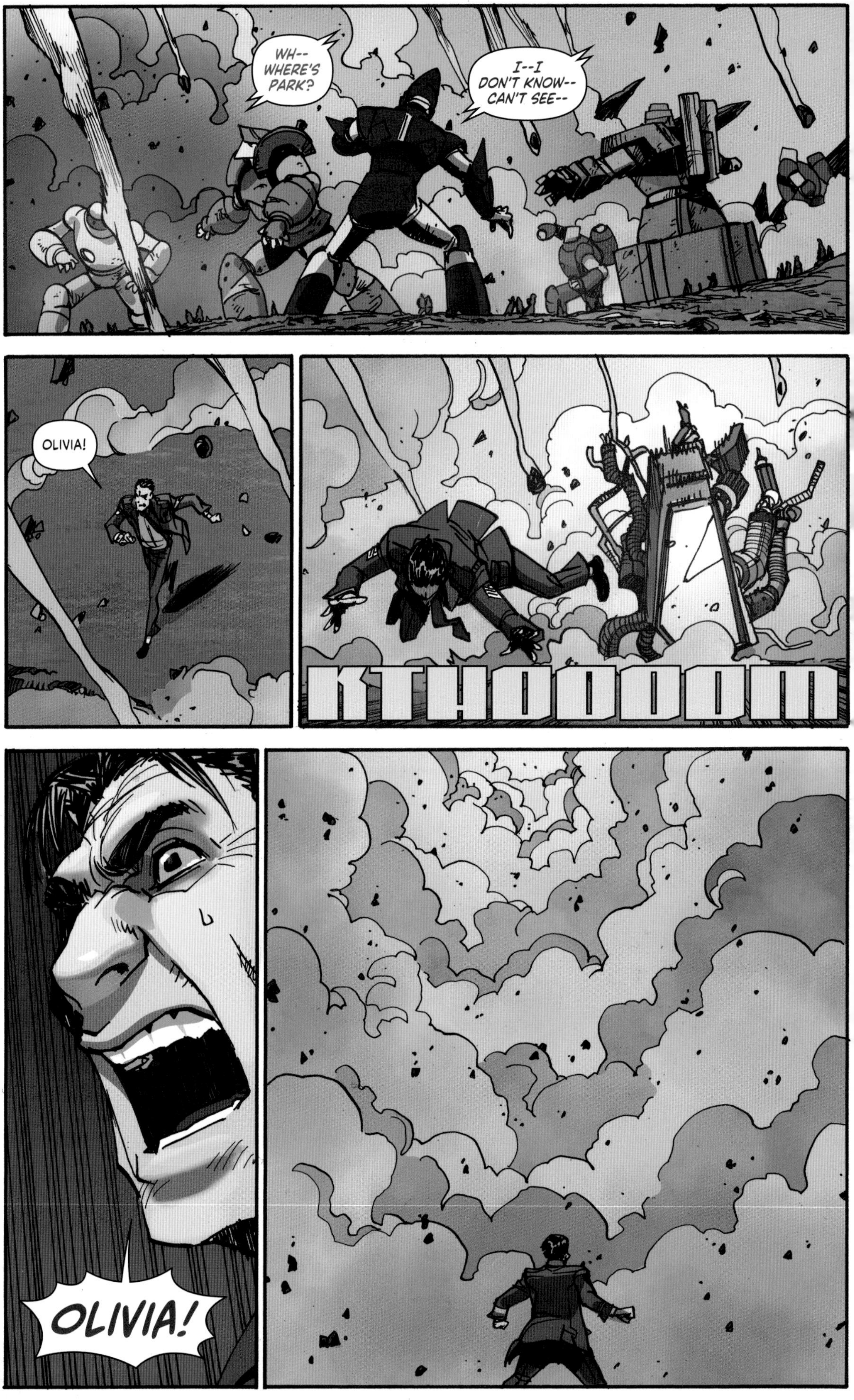
WH-- WHERE'S PARK?
I--I DON'T KNOW-- CAN'T SEE--
OLIVIA!
KTHOOOOM
OLIVIA!

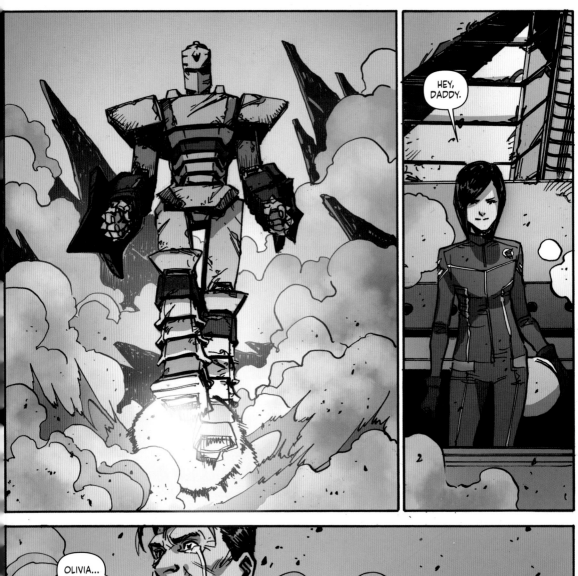

HEY, DADDY.

OLIVIA...

YEEEAAH!

THANK GOD.

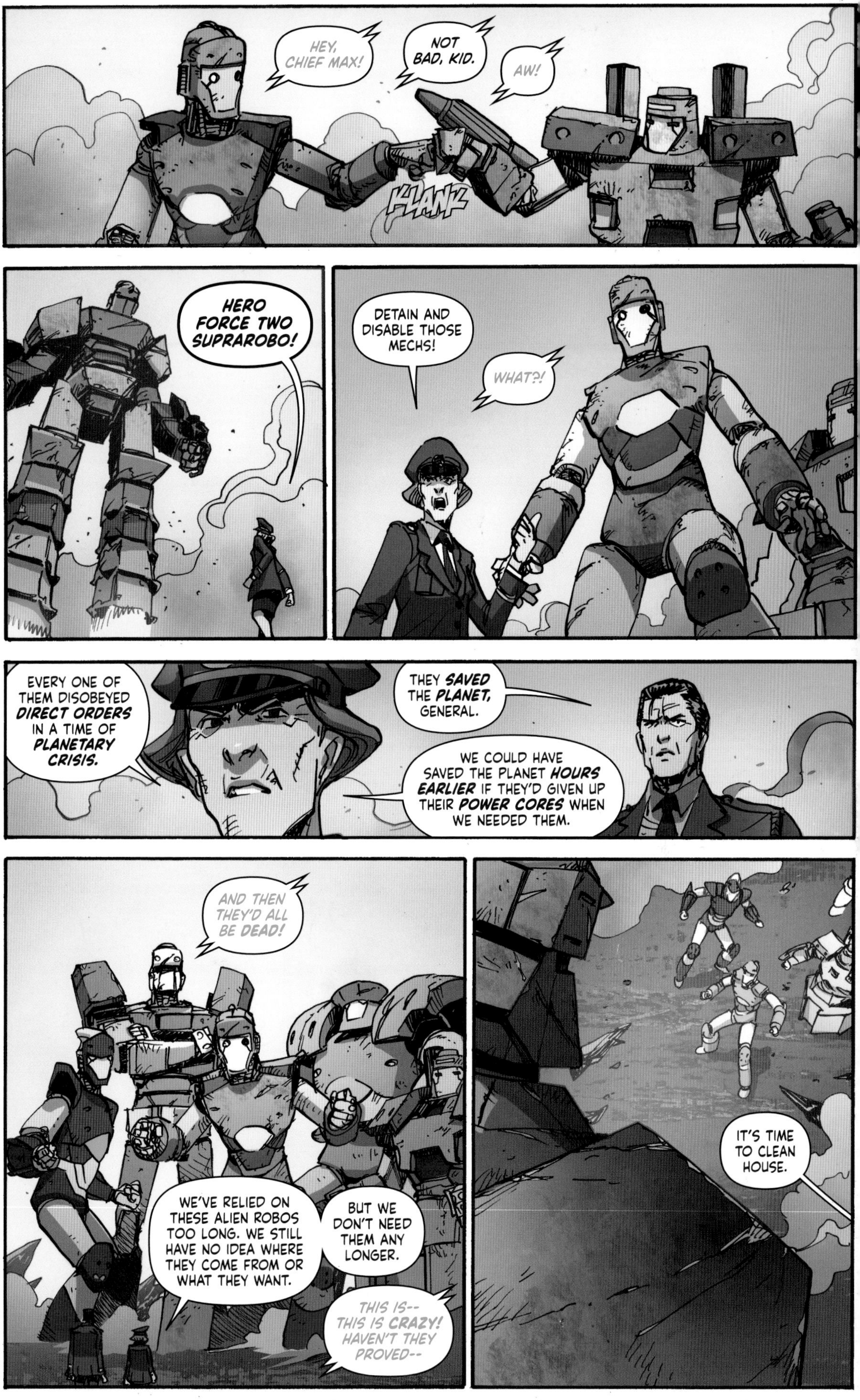
HEY, CHIEF MAX!
NOT BAD, KID.
AW!
KLANK
HERO FORCE TWO SUPRAROBO!
DETAIN AND DISABLE THOSE MECHS!
WHAT?!
EVERY ONE OF THEM DISOBEYED DIRECT ORDERS IN A TIME OF PLANETARY CRISIS.
THEY SAVED THE PLANET, GENERAL.
WE COULD HAVE SAVED THE PLANET HOURS EARLIER IF THEY'D GIVEN UP THEIR POWER CORES WHEN WE NEEDED THEM.
AND THEN THEY'D ALL BE DEAD!
WE'VE RELIED ON THESE ALIEN ROBOS TOO LONG. WE STILL HAVE NO IDEA WHERE THEY COME FROM OR WHAT THEY WANT.
BUT WE DON'T NEED THEM ANY LONGER.
THIS IS-- THIS IS CRAZY! HAVEN'T THEY PROVED--
IT'S TIME TO CLEAN HOUSE.

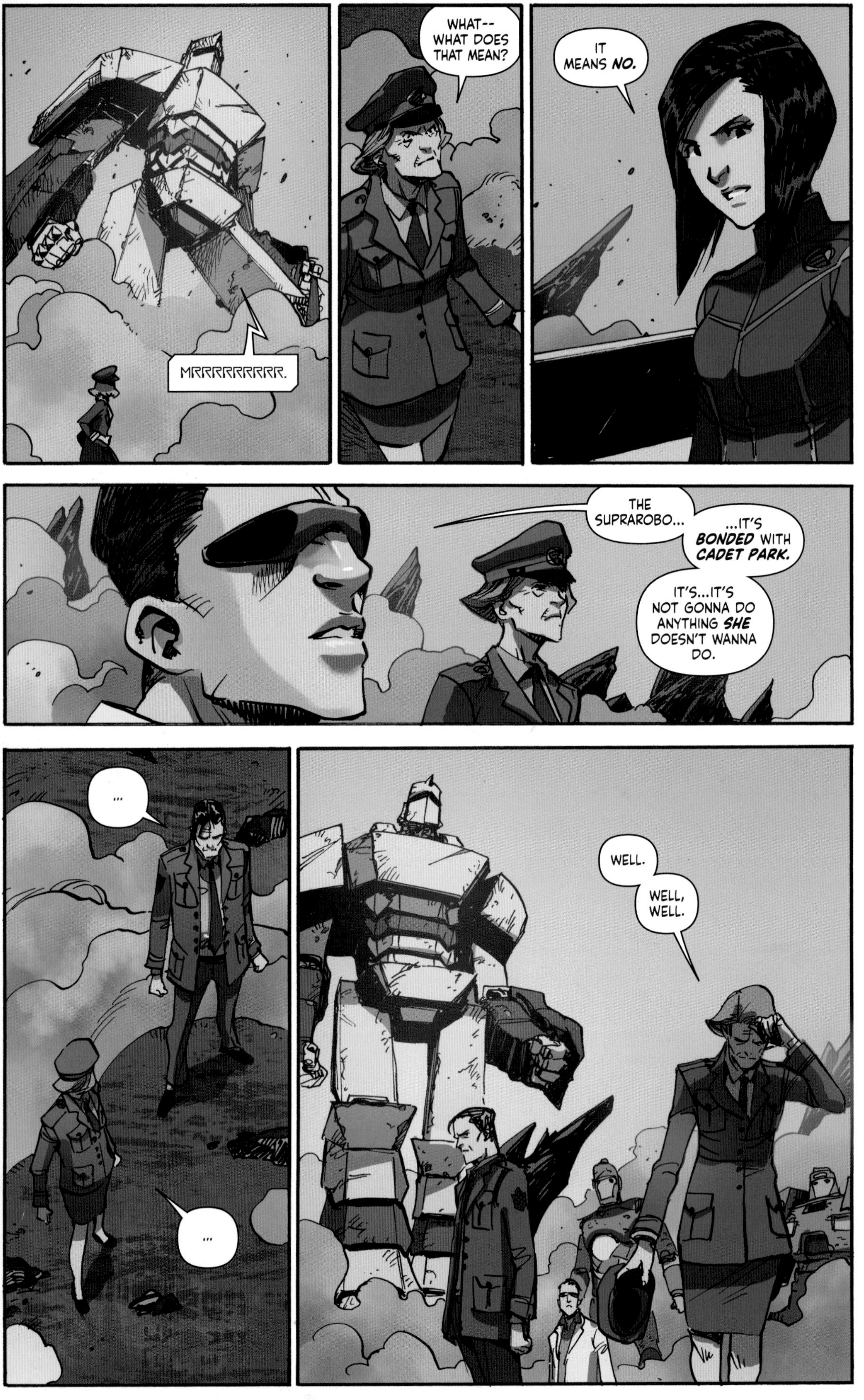
MRRRRRRRRRR.
WHAT-- WHAT DOES THAT MEAN?
IT MEANS **NO.**
THE SUPRAROBO...
...IT'S **BONDED** WITH **CADET PARK.**
IT'S...IT'S NOT GONNA DO ANYTHING **SHE** DOESN'T WANNA DO.
...
...
WELL.
WELL, WELL.

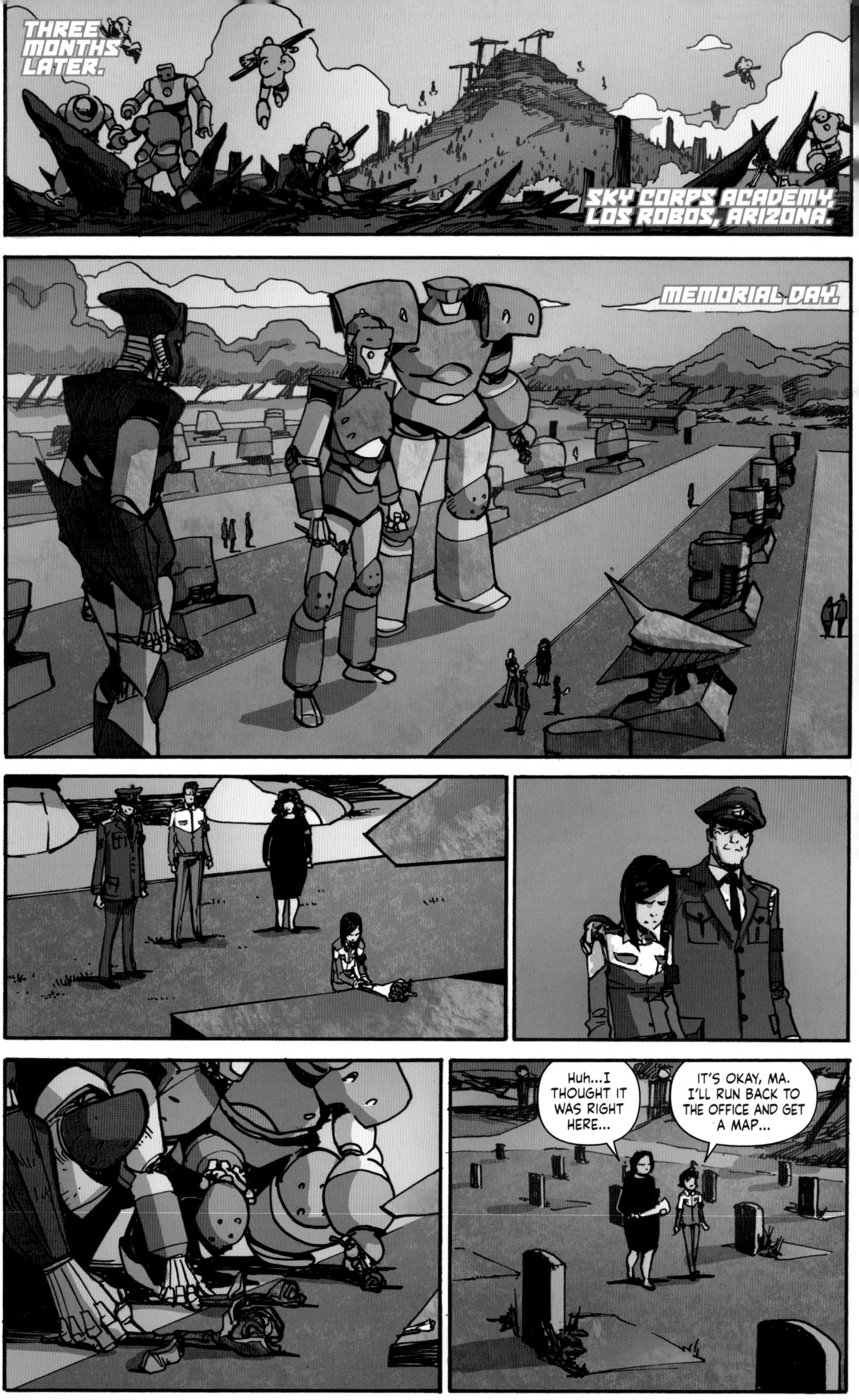
THREE MONTHS LATER.
SKY CORPS ACADEMY, LOS ROBOS, ARIZONA.
MEMORIAL DAY.
Huh...I THOUGHT IT WAS RIGHT HERE...
IT'S OKAY, MA. I'LL RUN BACK TO THE OFFICE AND GET A MAP...

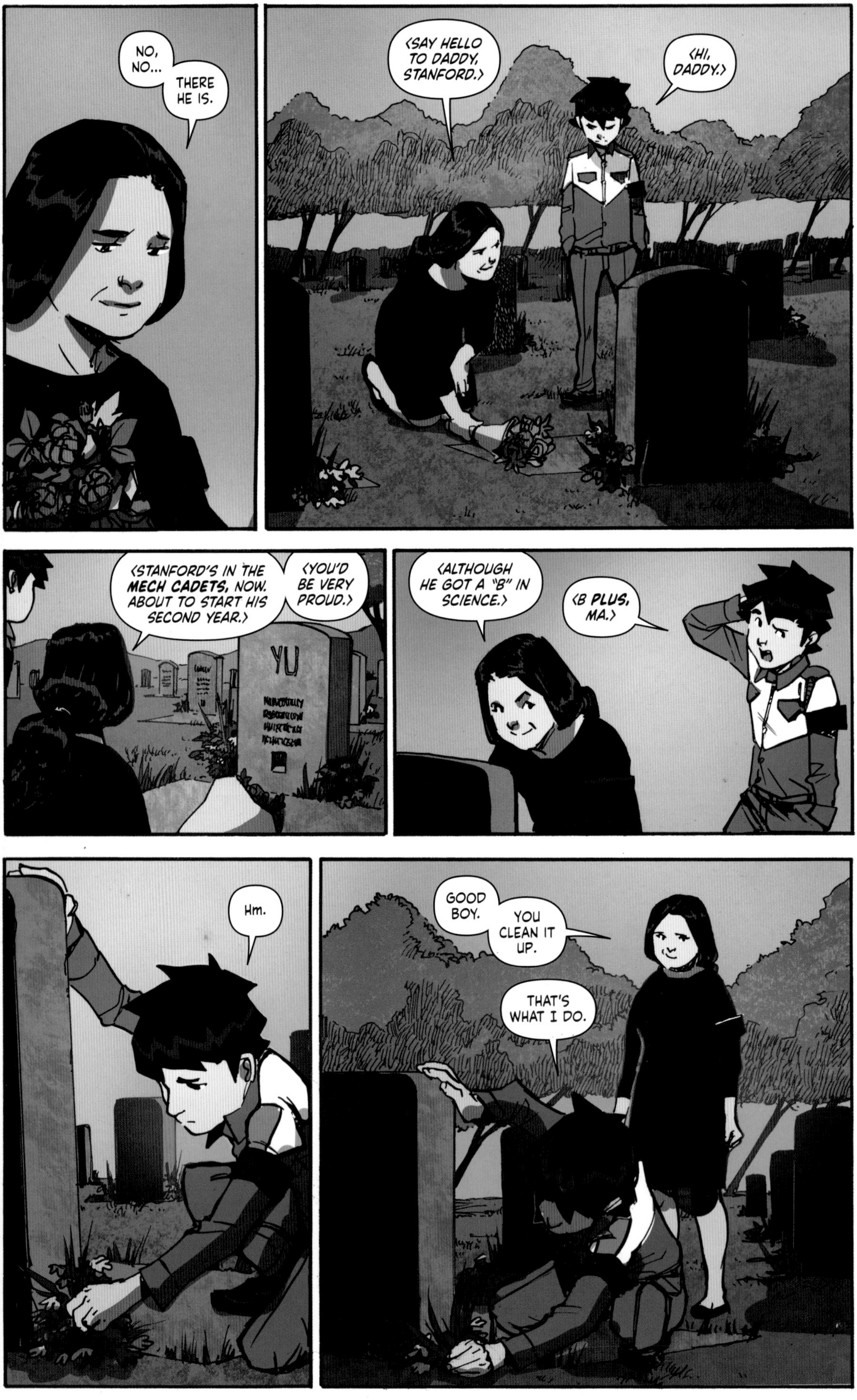
NO, NO...
THERE HE IS.
<SAY HELLO TO DADDY, STANFORD.>
<HI, DADDY.>
<STANFORD'S IN THE **MECH CADETS**, NOW. ABOUT TO START HIS SECOND YEAR.>
<YOU'D BE VERY PROUD.>
YU
<ALTHOUGH HE GOT A "B" IN SCIENCE.>
<B **PLUS**, MA.>
Hm.
GOOD BOY.
YOU CLEAN IT UP.
THAT'S WHAT I DO.

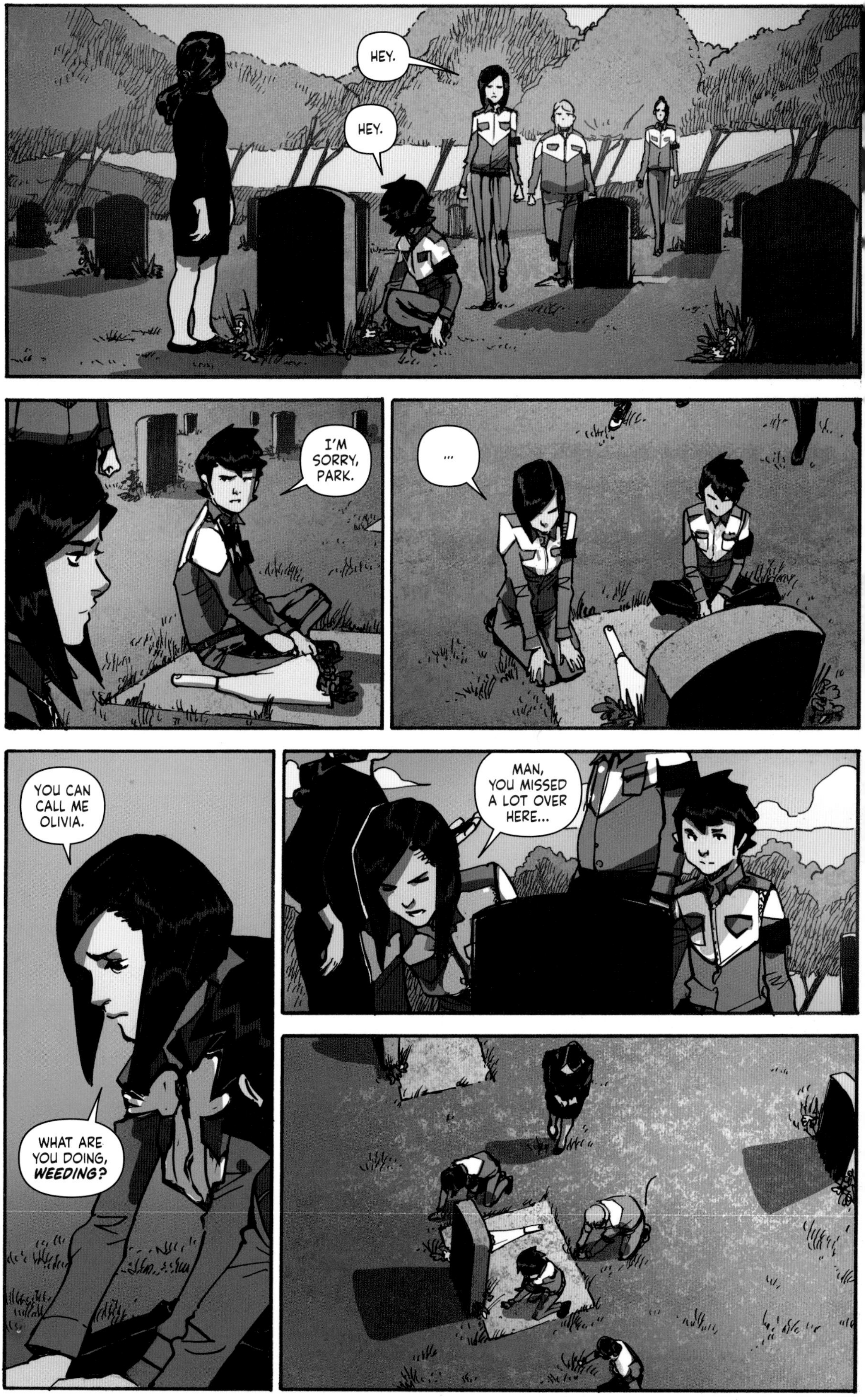
HEY.
HEY.
I'M SORRY, PARK.
...
YOU CAN CALL ME OLIVIA.
WHAT ARE YOU DOING, ***WEEDING?***
MAN, YOU MISSED A LOT OVER HERE...

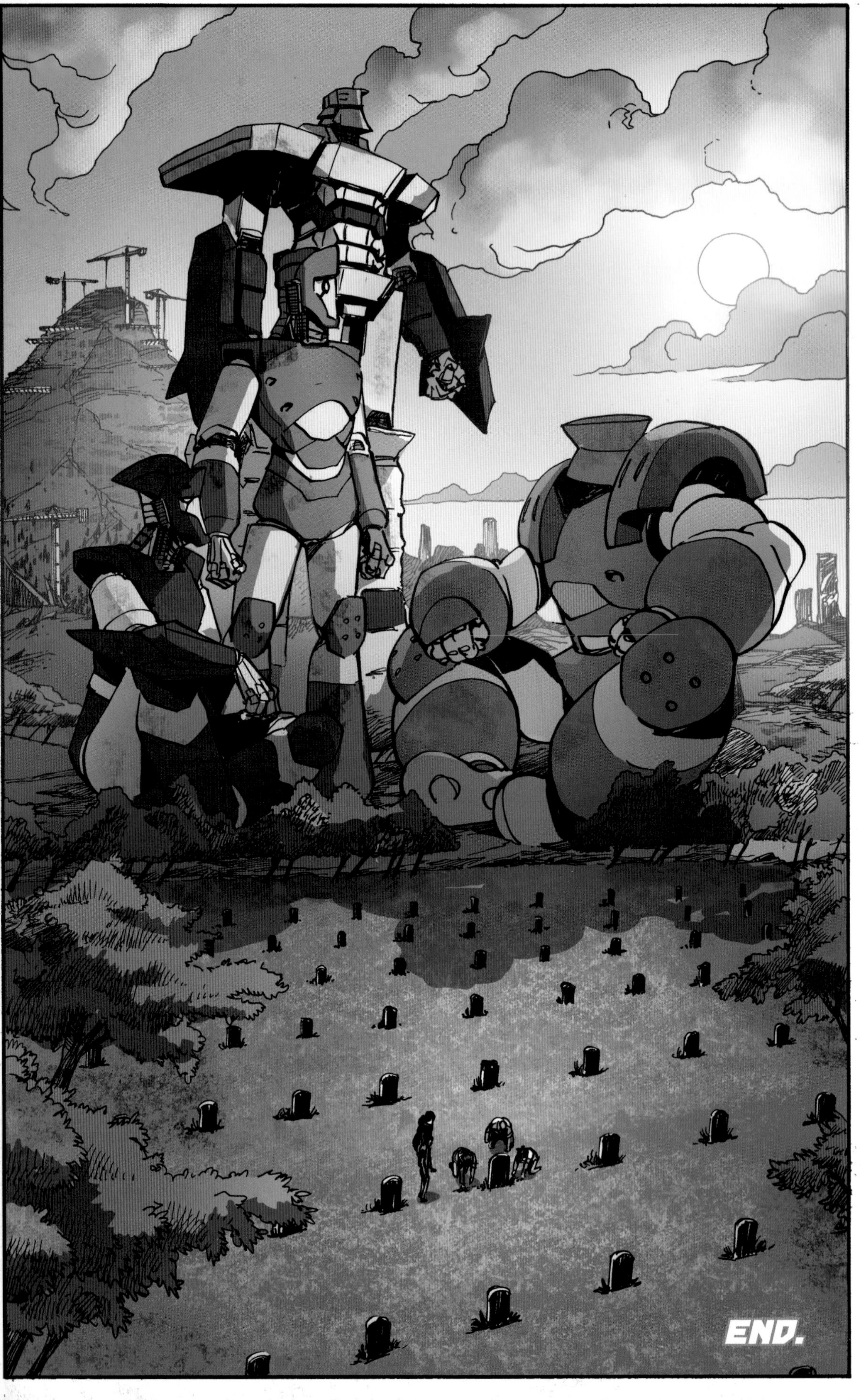
END.

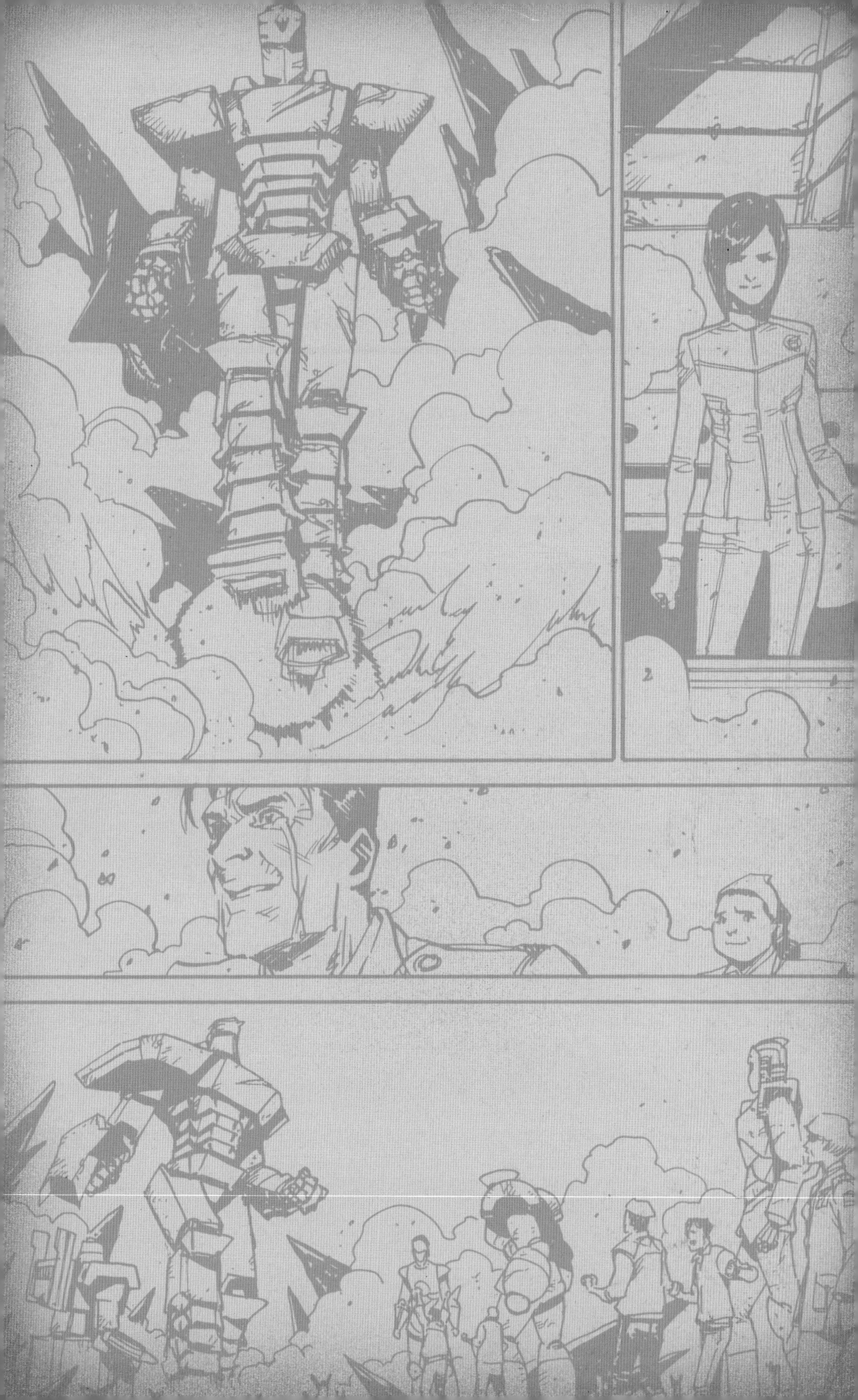

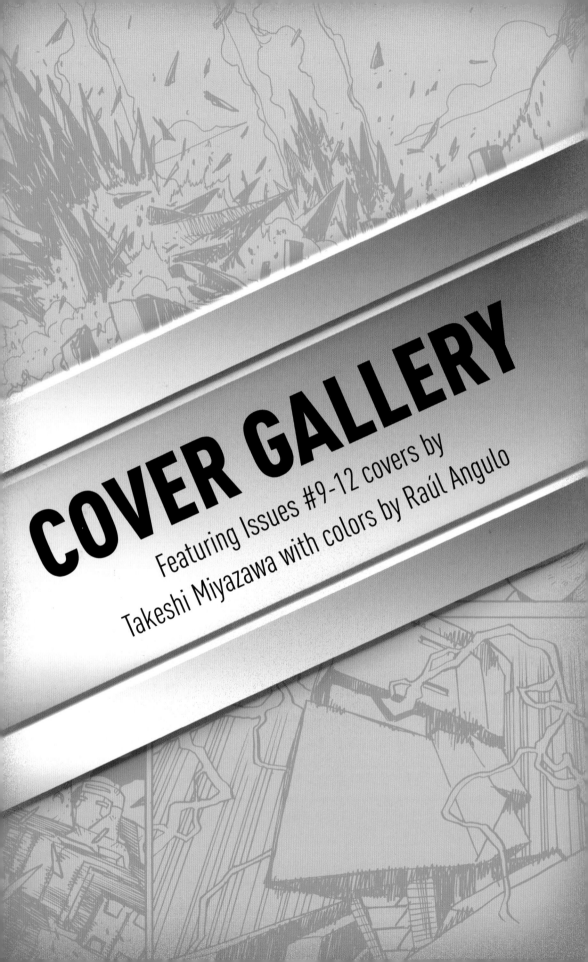

COVER GALLERY

Featuring Issues #9-12 covers by
Takeshi Miyazawa with colors by Raúl Angulo

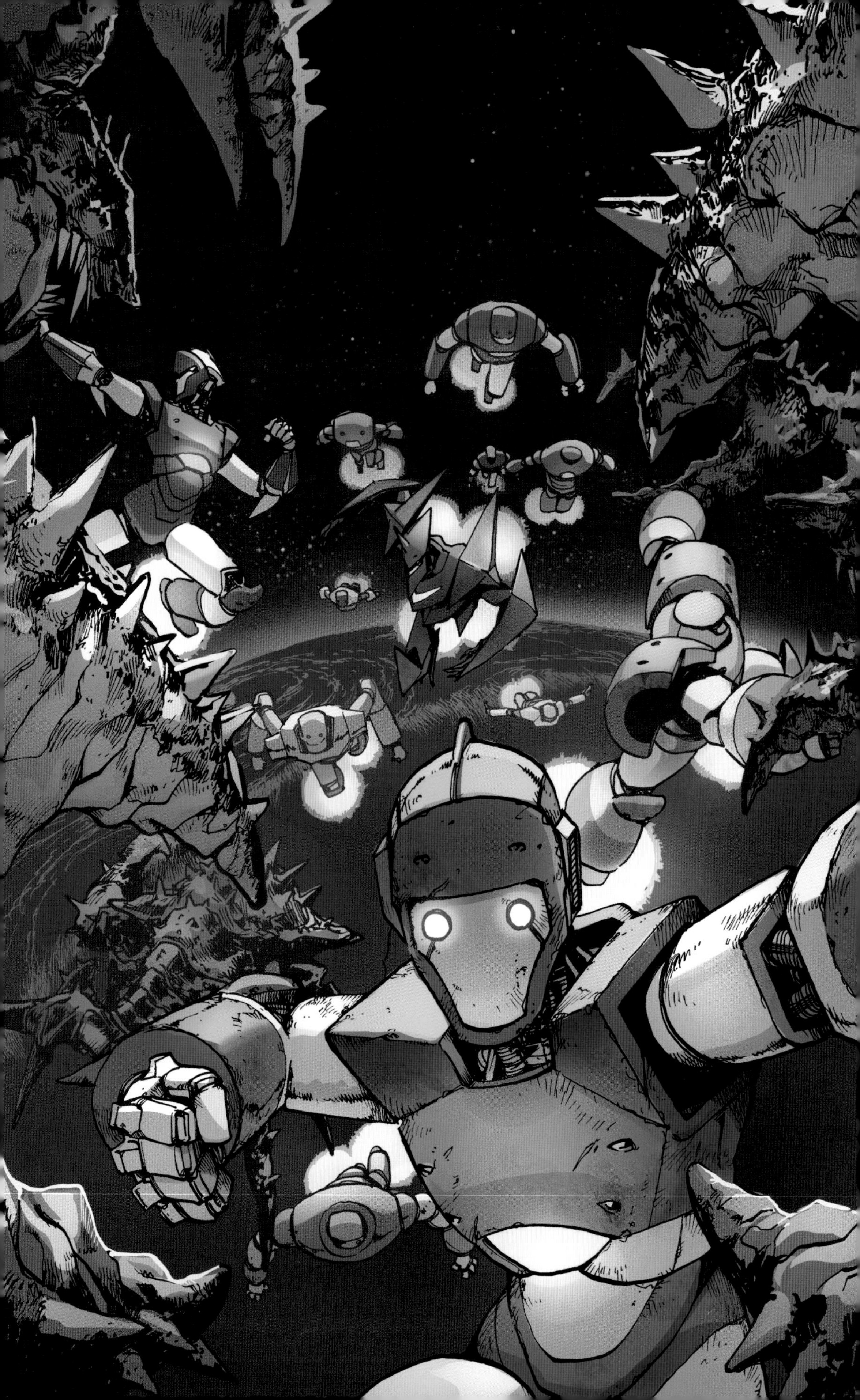

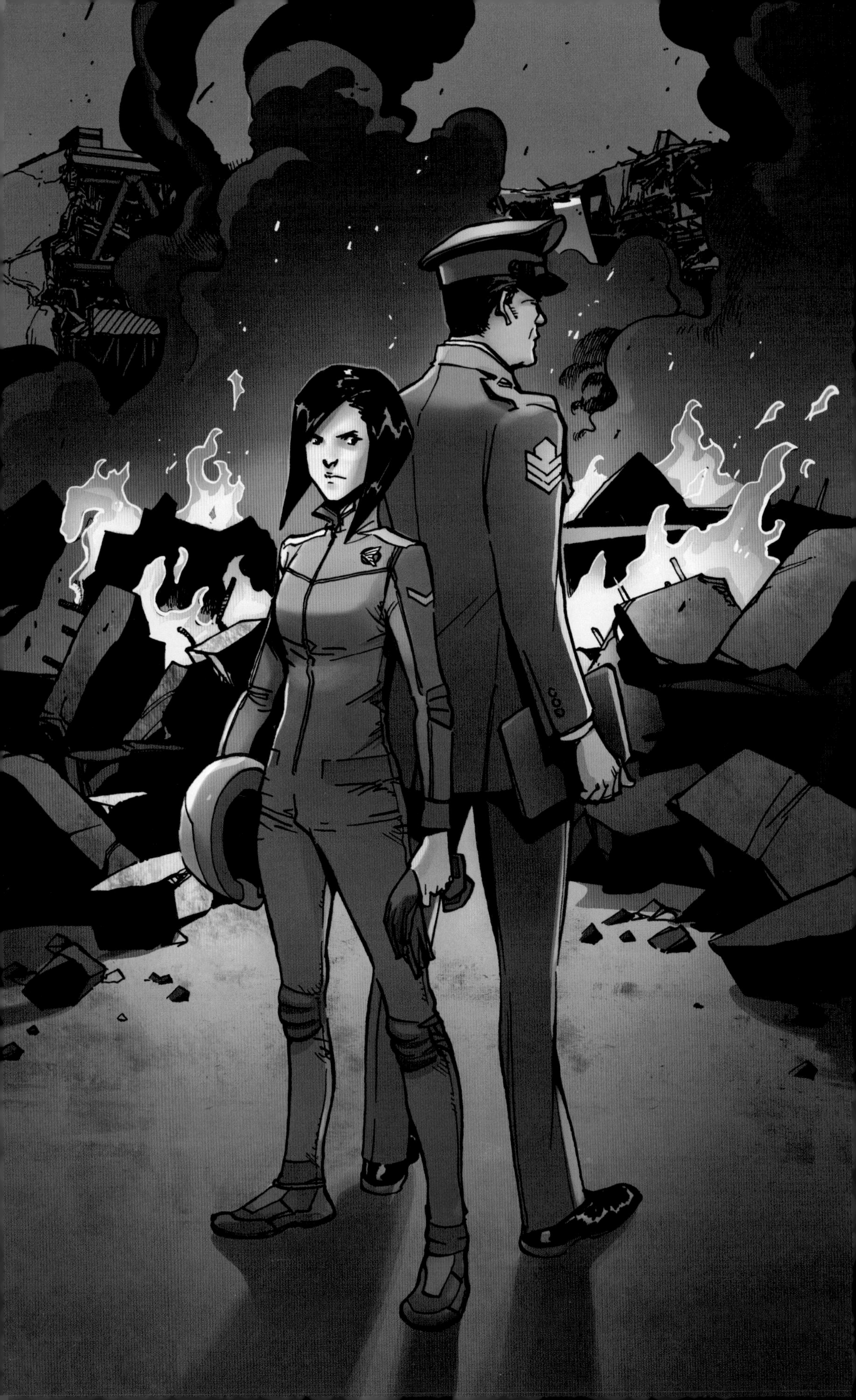

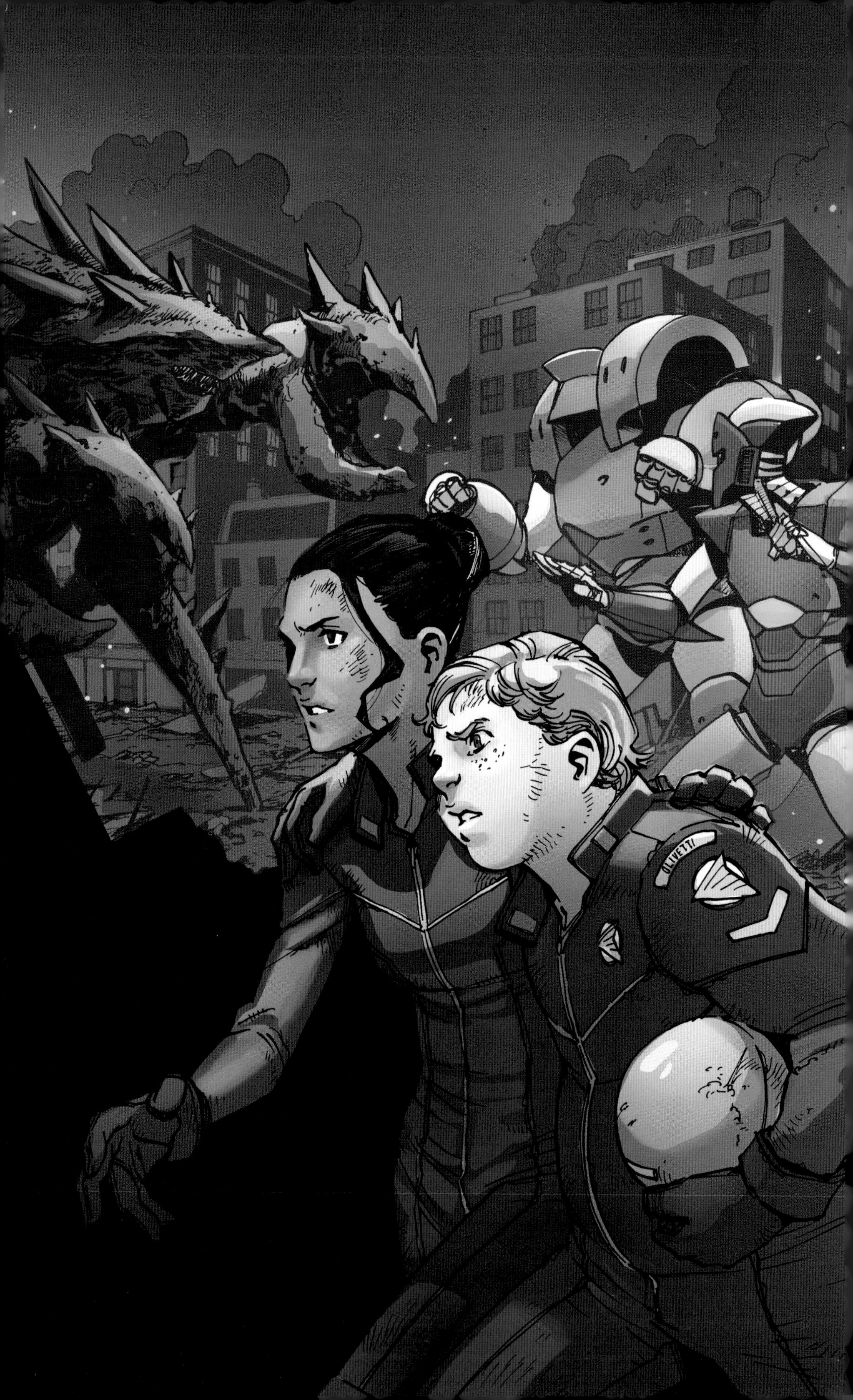
OLIVETTI

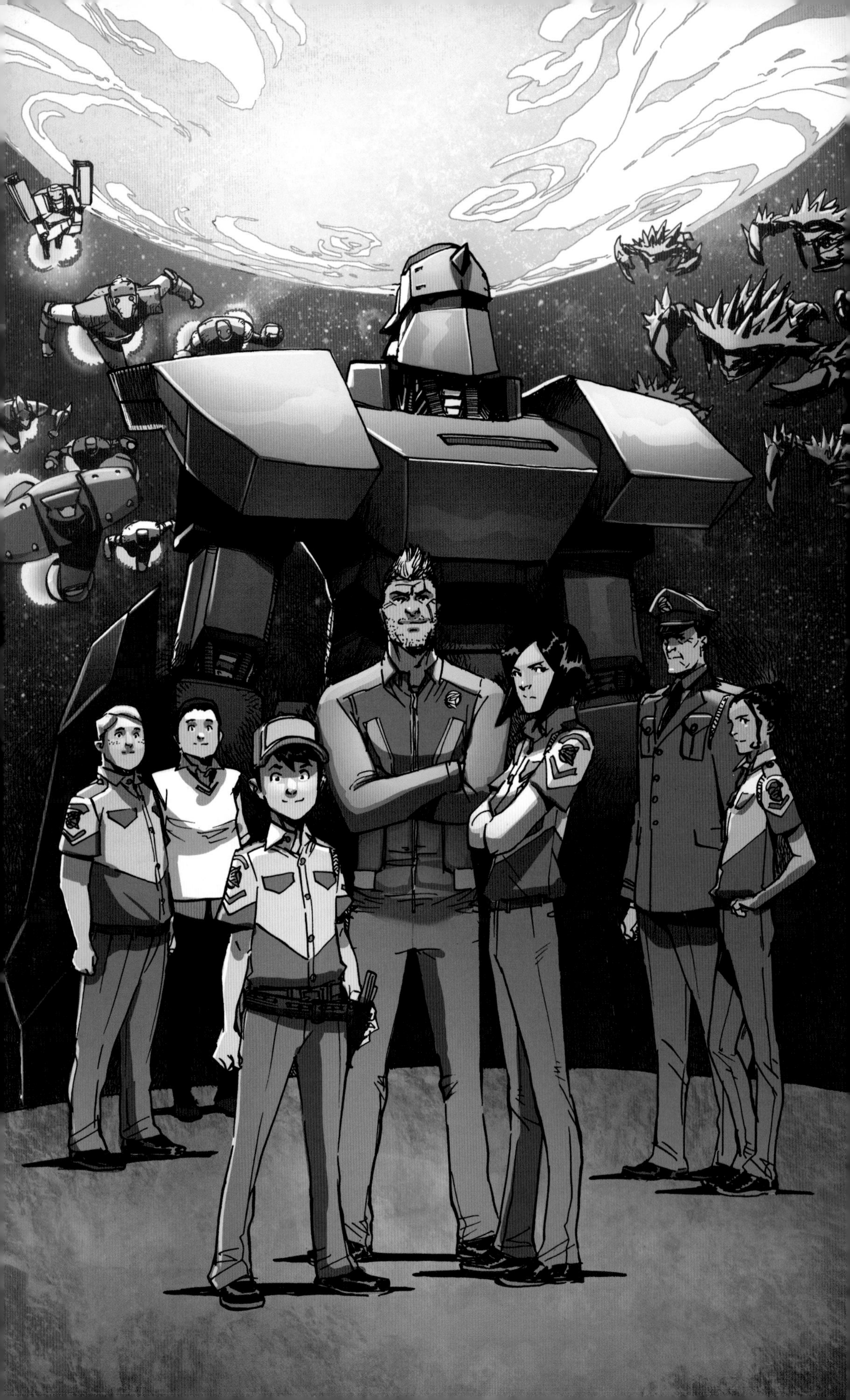

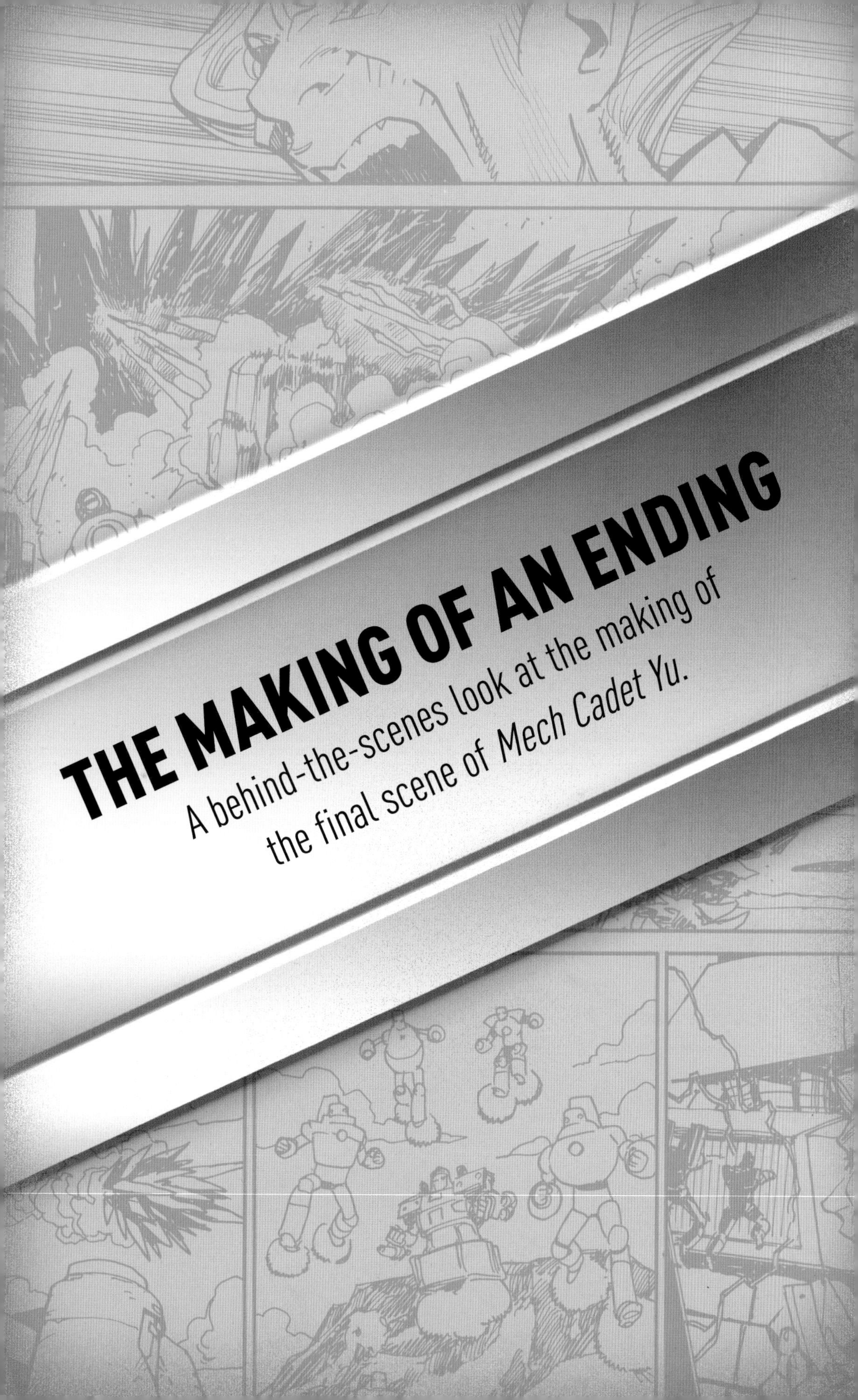

THE MAKING OF AN ENDING

A behind-the-scenes look at the making of the final scene of *Mech Cadet Yu*.

ISSUE TWELVE: PAGE NINETEEN

PANEL ONE: Sky Corps Academy. Worker robos flying around, rebuilding it. Lovely pink skies, glorious clouds.

    1. CAPTION: Three months later.

    2. CAPTION: Sky Corps Academy, Los Robos, Arizona.

PANEL TWO: Angle on a military graveyard in a green area in the desert. Long stretch of white tombstones. At the far edge of the graveyard, a group of robos and cadets stand over a big gravestone. Hero Force One's gravestone -- with a top part that's carved in the shape of Hero Force One's head. There are a number of other big gravestones in the area with other distinctive designs on their heads -- other fallen hero robos.

    3. CAPTION: Memorial Day.

PANEL THREE: Park kneels at Hero Force's grave, laying down a bunch of flowers. Red eyes. General Park, Skip, Chief Max behind her.

PANEL FOUR: Park steps back. General Park puts an arm around her shoulder.

PANEL FIVE: Wide shot. Buddy and the other robos kneel by the gravestone, laying down small scraps of metal twisted into lovely, flower-like shapes.

PANEL SIX: Stanford and Dolly walk down through the gravestones. Stanford's mom is holding a bunch of Gerber daisies.

    4. DOLLY: Huh...I thought it was right here...

    5. STANFORD: It's okay, Ma. I'll run back to the office and get a map...

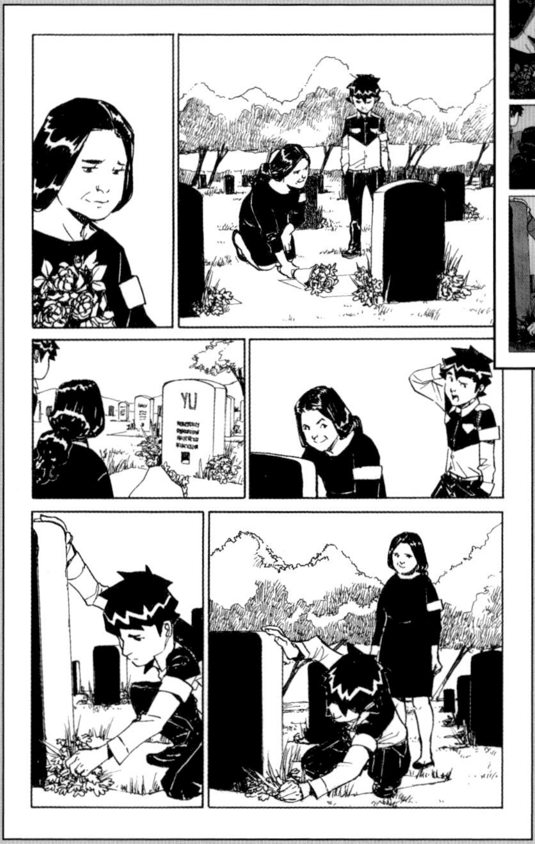
YU
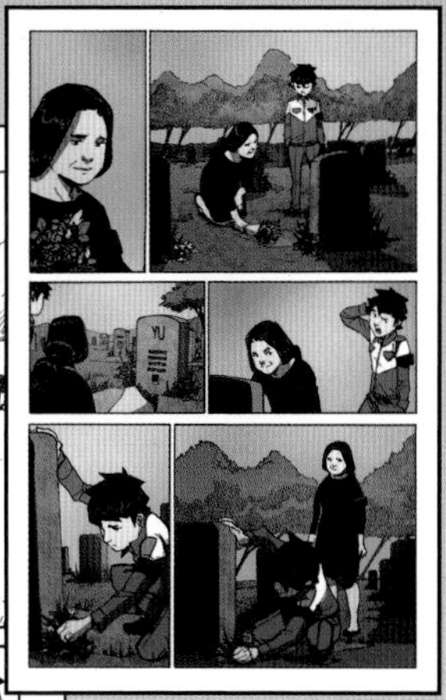
YU

ISSUE TWELVE: PAGE TWENTY

PANEL ONE: Dolly's face softens as she points at a grave.

1. *DOLLY:* No, no…
2. *DOLLY:* There he is.

PANEL TWO: She lays the flowers down on a grave. Stanford stands solemnly, respectfully, head slightly inclined.

3. *DOLLY:* <Say hello to Daddy, Stanford.>
4. *STANFORD:* <Hi, Daddy.>

PANEL THREE: Dolly kneels at the grave. Talks to the stone.

5. *DOLLY:* <Stanford's in the *Mech Cadets*, now. About to start his second year.>
6. *DOLLY:* <You'd be very proud.>

PANEL FOUR: She gives Stanford a look. He rolls his eyes a bit.

7. *DOLLY:* <Although he got a B in Science.>
8. *STANFORD:* <B *plus*, Ma.>

PANEL FIVE: Stanford kneels, pokes at some weeds at the edge of the gravestone.

9. *STANFORD:* Hm.

PANEL SIX: Stanford kneels, starts pulling the weeds while Dolly watches. Soft smile on her face.

10. *DOLLY:* Good boy.

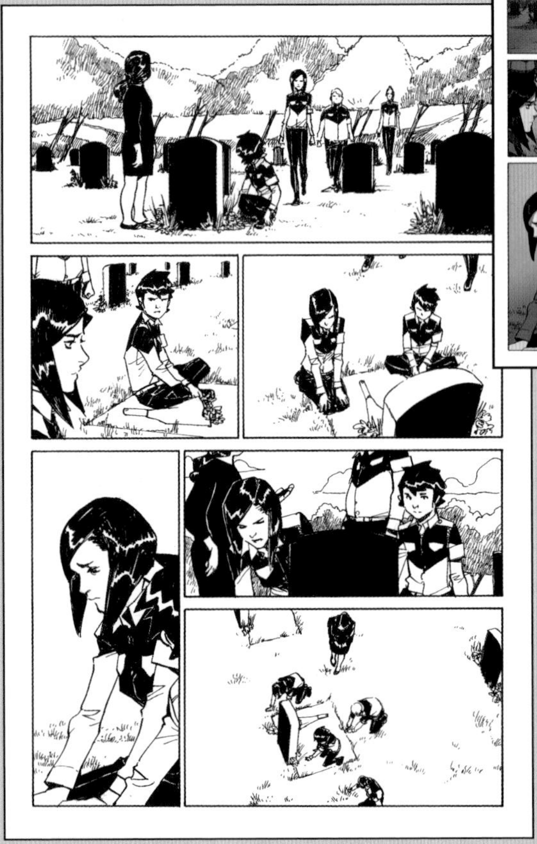

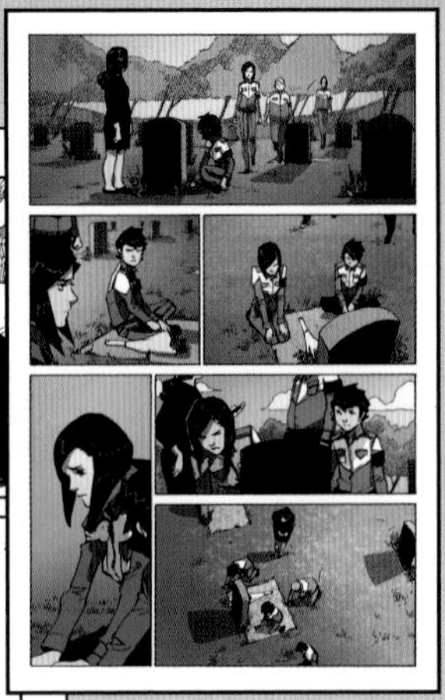

ISSUE TWELVE: PAGE TWENTY-ONE

PANEL ONE: Stanford's fellow cadets walk over. Park, Olivetti, Sanchez.

1. *PARK:* Hey.
2. *STANFORD:* Hey.

PANEL TWO: Stanford looks up at Park. Her eyes are red. She's been crying.

3. *STANFORD:* I'm sorry, Park.

PANEL THREE: She sits down next to him.

4. *PARK:* ...

PANEL FOUR: She fiddles with a blade of grass.

5. *PARK:* You can call me Olivia.

PANEL FIVE: Then she kneels, starts helping him weed. He gives her a small smile.

5. *PARK:* Man, you missed a lot over here…

PANEL SIX: Wide shot. Olivetti and Sanchez also kneel and start helping weed. All our young heroes, working together silently.

ISSUE TWELVE: PAGE TWENTY-TWO

PANEL SIX: Wide shot. The cadets continue weeding. But we pull back to reveal their robos are sitting, lying in the grass behind them. Gazing over the cadets at the sunset. Calm and solemn and relaxed. The Suprarobo sits behind them all, gazing towards the sunset as well.

    1. CAPTION: End.

    END.

DISCOVER
VISIONARY CREATORS

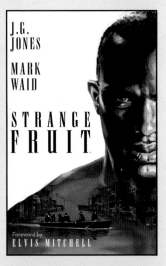

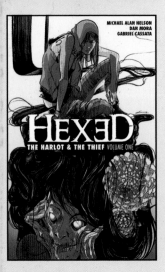